PRAISE FOR MARGARET COEL'S
THE EAGLE CATCHER

"The best parts of *The Eagle Catcher* are Coel's portrayal of the dual cultures that exist uneasily on the reservation and an uncanny sense of dialogue that makes her characters ring true."

—*The Denver Post*

"[*The Eagle Catcher*'s] native American theme will inspire comparisons to the work of Tony Hillerman, but its insights into the Arapaho way of life in our century are unique to this form."

—LOREN D. ESTLEMAN,
author of *Edsel*

"Insightful commentary about Arapaho culture ... Likable, well-drawn characters and a lively pace mark this novel—which seems poised for a sequel—for Hillerman fans."

—*Publishers Weekly*

"*The Eagle Catcher* is a beautifully plotted novel with tension that builds with the speed of a stone rolling down a hill."

—ANNE RIPLEY,
author of *Mulch*

"One can only hope that this is the beginning of a long and shining career for both Margaret Coel and Father John."

—*I Love a Mystery*

continued ...

THE EAGLE CATCHER

MARGARET COEL

BERKLEY PRIME CRIME, NEW YORK

THE BERKLEY PUBLISHING GROUP
Published by the Penguin Group
Penguin Group (USA) Inc.
375 Hudson Street, New York, New York 10014, USA
Penguin Group (Canada), 90 Eglinton Avenue East, Suite 700, Toronto, Ontario M4P 2Y3, Canada
(a division of Pearson Penguin Canada Inc.)
Penguin Books Ltd., 80 Strand, London WC2R 0RL, England
Penguin Group Ireland, 25 St. Stephen's Green, Dublin 2, Ireland (a division of Penguin Books Ltd.)
Penguin Group (Australia), 250 Camberwell Road, Camberwell, Victoria 3124, Australia
(a division of Pearson Australia Group Pty. Ltd.)
Penguin Books India Pvt. Ltd., 11 Community Centre, Panchsheel Park, New Delhi—110 017, India
Penguin Group (NZ), 67 Apollo Drive, Mairangi Bay, Auckland 1311, New Zealand
(a division of Pearson New Zealand Ltd.)
Penguin Books (South Africa) (Pty.) Ltd., 24 Sturdee Avenue, Rosebank, Johannesburg 2196,
South Africa

Penguin Books Ltd., Registered Offices: 80 Strand, London WC2R 0RL, England

This is a work of fiction. Names, characters, places, and incidents either are the product of the author's imagination or are used fictitiously, and any resemblance to actual persons, living or dead, business establishments, events, or locales is entirely coincidental. The publisher does not have any control over and does not assume any responsibility for author or third-party websites or their content.

THE EAGLE CATCHER

A Berkley Prime Crime Book / published by arrangement with the author

PRINTING HISTORY
The University Press of Colorado edition / 1995
Berkley Prime Crime mass-market edition / September 1996

Copyright © 1995 by Margaret Coel.

ISBN: 978-0-425-15463-2

BERLEY® PRIME CRIME
Berkley Prime Crime Books are published by The Berkley Publishing Group,
a division of Penguin Group (USA) Inc.,
375 Hudson Street, New York, New York 10014.
The name BERKLEY PRIME CRIME and the BERKLEY PRIME CRIME design are trademarks belonging to Penguin Group (USA) Inc.

PRINTED IN THE UNITED STATES OF AMERICA

26 25 24 23 22 21 20 19 18

DEDICATED WITH RESPECT TO THE ARAPAHOS,
PEOPLE OF THE PLAINS AND OF THE BLUE SKY

ACKNOWLEDGMENTS

Every author owes an enormous debt to those who believed, who encouraged, who championed, and I am no exception. I wish to express my deep gratitude to all who read this manuscript—some, several times—and suggested the ways to make *The Eagle Catcher* a better book than it otherwise might have been. My perceptive readers included Elaine Long, Karen Gilleland, Janis Hallowell, Julie Paschen, Bruce Most, and Ann Ripley, all exceptionally talented writers themselves; Carol Irwin, a fine teacher and editor; and Virginia Sutter, member of the Arapaho tribe and former tribal councilwoman.

My thanks to those who explained the many technical issues with which I had to grapple. They include Ben Binder, of Digital Design Group, Inc., who helped to clear a path through the thicket of oil leasing on reservations; William Irwin, special agent, Federal Bureau of Investigation, and Richard Gist, federal magistrate, who clarified many points on law enforcement on reservations; Scott Ratliff, member of the Shoshone tribe, and Miriam and Hugh Crymble, who suggested people to contact and places to see at Wind River Reservation.

Special thanks are extended to my good friend, the Rev. Anthony Short, S.J., for sharing his deep insights and understanding of Arapaho culture; to the Rev. J. Robert Hilbert, S.J., St. Stephen's Mission, for his hospitality during my numerous research trips to Wind River Reservation; to the many Arapaho people who have been kind and generous enough to share their thoughts and experiences with me, especially Mary Ann Duran, Bob Spoonhunter, Virginia Sutter, and Pious Moss.

My thanks also to my agent, Jane Jordan Browne, to Luther Wilson, director, University Press of Colorado, and to Judith Stern, senior editor, Berkley.

And to my husband, George Coel, who has always believed in me the most.

AUTHOR'S NOTE

Except for the fact that Wind River Reservation in Central Wyoming sprawls across two-and-one-half million acres, an area larger than the states of Rhode Island and Delaware combined, and

except for the fact that the Arapaho and Shoshone people call the Wind River Reservation home, and

except for the fact that, for more than a century, Euro-Americans have continued to devise a host of ingenious methods to defraud American Indian tribes across the West,

except for all of this, *The Eagle Catcher* is not based on actual events or situations.

Nor are the characters based on real people of any time. The people who move through this story are, in the words of Henry James, my dream people.

Margaret Coel

THE
EAGLE
CATCHER

∞ 1 ∞

A COLD GUST of wind whipped across the Ethete powwow grounds and flapped at Father John Aloysius O'Malley's windbreaker. He savored the warmth in the cloud of steam rising out of the foam cup a moment, then took another sip of coffee. His eyes searched the crowd of Arapahos: parents herding kids along, an occasional father with a child on his shoulders, grandmothers and grandfathers trailing behind, bands of teenagers—all headed toward the dance arbor. Father John recognized most of the faces. He didn't see Harvey Castle anywhere.

The sky was as gray as granite. It might rain today, but Father John considered it unlikely. It hadn't rained since June, the Moon When the Hot Weather Begins, by the Arapaho Way of marking time. Now it was the last Saturday in July, the Moon When the Chokecherries Ripen, and even the air felt cracked and brittle. The Arapahos kicked up little whirls of dust as they settled themselves into aluminum lawn chairs around the arbor. He had never figured out why they called it an arbor—there wasn't a tree in sight. Just a patch of scraped earth where the dances would take place.

Father John wondered what was keeping Harvey. The

dancers were already lining up outside the three-foot-high log fence that marked off the arbor, feathered headdresses bobbing in the wind. The Grand Entry would start any minute. It wasn't like the tribal chairman to be this late. He'd sounded worried yesterday when he'd called. "You goin' to the powwow this weekend?" he'd asked. Of course Father John was going to the powwow. It was the biggest celebration of the year at Wind River Reservation—he wouldn't miss it. And he intended to bring his new assistant at St. Francis Mission and introduce him around.

"Meet me at the brush shade at nine o'clock tomorrow. I got something important to talk over." There was urgency in Harvey's voice. Father John had almost asked what was going on. But he had shoved the impulse aside and muttered something like, "See you tomorrow." He'd been pacing in front of the brush shade a good thirty minutes now. He was drowning in coffee, and Harvey was nowhere around.

"You lookin' for somebody, Father?" It was a woman's voice behind him, but Father John turned quickly, half expecting Harvey to be there, too. Alva White Bull was leaning over the metal table in the center of the brush shade, which he would have called a food booth back in Boston. She looked up, sent him a quick smile, then went back to flattening a wad of dough on the table with the palms of her hands.

"Now what makes you think so, Grandmother?" He used the Arapaho term of respect for the old woman, but he couldn't resist teasing her a little.

"You pawin' the ground like some bronco locked up in a chute." Alva White Bull scooped up the dough and flopped it into a pan on the cookstove at the end of the table. Grease popped and spit in the air.

"Just waiting for you to pour me some more coffee," Father John said. Pushing his cowboy hat back, he bent his six-foot-three-and-one-half-inch frame under the sloping roof of the brush shade and set the empty Styrofoam cup on the plank counter. He'd already had four or five cups of coffee this morning—he'd lost count—but coffee beat the vodka tonics he had once used to jump-start the day.

The old woman swung an aluminum coffee pot off the cookstove and refilled his cup. Then she pushed a paper plate stacked with fry bread toward him. Rivulets of grease ran from the plate, leaving wet tracks along the counter.

He wasn't hungry; he'd had toast and a couple of eggs at the priests' residence earlier, but he took a chunk of fry bread to be polite. It tasted crusty and warm.

"Have you seen Harvey Castle this morning?" he asked.

"No. You s'pose to meet the tribal chairman?" The old woman's voice rose with expectancy as she cast out a line for some gossip.

"Supposed to," he said.

"He must've forgot."

Father John laughed, nearly choking on the fry bread. "Not likely, Grandmother. The Arapahos and the Irish are alike, you know. We never forget anything. It's a blessing."

"Yeah, yeah," she said, flapping one hand as if to wave off a pesky mosquito.

Suddenly the loudspeaker began whistling back on itself, and the announcer's voice boomed over the crowd. "Good morning, folks, and welcome to the Ethete powwow." He was seated at the judges' table inside the arbor.

"We got the best dancers on the Great Plains gonna dance for us this weekend." The voice rose over the whistling sounds. "This weekend we're gonna get in touch with the harmony and peace that us Arapahos know is important for a good life. That's what the powwow's all about. Dancers say they're ready now, so we're gonna start the Grand Entry."

The drums started beating, and the loud thuds rolled through the air like thunder. Then the singers began chanting in high-pitched voices as the dancers flowed into the arbor, turning it into a sea of colors. The women were in dresses, blues and reds and purples and golds. Some wore buckskin dresses with long fringed sleeves and skirts. The men wore silk shirts and shorts topped with breastplates of polished bones and aprons covered with shimmering glass beads. All the dancers had on beaded moccasins and ankle cuffs of white angora. Some had wheels of red and orange feathers twirling on their arms and backs. Long yellow feathers, like stalks of prairie grass, sprouted from head-dresses and bent in the wind.

Father John considered going back to his lawn chair to enjoy the dances. He was feeling a little guilty at leaving his new assistant alone for so long. Father Brad Jansen was easy to spot in the front row of spectators. His was the only blond head among the cowboy hats and baseball caps, and nobody else had on black clericals. But something held Father John in place. It wasn't like the tribal chairman to schedule a meeting and not show up. Harvey had been worried. There had been something in his voice—unspoken, but unmistakably there. Father John was starting to feel uneasy.

Then it hit him. Harvey could be in his tipi. Maybe he didn't feel well this morning and was taking his time getting ready for the powwow. Or maybe some tribal business had come up that demanded his attention.

"Thanks for the refills, Grandmother," Father John said. Setting the half-empty cup on the counter, he started for the campground which abutted the western edge of the pow-wow grounds. In the distance, the brown humps of the Wind River Mountains rode against the sky like a herd of giant buffalo. Most of the Arapahos would stay here over the weekend. The campground was filled with pickups and aluminum trailers parked next to white canvas tipis with lodgepoles jutting upright like bundles of kindling wood set on end. The tipis all looked alike, the flaps facing the east so that the first thing Arapahos saw each day would be the rising sun. He was pretty sure Harvey had pitched his tipi where he usually did, next to the access road.

"You goin' the wrong way, Father. Dancin's over that way." Leon Wolf had just stepped out of a trailer and was adjusting a baseball cap on his head, grinning. A row of white teeth flashed in his brown face.

"Thanks a lot, Leon," Father John hollered back. The simple, good-natured exchange made everything seem normal and in place, but the uneasy feeling still gnawed at him. The minute he spotted Harvey's tipi, he knew something was wrong. The flaps on the other tipis were closed, tied securely in place, but the flap on Harvey's hung loose, jumping sideways in the wind. Father John started running, the thud of the drums reverberating in his chest. He reached the tipi, threw the flap back against the canvas, and ducked inside. In the slim shaft of daylight, he saw the army-green sleeping bag on the dirt floor. Someone was in it.

"Harvey," he called. "You okay?"

Then Father John saw the black stain on the bag. He dropped down on one knee, wincing as the hard ground bit through his blue jeans and into his kneecap. He pulled back the top of the bag. Harvey's eyes were open, staring up into nothingness. Father John laid a finger alongside the Indian's neck. The skin felt stiff and cool. There was no pulse.

Suddenly Father John was aware that someone had come in behind him and was blocking the thin stream of daylight.

∞ 2 ∞

"**W**HAT'S WRONG WITH Harvey?" Leon sounded scared.

Father John pivoted slightly, his kneecap burrowing farther into the earth. Glancing up, he said, "Get the medics, will you?"

"What happened?" Leon persisted.

"I don't know," Father John said. "Just get the medics."

Leon backed out of the tipi, his boots making a slap-slap sound against the earth as he ran away. The noise of the powwow filtered through the canvas: pounding drums, high, scratchy singing, humming loudspeakers, a wailing child somewhere.

Father John looked down at the still figure in the sleeping bag. He felt a chill crawling over him like an army of ants. Based on the number of times he'd been called to emergency rooms, he could make an educated guess as to what had happened. The tribal chairman had been stabbed in the chest. A bullet would have produced a lot more blood than the tidy stain that had soaked through the sleeping bag. Leaning closer, Father John saw the small slit in the bag, neat, clean, and precise as a surgeon's cut.

But where was the weapon? There was a suitcase pushed against the slanted tipi wall, and tossed on top a dark windbreaker, a shaving kit, and some keys splayed on a metal circle. Nothing that could have done this. The ground was churned into little mounds of dirt, and in the filtering daylight he thought he could make out a footprint. Perhaps a moccasin print. There, at the foot of the sleeping bag, was what looked like an eagle feather half hidden in the broken dirt. Father John couldn't take his eyes off it. Harvey would never have allowed the sacred eagle feather to touch the ground.

Looking back at the still body, Father John began slowly tracing the sign of the cross on the Indian's forehead, speaking the words of the ancient prayer: "May your soul rest in the mercy of God, and may the perpetual light shine upon you." Then he added, "May you dwell with the Star Nations, my friend. May you walk in the Milky Way."

Suddenly Leon burst into the tipi, two medics right behind. "Here he is, like I told you." The Indian was breathing hard. Father John got to his feet as one of the medics leaned over the sleeping bag and placed his fingers below Harvey's right ear. "Jesus," the medic said.

"Is he dead?" Leon asked.

"Dead as he's ever gonna be," said the medic, pulling a radio out of the clip on his belt. "Get the Bureau of Indian Affairs police over to Chairman Castle's tipi," he barked into the radio. "We got ourselves one hell of a problem."

A crowd of Indians had started to gather outside the tipi, their whispers like the soft swoosh of the wind in the cottonwoods. They began filing inside—three or four men, a couple of women, two little boys crowding into the small space. Father John kept expecting Harvey's family to rush inside—his mother, Maria, or his sister, Rita. And where was Anthony, Harvey's nephew? Surely they were at the powwow somewhere. Then he remembered he hadn't spotted them in the crowd when he was waiting for Harvey.

At that moment Charlie Taylor, one of the tribal councilmen, burst through the opening and shouldered his way to the sleeping bag. He looked down at Harvey's body, not saying a word, then abruptly swung around and darted outside. Father John watched him through the opening. He was running.

"Jesus H. Christ. Never thought I'd see this," said Art Banner, the Arapaho chief of the Bureau of Indian Affairs police force at Wind River Reservation. The armpits of his light-blue uniform shirt were rimmed in sweat. One hand rested on top of the holster attached to the wide black belt of his navy trousers. He glanced back at the policemen looping yellow tape around stakes driven into the ground outside of Harvey's tipi.

The drums had stopped beating, and the air was heavy with silence. The sky had turned luminescent blue, as if the gray sky had rolled away to reveal another sky above. The sun was out in full force now, bathing the powwow grounds in golden light and burning through Father John's plaid cotton shirt and blue jeans. He had taken off his windbreaker and swung it over one shoulder. Now he pulled his cowboy hat forward. What a curse on the Great Plains — red hair and pale, freckled skin. No one who looked like he did belonged here, he sometimes thought. His nose was permanently sunburned.

"Who the hell did this?" The BIA police chief looked off into the distance, his black eyes squinting in the sun. He seemed to be talking to himself. "It wasn't robbery. Nothin's been messed with."

Father John wished there was something he could say. Art Banner, he knew, had been a lifelong friend of Harvey's. Words were so inadequate. Finally he mentioned the footprints. It was more comfortable to keep the conversation on facts.

"Yeah. I saw 'em. We'll get casts," said the chief.

"How about the eagle feather?"

Banner met Father John's eyes. "You thinkin' the murderer dropped that eagle feather? Nothin's ever that easy, John. Most likely Harvey dropped it and didn't know it. His dance regalia's in the suitcase. We'll look over the headdress for any missing feather."

Father John let his eyes roam over the powwow grounds a moment. Less than an hour ago, the Grand Entry had started, and the rows of lawn chairs around the arbor had been filled with Arapaho families. Now the arbor was deserted, and dancers and spectators were lugging coolers and folded aluminum chairs toward the campground. The sound of metal clanging against metal filled the air as tipi stakes were hammered out of the ground. News of Harvey's murder had spread like prairie fire, even before the announcers had officially declared the powwow canceled. In another hour, Father John knew, Arapaho families would be tearing down the highway in pickups and trailers piled high with camping gear, getting away from the Ethete powwow grounds as fast as possible. Evil seeped into a place, contaminated it, destroyed its spirit.

Father John drew in a long breath. "I haven't seen Harvey's family," he said.

"A couple of my boys are on their way out to the ranch to tell 'em. God, it's gonna be tough." The chief lifted one arm and dipped his forehead into his shirtsleeve, leaving long, wet streaks on the blue cotton. "How come you happened to find him?"

Father John explained how he was supposed to meet Harvey this morning and went looking for him in his tipi. Banner seemed to listen with one ear while he watched his men finish cordoning off the area. As soon as Father John mentioned Leon Wolf, the chief motioned to two policemen. "Get some boys talkin' to everybody who was camping in the vicinity before they're all out of here. And get a detail out searching every inch of the grounds," he ordered.

"So you and Harvey s'pose to have some kind of meeting?" Banner turned back to Father John.

"He called yesterday and said he had something important to talk over."

The police chief's eyebrows shot up. "What d'ya think it was about?"

"I wish I knew." Father John lifted his cowboy hat and ran his fingers through his hair. It was wet with perspiration. He could feel the guilt burning through him like the sun. Harvey hadn't sounded like himself. Father John had sensed the different tone in his voice, but he had pushed it aside. What if Harvey had been killed to keep him from talking? Why hadn't he driven out here last night? Found out what was bothering Harvey? If he had, maybe his friend would still be alive. Why hadn't he? Because he'd wanted to watch the Red Sox, for God's sake.

"Maybe that Arapaho history he was working on?"

Father John stared at the police chief in astonishment. He hadn't even considered the possibility that Harvey had wanted to talk about Arapaho history.

"You was helpin' him with it, ain't that right?" the chief persisted.

It was true Harvey often dropped by St. Francis Mission to discuss the latest nuggets he'd dredged out of some archives. The warriors killed in a battle in the Old Time. The fine print in some treaty. The grand promises whites had made to get Arapahos to follow the White Man's Road. History was Father John's field. He had taught American history at Jesuit prep schools back east for six years before what he called his Great Fall—when his alcoholism became common gossip in the hallways and cafeteria.

"It wasn't history Harvey wanted to talk about," Father John said after a moment. "He was worried about something. I think it was something going on now, not something that happened in the past."

The chief nodded slowly, lost in thought, as a tan jeep wheeled across the grounds, threading its way among the Indians breaking camp. It stopped behind the white BIA patrol cars in the access road, and a man about six feet tall jumped out. He had on tan slacks and a navy blazer that swung open as he strode across the road. A red tie was knotted at the collar of his white shirt. Without missing a step, he hurdled the yellow plastic tape and ducked into Harvey's tipi.

"There goes the Lone Ranger," Banner said. "Jeff Miller, new FBI man in these parts. You met him yet?"

"Not yet."

"He used to be down on the Big Reservation," Banner went on. "Then last spring, some Navajo told him all about how he was gonna shoot some other Navajo. Miller said the guy was a blowhard, so he didn't take it seriously. What d'ya know, the guy went out and did just like he said. So the powers that be sent Miller up here to Central Wyoming. Exiled, he calls it. How d'ya like that? Exiled up here with us!"

Father John nodded. He'd felt exiled, too, six years ago.

Banner drew in a long breath, then said, "Well, this is gonna be fed business, that's for sure. But Miller's gonna have himself a partner whether he likes it or not. Harvey was my friend. Screw the rules."

Father John understood the police chief was talking about the wavy line between tribal and federal jurisdictions on Indian reservations. The Bureau of Indian Affairs police handled the everyday, run-of-the-mill stuff, but major crimes, like murder, went to the FBI. This was one murder case Banner was going to be involved in, probably up to his eyeballs.

"Better stick around," the chief said. "The Lone Ranger's gonna want to talk to you."

"Murder happen around here very often?" Father Brad Jansen was sipping a Coke and leaning against the counter of the brush shade where Father John had waited to meet Harvey earlier.

"This isn't Chicago," Father John said, immediately regretting the edginess in his voice. He felt a full-blown headache coming on, and his heart was racing. That was no reason to take it out on this young priest.

"Want a Coke, Father?" Alva White Bull was still inside the shade, only now she was stacking plastic bags of hamburger buns into cardboard boxes scattered around the dirt floor.

"Sounds good, Grandmother." He stopped himself from saying "Hurry" as the old woman stooped over, lifted up the lid on a cooler, and fished out a Coke from the cans wedged among melting cubes of ice.

Father John popped the tab and took a long gulp. The cold, syrupy liquid slid down his throat. He was thirsty, that was all. The shock of finding a friend murdered would make anyone thirsty. And it had gotten so damn hot all of a sudden. That was the whole of it, except he knew it was only a small part. The big part was that every day, no matter what happened, he wanted a drink.

"Well, maybe it's not Chicago." Father Brad's voice droned on. "But it looks like you've got a professional hit here."

"What are you talking about?" Father Brad had his full attention now.

The younger priest crossed one leg over the other and dug the toe of a wing tip into the ground. "People are saying the tipi looks like Harvey had just tucked himself in for the night. It's not as if some thief came sneaking in to steal his wallet."

"You're saying somebody set this up? Planned to . . ."

"Hit him," Brad said.

"On the first night of the powwow weekend with a couple hundred people camped here, any one of whom could have seen him or her—whoever this professional murderer is? Why not plant a bomb in Harvey's pickup or pick him off with a rifle out on his ranch? Isn't that how it's done on TV?"

The young Jesuit slumped against the counter of the brush shade. "I watch the same TV as you."

"I watch the Red Sox," said Father John. He could feel his anger at full boil beneath the surface.

"Harvey was the tribal chairman, wasn't he?" Father Brad went on, squaring his shoulders. "There's oil here, right? I'd be willing to bet that Harvey isn't the first tribal chairman murdered for oil." The young priest held up his empty Coke can and sighted the trash barrel. Bull's-eye.

It was hard to stomach, this new assistant's confidence, the earnest confidence of the immature. He'd been on the reservation a total of two weeks, and he had everything figured out. Just what we need, thought Father John. Somebody with all the answers.

Father John turned away. Harvey's tipi was the only one still standing. The FBI agent had stationed himself just outside the yellow tape and was talking to Leon Wolf and a couple of other Arapaho men. Several BIA policemen were talking to the few other Indians still milling about.

"Does that mean Anthony's not gonna get into trouble?" Alva White Bull asked.

Slowly Father John looked back toward the old woman. The idea that Anthony was somehow connected to his uncle's murder was even more outrageous than Father Brad's hit-man theory. "What are you getting at, Grandmother?"

The old woman looked as if she was biting back tears. "I been awful worried ever since I heard about poor Harvey 'cause of that big fight him and Anthony got into last night," she said. "But I been thinkin', well . . ."

She hesitated, and Father John waited for her to go on. It was polite to be patient until the elders felt like continuing their stories. That had been the hardest thing for him to learn in the six years he'd been at St. Francis Mission. Patience had never been one of his virtues.

Finally Alva White Bull said, "I been thinkin' that it's a good thing Vicky Holden's come back. She's one of them lawyers now, and she can help Anthony if he went and done anything crazy."

Father John drew in a long breath. He hadn't seen Vicky Holden this morning either, and now it struck him as odd she wasn't here. He'd been so preoccupied looking for Harvey he hadn't realized a lot of other people weren't around, that this wasn't the usual powwow weekend, not usual at all. Now this elderly Arapaho woman was suggesting that Anthony was going to need Vicky's help.

Father Brad leaned on the counter, obviously intrigued by the old woman's developing story. He plunged ahead. "So what about the fight last night?"

Alva White Bull hesitated, then lowered her voice and turned to Father John, as if to tell him alone. "Everybody was settin' up camp, and Harvey was poundin' in the stakes for his tipi," she began. "All of a sudden, Anthony comes speedin' in the campground in that jeep of his. He jumps out and starts shoutin' at Harvey. Well, Rita got real upset. Tried to calm him down, but Anthony don't pay no attention to his mother or anybody else. He forgot all about respect since he went off to college, you ask me. Acts just like a white man. No offense, Father John," she said, still ignoring the younger priest.

"Next thing you know, Anthony gets back into his jeep and takes off same way he drove in. Crazy, I call it." The Indian woman made a little clicking noise with her tongue.

Father John felt as if he'd been hit with a bucket of cold water. He stepped back from the brush shade, instinctively wanting to put some space between himself and the old woman's suspicions. Anthony Castle was one of the sharpest kids he had ever met, white or brown or any other color. He was set to start medical school in Denver in the fall, after he finished up at the University of Wyoming. All he talked about was becoming a pediatrician and helping his people on the reservation. But he was a hothead, Anthony. He was such a damn hothead.

After a moment Father John said, "Anthony didn't have anything to do with his uncle's murder, Grandmother. I'm sure of it." He heard the hesitation in his own voice and wondered whom he was trying to convince.

∞ 3 ∞

FATHER JOHN POUNDED one fist against the steering wheel of the old red Toyota pickup. Jesus, Harvey Castle was a good man. Why did this have to happen to a good man? What possible motive could anyone have for murdering a man like Harvey? Nothing made any sense.

Ahead the gray asphalt of Little Wind River Bottom Road shimmered in the afternoon sun. The rounded foothills of the Wind River Mountains loomed to the west, but in every other direction the golden plains rolled into the distance as far as he could see. Here and there an oil pump appeared on the horizon, like a great black hawk pecking the earth.

Keeping his eyes on the road, Father John opened the glove compartment and pulled out an opera tape. He set the tape into the portable player wedged in the middle of the front seat and pushed a button. The plaintive swells of *La Traviata* filled the cab and drowned out the sound of the wind crashing over the half-opened windows. He allowed the music to spread through the spaces of his mind, hoping it might hold the anger and sorrow at bay for a little while.

It had been past noon before he and Father Brad had left the powwow grounds and headed back along Seventeen-

Mile Road to St. Francis Mission on the eastern edge of Wind River Reservation. He had made an effort to be more patient with his new assistant. Not that long ago he'd been cocksure and full of himself, too, and that image of himself that he glimpsed in the younger priest—that was what grated on him. Father John had spent an hour answering the telephone in the priests' residence. Yes, Harvey Castle was dead. Yes, it looked like murder. No, he didn't know anything else. After nibbling on part of a sandwich and finishing another cup of coffee, he'd left Father Brad to man the phone and had set out for Harvey's ranch.

He couldn't get Father Brad's hit-man theory out of his mind. It would have been ridiculous, if only the logical conclusion weren't so terrible. What if Harvey had been working on something important—there was that word again—on the tribal council—the business council, as Arapahos called it. And what if someone had hired a hit man to stop him? Wouldn't that mean the other five tribal councilmen were also in danger? Wouldn't that mean there could be more murders on the reservation? Oh, the relentless logic of the Jesuit system—once locked onto your thought processes, it never released its grip. Sometimes he wished he could think in another way, forget about logic.

Easing down on the accelerator, Father John glanced at the speedometer needle jumping at sixty-five. The Toyota shivered and balked, but he didn't let up. He liked the sense of hurtling down the road, the illusion of outracing whatever demons might be in pursuit. His new assistant was right about one thing, and that bothered him, kept him from dismissing the theory altogether. There was oil on Wind River Reservation. The irony never failed to amaze him. A hundred years ago nobody had wanted this desolate piece of real estate, windblown and sun-scorched all summer, adrift in freezing snow all winter. So the federal government had sent the Shoshones to live here first, and then the Arapahos.

Shoshones had settled up north around Burris and Crowheart, while Arapahos lived in the south around the fork of the Wind River and the Little Wind River. The Middle Earth, Arapahos called the land. Sacred space where human beings could *be*. A gift of *Nih'a'ca'*, the Shining Man Above. Then somebody had hit a gusher, and ever since, whites had cast greedy eyes on the reservation.

Lucky they couldn't get their hands on it, Father John thought, or they'd have it. True, Arapahos had sold large portions just to keep from starving to death, before laws prohibited such sales. But in recent years, they'd bought back some of the original lands with royalties from tribal oil wells.

Now it was mostly Arapaho land as far as Father John could see, across the plains and into the foothills, except for the 100,000-acre Cooley ranch that butted against the southwestern edge of the reservation. Mathias Cooley, the first government agent, had bought it from Chief Black Night more than a hundred years ago. Rumor on the moccasin telegraph was that Ned Cooley, the agent's great-grandson, intended to sell the ranch, now that he had his sights set on the statehouse.

"Damn," Father John said out loud, hitting the rim of the steering wheel again. He'd forgotten about the annual pig roast at the Cooley ranch tonight. He'd only attended once, his first summer at St. Francis. White-only events around here weren't for him. But his new assistant had pounced on the invitation when it arrived last week, and Father John had agreed to go.

He'd rationalized it, he had to admit. Ned Cooley would be announcing his candidacy to a lot of important people from Lander and Riverton, and Father Brad might have better luck than he'd ever had in getting important people to contribute to St. Francis Mission once in a while. "The chance of a rookie pitching a no-hitter." Father John was used to talking to himself out loud in the Toyota. "Brad can go if he wants. I'm counting myself out."

Little Wind River Bottom Road bent to the east like a broken arrow, and as Father John slowed the Toyota into the turn, he thought about his interview with the FBI agent. He'd told him everything he knew. Well, almost everything. He hadn't mentioned Alva White Bull's story about Anthony and Harvey quarreling last night. But he hadn't witnessed the quarrel himself, and the fed hadn't asked about it, so it wasn't as if he'd lied. What was that old Jesuit maxim? A wise man never has to lie. Thinking about it made him smile.

He felt calmer now, with the notes of "Di Provenza il mar" filling the cab. The open spaces always calmed him. He never minded spending a large part of every day in the Toyota, awash in the music of *La Traviata* or *La Bohème* or *Don Giovanni*, crisscrossing the reservation, fifty miles here, thirty miles there, twenty-five over there. Arapahos lived on ranches miles from their nearest neighbors.

So different from Boston where he'd grown up. People lived on top of one another there, encased in brick and asphalt, with no space around them. He and his brother had slept on the foldaway in the front room of a third-floor walkup that jutted over the traffic on Commonwealth Avenue. Only on the sandlots had he felt the earth stretching into the vastness, felt himself part of the sky and the infinite space. By the time he was twelve, he could throw a fastball that curved around home plate. He could still throw a decent fastball and trot around the bases at a pretty good run. Baseball had been his ticket to Boston College, and after graduation he had gone into the Jesuit seminary.

He hadn't intended to stay at St. Francis Mission long. The assignment had come while he was still in treatment at Grace House. He had figured he'd be here long enough to take his lumps, to be duly humbled, as only the Jesuits could humble one of their own. Then it would be back to teaching American history—with some fresh insight into the American Indian—at one of the Jesuit prep schools before moving on to a university, perhaps Fordham or Georgetown. He had actually said as much to old Father Peter, as if St. Francis Mission were the Siberia of the Jesuit order. Dear God, what an arrogant SOB he'd been.

But the months had gone by, then one year, then another. And Father Peter had had his heart attack and gone to the Jesuit retirement house in St. Louis, and he had taken Father Peter's place as superior. He'd been here almost six years now, three years as superior. And he'd had numerous young Jesuit assistants. One had stayed most of a year, but the others had hardly unpacked their bags before leaving. He wondered how long Father Brad would stay around. Life on an Indian reservation—the emptiness, the loneliness—well, it wasn't for everybody.

The Toyota started up a rise so gentle he was hardly aware of the pull until the pickup began slowing. He jammed down the gas pedal feeling the bed fishtail on the asphalt. Suddenly Harvey's white frame ranch house hove into view. Behind it a field of hay moved in the wind like the surface of a green sea, while a line of gray-green cotton-wood trees marked the banks of the Little Wind River in the distance. Easing on the brakes, Father John wheeled in behind the pickups at the side of the road.

Arapaho families were milling about in the driveway, and a group of men had congregated at the gate. Overhead, an arch of black iron floated against the blue sky forming the words "White Eagle Ranch." Father John knew that White

Eagle, Harvey's great-grandfather, had ridden with Chief Black Night in the Old Time.

Charlie Taylor stepped back from the group and came toward the road, just as Father John slammed the door of the Toyota. "How're you doing?" he called to the Indian, remembering how Charlie had run away from Harvey's tipi, as if he couldn't stand what he had seen.

"Hell, I'm okay." A brown Stetson shaded the councilman's eyes which were busy searching the road. Father John realized Charlie hadn't walked out to greet him—he was leaving and he was in a hurry.

"We don't scare easy," Charlie added as he reached Father John. The silver bolo tie hanging down the front of his crisp white shirt glinted in the sun. His pace barely slowed.

"Any reason to be scared?" The hit-man theory still crouched in Father John's mind, like an animal waiting to spring out of a cage.

"No. Hell, no," Charlie said over his shoulder, hurrying past. "I gotta get goin'. There's gonna be lots of work on the business council with Harvey gone, and I'm gonna fill in as chairman till we elect somebody permanent." The councilman strode toward the line of pickups. Father John looked after him a moment before starting down the driveway. He stopped at each group, shaking hands, patting the men on the back in a half-hearted attempt at encouragement. Nobody said anything, and Father John felt the same helplessness and sadness that he knew was gripping them.

Just as he mounted the steps to the concrete stoop in front of Harvey's bi-level house, Charlie's pickup roared out into the middle of Little Wind River Bottom Road trailing a cloud of exhaust and sounding like an eighteen-wheeler pushing eighty. Suddenly it veered across the road just as an oncoming automobile topped the rise. Father John grabbed the metal railing on the stoop and braced himself for a head-on collision. Miraculously the pickup swerved back into its own lane just as the car passed.

Father John let out a long breath and glanced back at the driveway. The Indians stood riveted in place, staring at the road. Finally one of the men turned and caught his eye. "What's that fool Charlie thinkin' of?" the Indian shouted. "He's gonna get hisself killed one of these days if he ain't careful."

∞ 4 ∞

FATHER JOHN RAPPED on the metal screen door.
The front door stood open into the shadows of the entryway,
and he could see people moving about on the landing at the
top of the stairs. Their voices sounded like rain skittering
over the roof. After a moment Rita came down the stairs and
out of the shadows.

"I been hopin' you'd get here," she said, holding the
screen door for him with one hand while dabbing a tissue at
her eyes with the other. Her long black hair swung about her
shoulders like a nun's veil. She wore faded blue jeans and an
orange blouse that hung below her waist and tugged at her
hips, giving her a squared-off look. Her face had a blotched
puffiness about it, but her eyes were the dusky gray of
dawn. It struck him that she was probably not many years
away from having been beautiful.

"I'm terribly sorry about Harvey," he said, stepping into
the small entry and waiting for his eyes to adjust from
the bright sunlight outdoors. There was a hollow ring to the
words that hung in the air between them. He wished he
could think of something to say that might console her.

"You were a good friend to my brother," Rita said, still dabbing at her eyes. "He trusted you."

He'd always hoped Harvey trusted him, but he had never taken it for granted. Arapahos didn't trust whites easily. He tossed his cowboy hat on the bench behind the door and followed Rita's broad figure up the half flight of green carpeted stairs, grateful for the little miracles. Here he was, hoping to console Harvey's family, and Rita had said something that consoled him.

Odors of the beef stew and percolating coffee drifted out of the arched doorway to the kitchen just off the landing. Several Arapaho women buzzed about, stirring a pot on the stove and shuffling casserole dishes, plastic food containers, loaves of bread, and bags of hamburger buns around on the counters. The green carpeting trailed down a long hallway to one side of the landing and spread across the living room on the other side.

Rita turned and planted herself in the kitchen doorway. "After you seen Mother," she said, nodding toward the living room, "there's something important I wanna talk to you about." Then, "What's the matter?"

Father John shook his head. That's what Harvey had said the last time he'd spoken with him. "There's something important I wanna talk over." He wondered if what Rita had to tell him was related to whatever had been bothering Harvey. It would have to wait.

He took in the living room at a glance. Five grandmothers occupied the sofa and two upholstered chairs along the far wall. Six tribal elders sat on straight-backed kitchen chairs against the half wall that divided the stairwell from the living room. Maria was in a rocker in a far corner, near a window that framed the snow-tipped peaks of the Wind River Mountains. An Arapaho couple and two teenagers hovered over the old woman, paying respects.

Father John made his way down the line of elders, saying a few inane words about being terribly sorry, shaking their hands. Their grasp was stronger and firmer than their wiry, frail-looking bodies would suggest. He stepped across the room and greeted the grandmothers. Next to the sofa stood a table covered with wood-framed photos of Anthony. Anthony racing down court, sighting the basket, going for a layup, stopped by the camera in midair.

Father John still felt a twinge of regret that the most talented player he'd ever coached, definitely the MVP of the mid-Wyoming baseball circuit, had defected to basketball. Anthony had hit so many home runs the summer he'd played for the St. Francis Eagles that the other coaches had sent Father John a three-page letter, the gist of it being that the Castle boy demoralized their pitchers. The next summer, when Anthony decided not to come out for the Eagles, the other coaches had probably had a party.

Anthony had turned into the best center the Indian High School basketball team had ever seen. The Indian kids brought home the state championship two years in a row, and the University of Wyoming coach had come to the reservation to recruit him. Father John shrugged off the memory. It had all turned out for the best, anyway. Basketball meant that Anthony was able to go on to school, and Father John was glad of that.

He was amazed at how much of Anthony the stop-action shots had caught. Quickness, skill, determination, hotheadedness, it was all there. Shoot from the outside, fake out the defense, love the risks. Anthony was like the young warriors in the Old Time who had no patience with the talking ways of the chiefs. Action was what they had demanded, even if it brought soldiers to the villages. Father John wondered what Anthony and Harvey had quarreled about. Something Harvey had wanted to turn over and look at from all sides, thoughtfully, considering all the consequences, while Anthony had wanted action?

Father John felt a tug at his shirtsleeve. One of the grandmothers was motioning him toward Maria who was now alone, her black oxfords pushing against the carpet. The squeak of the wooden rocker cut through the buzz of voices that filled the room.

Her grandmothers had howled with grief at the deaths of their children. They had taken knives and gashed their arms and legs and cut off their hair. Somehow that seemed appropriate, Father John thought now. More equal to the terrible fact of a child's death than Maria's quiet containment of grief.

Someone opened a folding chair, and he sat down next to the old woman. Will Standing Bear scooted his chair over from the other elders, then settled back, knobby hands clasped in his lap. Father John took Maria's hand. It was as small as a child's and as smooth and cool as a rose petal. A red sweater was draped over her shoulders, even though the house was hot and stuffy. She seemed sunk into herself, already in the half-life—half with her dead son, half with the living.

"Hana je nahadina," the old woman said, her words almost lost among the murmuring voices.

Will leaned forward. "She says the commandment. 'Thou shalt do no murder.' She don't know why the commandment was broke."

Father John was quiet a moment. "I don't know either," he said finally. "Harvey was a good man." He saw by the flash of light in the old woman's eyes that she understood he meant good in the Arapaho Way. A good man was generous and kind, thoughtful of others. Only a few could be called good.

"We must bury my grandson on the third day. You take

care of it, *Teenenoo Hiinooni'it*," Will said, calling Father John by the Arapaho name he had given him three years ago. It meant Touch-the-Clouds. It symbolized what he did as a priest, and, Father John suspected, the fact that his head rose above the heads of most other men around here.

He promised the old people that the wake would take place Monday evening, the funeral first thing Tuesday. Everything else at St. Francis, the sodality and ladies aid meetings, the religious education classes, the daily Mass, would give way to the rituals of Harvey's funeral. Aware of other people filing into the living room and waiting to speak to Maria, he patted her hand before he let it go. "I'll be back," he said.

Rita was on the landing outside the kitchen. She wheeled around and started down the hallway, and he followed. Halfway along, she stopped, turning to look beyond him toward the living room as if to make sure no one else had followed.

"You heard about the fight last night?" Rita's voice cracked with anxiety.

Father John nodded.

"That's all the grandmothers are talking about. Not so I can hear, of course." Rita pressed the tissue against her mouth, stifling a cry.

"Is that what you wanted to tell me about?"

Rita took a deep breath and nodded. "Anthony got home from school yesterday afternoon. He was gonna dance at the powwow. He does the Fancy Dance, you know. Harvey taught him when he was little." She closed her eyes a moment, fighting for control. "Soon as Anthony got in the house, him and Harvey got into a big fight. Then last night, when Anthony came out to the powwow grounds, they started up again. Next thing I know, Anthony takes off in his jeep."

"What was it all about?"

Rita shrugged. "Probably the Cooley ranch. No big deal. Anthony thinks Our People should buy it back. Harvey was against it, that's all."

"They argued about the Cooley ranch?" Father John could have come up with a dozen things a headstrong twenty-two-year-old might argue with his uncle about. Dropping out of school before finishing his degree. Deciding not to go on to medical school. Getting mixed up with the wrong girl. But a piece of real estate? Whether Arapahos should buy back land that had once been part of the reservation? Besides, as far as he knew, Harvey had always been in favor of buying back the old lands. Why wouldn't he want to get the Cooley ranch back?

Rita lowered her voice to almost a whisper and, as if she had read his mind, said, "Oh, Harvey was all for it at first. Then he talked to Will Standing Bear and the other elders. They told him, 'Don't trust the agent.'"

"The agent?" Father John knew Arapahos still referred to the first government agent as 'the agent.' "What were they talking about? Mathias Cooley's been dead a hundred years."

"All I know is Harvey changed his mind." Rita leaned against the opposite wall. "He was gonna make a big presentation to the business council next Tuesday. Charlie Taylor was backing him. He always went along with Harvey."

Father John hooked his thumbs into the pockets of his blue jeans. Maybe this was what Harvey had wanted to talk to him about, but he doubted it. He and Harvey rarely discussed matters before the business council. Anyway, if Harvey had changed his mind about the Cooley ranch, it probably had more to do with finances than with anything the elders had said.

"Maybe Cooley wants too much money," Father John suggested.

"Five million? That's too much all right. But we could've done it. We got oil money."

Father John didn't want to argue with her. There were oil wells across the reservation, all owned by the two tribes. Part of the royalties were paid out to the people, in what they called their per capitas. The per capitas gave Arapaho and Shoshone families a modest income, which they relied upon. But some royalties were reserved to buy back the old lands. Those, he knew, were already committed to certain lands. Maybe there wasn't enough left for a major purchase like the Cooley ranch. After a moment he asked, "Where's Anthony now?"

Rita was staring down the hall, and he realized she had been expecting her son. "I thought for sure he'd come home last night, but he never showed up," she said. "Mom and I were here all night—Mom's too old for campin' out, and I'd just as soon sleep in my own bed. But Harvey loved the camp life. Part of him was living in the Old Time, you know."

She dabbed at her eyes again before hurrying on, her voice rising. "When Anthony didn't come home, I figured he must've gone back to the powwow grounds to fix things up with Harvey. I was gettin' ready to take Mom out there this morning when the grandmothers and Will Standing Bear and a couple policemen came drivin' up, and they told us what happened . . ."

Rita lowered her face into her hands and began sobbing. Father John stepped across the hall and put his arms around her. "I'm so sorry," he said, feeling his own grief and anger wash over him like a hot breeze, trying to comfort himself as well as her with the words.

After a moment she pulled away and, leaning against the

wall again, let out a long breath. "I'm scared the police are gonna think Anthony—" She stopped a moment. "Anthony would never hurt Harvey. I mean, Harvey was the only father he'd ever had, you know." There was a question in her voice, as if she were wondering if he *did* know.

"I understand," he said. A look of relief crossed Rita's face. She had never told him about it, but Harvey had. How Rita had run off with some Indian who had been passing through the reservation. How he had left her in Denver, pregnant and scared out of her wits. And how Harvey had gone to Denver and brought her home. It was right after his divorce, he'd said, and he'd been happy to help his sister raise her child.

"The police aren't going to blame Anthony, not without witnesses, or some evidence that Anthony was in the tipi at the time Harvey was killed," Father John said, hoping to allay her fears and, at the same time, reassure himself. "They need hard evidence that would stand up in court, like fingerprints or hair samples or—"

"The knife," Rita interrupted. She was twisting the tissue into a rope, and her hands were shaking. "The grandmothers said he was knifed."

"That's what it looks like," Father John said softly. There was no telling what gossip the grandmothers had passed on.

"Oh, my God," Rita said, dropping her face into her hands. Just as he was about to put his arms around her again, the screen door slammed, and heavy footsteps bounded up the stairs.

"Anthony!" Rita screamed, flinging herself past Father John and rushing down the hallway.

"Who killed him?" Anthony said, demanding an instant answer, an explanation that would make sense out of the senseless. His voice was low and hoarse. Close to six feet tall, muscular and lanky at the same time, he seemed to fill up the landing at the top of the stairs. Except for his yellow T-shirt and ragged blue jeans slit open at the knees, he could have been a warrior in the Old Time, with eyes as black and determined as slate, a hooked, defiant nose, prominent cheekbones, and blue-black hair that fell over his forehead with its own insistency. He scanned the elders and grand-mothers in the living room, the women crowding around the kitchen doorway, before fixing his eyes on his mother.

Rita stopped and stood still, as if to take him in and make sure he was really there. Then she ran forward again, stretched out her arms and gathered him to her, cradling him like a little boy. Her head and shoulders were shaking, and Father John knew she was sobbing silently.

"I stopped for gas up at Ethete," Anthony said, pulling slightly away from his mother's grasp while still patting her shoulder, "and Jake Littlehorse told me . . ." He stopped abruptly. The words refused to be uttered.

After a moment, he said, "I'm gonna get whoever did this, Mom, no matter what I have to do." The house had gone quiet except for the faint clack-clack-clack of the screen door knocking in the wind.

∞ 5 ∞

FATHER JOHN DESCENDED the stairs and retrieved his cowboy hat from the bench. He had promised to come back later. Now Anthony needed to be with his family. In any case, Father John didn't know what he would say. He didn't understand why Harvey had been murdered in his tipi. He didn't have the answers. Just platitudes, that's all he had, about being sorry, about Harvey being a good man, a damn good man. Harvey and his family deserved more than platitudes.

He squinted into the fiery sunlight as he stepped outside onto the concrete stoop, setting the screen door firmly in place behind him. The sky had turned sapphire blue with wisps of white clouds floating and banking against one another, like sailboats skimming the surface of the sea. The afternoon sun spilled its heat over the stoop, and a hot, steady breeze rustled the leaves of the lone cottonwood tree in the front yard and swept across the small patch of grass.

The grandmothers still clucked over Harvey's patch of grass. Father John had often overheard them as they stitched patterns of beads onto shirts and moccasins at the St. Francis meeting hall. The idea of pouring water onto something that didn't belong here and didn't want to grow here! He thought of what Harvey had told him: how he'd planted grass around the cottonwood so Anthony could have a cool, shady place to play when he was little, until he got tall enough to ride the horses out on the ranch.

Father John made his way down the concrete steps and along the driveway, his boots scrunching against the gravel. Anthony's jeep blocked the driveway, like a marker hugging its place on a Monopoly board. Arapahos were still milling about, although the crowd seemed smaller and the line of pickups shorter out along Little Wind River Bottom Road. His throat felt as dry as the little puffs of dust he was kicking up, and as scratchy as a tumbleweed. He needed a drink. He wished he'd helped himself to a cup of coffee in the kitchen.

A few years back he would have had the answers, and they would have tripped off his tongue as easily as the sunlight glinted off the pebbles in the driveway. Smooth and glib he'd been, full of the certainty and clarity of fifteen years of Jesuit training. Shored up with all the arguments of the great philosophers from Aristotle to Aquinas, Kant to Kierkegaard. Tested in monographs and disputations, in endless discussions over dinner in the refectory every evening. He could have expounded at length on how God was First Mover and Creator, how all created things acted according to their natures, how free will defined the nature of human beings. He could have explained philosophically how someone, acting with free will, had chosen to murder Harvey.

So what? Harvey was dead—that was the fact of the matter, and no philosophical theory on how murder comes into the world would have comforted Harvey's family. It didn't even comfort him. He'd learned a lot about faith since he'd been at Wind River Reservation, mostly about how it was something other than an intellectual exercise. There were no words, no lofty concepts, that could take away the pain. Faith was living with the pain.

He was about to get into the Toyota pickup out on the side of Little Wind River Bottom Road when a BIA patrol car slowed alongside him. Its red brake lights flashed on and off as the car turned in to the driveway and rocked to a stop. The jeep he'd seen this morning at the powwow grounds pulled in behind, its rear bumper hanging into the road. Doors flung open, and Art Banner lifted himself from the patrol car as the FBI agent, Jeff Miller, jumped from the jeep.

The two agents of law and order walked back onto the road toward him, their arms swinging like martinets: Miller in dark suit with jacket open and red tie hanging dead center; the police chief in light-blue shirt and navy-blue slacks wrinkled with sweat, as if he'd been wearing them for days.

"Anthony Castle inside?" The agent threw his head back toward the ranch house.

Father John felt his muscles tense, the way they had on the pitcher's mound, when everything depended on the next throw of the ball. All his senses shifted into high gear as he gripped the rim of the opened door on the Toyota. "Anthony's with his family." He drew out the words, giving himself time to assess the situation.

"We've got some questions. It's best he comes to Lander," Miller said, squaring his shoulders and looking steadily at Father John.

"Why Lander?"

Banner wedged himself between the fed and Father John. "We just need some questions answered, that's all. No sense disturbing the family."

"Anthony doesn't know anything about his uncle's murder." Father John stepped out from the door and slammed it hard, deliberately punctuating his words. He walked to the front of the pickup, eyes locked on Miller. It was this FBI agent who needed convincing. "Anthony wasn't even around."

Miller folded his arms across his middle. "Oh, he was around all right. No doubt you know all about that big fight he and his uncle got into last night. Twenty, thirty witnesses saw it. Big coincidence, wouldn't you say, that Harvey got stabbed afterward? Coroner estimates time of death sometime between midnight and six this morning."

"Anthony left the powwow grounds," Father John said, keeping his voice steady, reasonable.

"We think he came back," said the agent.

Some of the Arapaho men who had been standing in the driveway walked out onto the road and lined up like bodyguards behind Banner and Father John.

Miller ignored them. "We got the murder weapon. BIA police found a hunting knife out on the grounds behind Harvey's tipi. Hidden in some sagebrush."

"We think it might be the murder weapon." Banner jumped in. "We won't know for sure 'til the lab tests it."

"Maybe Anthony can identify it," Miller said, his voice thick with sarcasm. "It's got his initials on the handle."

A strong dislike for this white man rose like bile in Father John's throat. He heard the Arapahos behind him gulping in air, and he hoped everybody stayed calm. "Could be a coincidence," he said hurriedly.

"Yeah. Coincidences all over the place." Miller kept his eyes locked on Father John's.

"Will you do us a favor and tell Anthony we wanna talk to him?" Banner took another step in front of the fed, almost blocking him altogether.

Father John switched his gaze to the police chief. He understood what the Indian was about. Banner didn't want to insult Harvey's family by coming into their home with some cockamamie suggestion that Anthony had something to do with the murder. And there was no way he wanted to deal with the wrath of Anthony's grandmother. Arapaho grandmothers would put a she-wolf to shame when it came to protecting their young.

"Okay," Father John said almost under his breath. There was only one reason he would do this: maybe he could soften the blow a little for Anthony, explain the situation to Maria and Rita. He didn't want the family upset any further.

"There's an explanation for all this," he said, starting toward the driveway. He said it for the fed's benefit.

Father John took the stairs two at a time. From the landing he spotted Anthony sitting cross-legged on the living room carpet next to Maria's rocker. Catching the young man's eye, he motioned to him.

Anthony sprang upward like a whipcord unknotting itself. He strode across the living room, his eyes on Father John. "What?" he asked.

Father John turned and walked halfway down the hallway to where he and Rita had stood a few minutes ago. Then he faced the young man. Keeping his voice low, he said, "Banner and the new FBI agent want you to come to Lander for questioning."

Anthony blinked and shifted his weight from one foot to the other. "They think I had something to do with Harvey's murder?"

Father John placed a hand on the Indian's shoulder to steady him for what he had to say next. "They found a hunting knife with your initials on it."

"No." Anthony rocked backward as if he'd been hit by a strong gust of wind. Shaking off Father John's hand, he whirled around and drove one fist against the wall. Several women poked their heads through the kitchen door, eyes wide with surprise and fear.

"Take it easy," Father John said, gripping the young man's shoulder again. He could feel the tenseness there.

Anthony's breath came fast and hard. "Give me a couple more minutes with grandmother," he said.

"What's going on?" Rita asked. Father John could hear her puffing as she followed him down the stairs. He stepped back and pushed open the screen door for her. He saw the fear in her eyes as they stepped out onto the concrete stoop.

He began explaining how the police had to question everybody and wanted Anthony to come to Lander, when suddenly Banner sprinted across the lawn, radio in hand, antenna pulled out. Father John felt as if he'd been hit by lightning. Jesus, why hadn't he seen it coming? He swung himself over the metal railing and dropped about five feet onto the ground, sending shock waves reverberating up his spine. Then he started running after the chief.

Rounding the corner of the house, Father John saw Anthony zig-zagging through the hay field out back with Miller right behind. The agent was losing ground, his legs pedaling furiously through the stalks of hay. He would never catch Anthony. All of a sudden the Indian stumbled and pitched forward, as if one foot had caught the edge of a prairie dog hole. He was scrambling to right himself when the agent tackled him, and they both went down. Banner caught up and threw himself onto the pile. A cloud of dust rose over the three figures in the flattened hay.

Just as Father John reached them, his heart pounding against the walls of his chest, they struggled to their feet, the older men pulling Anthony up. Anthony's face had turned the dark red of dead leaves about to drop off an aspen tree. Both Banner and Miller were huffing. A couple of buttons on Banner's shirt had popped off. His shirttails hung loose over his uniform slacks, and little beads of sweat stood out on his forehead. Miller's navy blazer, smeared with gray-green dust, was bunched under his armpits. His red tie looped over one shoulder.

"I'm arresting you," Miller said, gulping air between his words, "on suspicion of murder."

Banner pulled a set of handcuffs out of his pocket and snapped them around one of Anthony's wrists. It took both Banner and Miller to pull Anthony's other arm around in back and close the handcuffs on that wrist.

"What's going on?" Father John tried to keep his voice calm, but he knew he was shouting. "He's got rights here."

"Yeah, he's got rights," Miller said, planting himself directly in front of Anthony. Then he began rattling off rights with about as much involvement as a printer zapping inked words onto a sheet of paper.

Rita pushed past the small crowd of Arapahos gathering around. "Don't take him away," she screamed, locking one hand on Banner's arm.

"Don't make this any harder than it is, Rita," the police chief said under his breath. He shook off the woman's hand as he and Miller propelled Anthony around the house and toward the driveway.

"Figured he'd make a break out back," Miller said to the small crowd circling them. He seemed well satisfied with himself. Father John pushed his way past the others and strode alongside the fed, looking beyond him to the young Arapaho, as if the white man weren't there. "You don't have to say anything," he said to Anthony. "Not without a lawyer."

Suddenly Anthony jerked away from his captors, squared his shoulders, and threw his head back. Father John half expected him to bolt down the driveway. He felt his own muscles tense before he realized that wasn't Anthony's intention. He was merely claiming, if not his liberty, his freedom. "Call Vicky, will you?" Anthony asked.

"You got it," Father John said, hoping the Arapaho lawyer was around this weekend. It wasn't like her to miss a celebration like the powwow.

Nobody spoke as the group continued past the small, silent knots of Arapahos in the driveway, stunned looks on their faces. Banner steered Anthony into the back seat of the patrol car, then slammed the door. Before he could get in behind the steering wheel, Rita burst past the others. "You can't take him," she screamed.

The chief stopped, one foot still on the driveway, the other in the car, and leaned over the top. "Take it easy, will ya, Rita? We're gonna get this cleared up fast as we can."

Exchanging a quick glance with Father John, Banner slid into the driver's seat. The FBI agent hurried to his jeep a few feet behind. Several women gathered around Rita as the vehicles backed out of the driveway, spitting gravel from under the rear tires.

Maria and Will stood on the concrete stoop gripping the railing like a rope between their hands. "Where they takin' my grandson?" the old woman asked as Father John mounted the stairs.

"Lander." He didn't want to say "jail."

"He'll be with white people," Maria said. Father John understood her fear. Anthony was about to be swallowed into an alien, official white world. Suddenly the old woman straightened herself upright and took a long breath as she reached for Father John's arm. "You gotta help him."

"I'll do everything I can," Father John said, hoping the old people wouldn't sense how scared he felt right now. It occurred to him that the fed had intended to arrest Anthony all along. Taking him to Lander for questioning—that was just a ploy. Miller would have arrested him as soon as they got there. But Anthony had forced his hand by running out the back door. God, what if Miller had gone for his gun? Anthony could've been killed.

"We've got to get a lawyer," Father John said. "Anthony asked me to call Vicky Holden."

Maria dropped her hand from Father John's arm. Both she and Will were quiet a moment. Finally the elder spoke, measuring out his words. "Yes. *Hisei ci nihi* is the granddaughter two generations away of Chief Black Night. You call her, *Teenenoo Hiiinooni'it*. Tell her that Our People need her now."

∞ 6 ∞

VICKY HOLDEN HEARD the muffled, distant sound of the phone ringing as she lifted her suitcase through the tailgate of the Bronco. She hurried up the sidewalk, pulling the suitcase on its little metal wheels while, at the same time, fitting the strap of a leather bag into the crook of her shoulder. The ringing stopped just as she reached the porch that fronted the small brick bungalow she'd called home the last couple of years. To hell with it, she thought. Whoever it was could call again. She wasn't ready to talk to clients yet. Four days in downtown Denver at a trial lawyers' meeting hadn't exactly been a snooze on the beach.

She dropped the suitcase on the wooden floor of the porch and riffled through her purse for the house key. The ringing started again. "Hold on," she said under her breath, jamming the key into the lock. It crossed her mind it could be Larry, even though she'd let him off at his law office ten minutes ago. It would be like him to want to know if she'd made up her mind yet. Was she coming to L.A. with him? What was it to be? He'd pushed for an answer the entire time they'd been in Denver. Not the makings of a relaxing trip. Not when she didn't know the answers, did not have a clue as to what she wanted to do. They'd taken the flight back to Riverton this afternoon in almost total silence.

Leaving the suitcase on the porch, she hurried across the gray carpet in the small living room. Another long ring. The phone looked as if it might jump off the table next to the blue, flower-printed sofa. Tossing her bag onto one of the cushions, she sat down and picked up the receiver.

"Hello? I'm here." There was no longer any attempt to conceal the irritation she'd bottled up the last few days. She kicked off her sandals and scrunched her toes into the carpet, steeling herself against another plea for an answer, against an earnest apology for how things had gone down in Denver.

"Vicky? I've been trying to reach you."

The voice at the other end caught her by surprise. She recognized it immediately. Father John O'Malley was the only man in these parts with that way of drawing out the first syllables of his words, as if he had a wad of cotton in his mouth. Straight out of Boston, she knew, although she had never been to Boston and had no intention of going. Denver was big enough, thank you, too big. And L.A. God, the thought made her stomach churn.

This was her place, the Wind River Reservation where she'd been born almost forty-two years ago. The biggest concession she'd made to city life had been to rent this brick bungalow at the edge of Lander, halfway between the open spaces of the reservation and her law office on Main Street.

"You okay?" There was no mistaking the anxiety in Father John's voice.

"What's going on?" Vicky had worked with the superior at St. Francis Mission on a number of cases ever since she'd returned to the reservation two years ago: bailing some Arapaho teenager out of jail, getting some Arapaho alcoholic into rehab, arranging for some grandparents or aunts and uncles to adopt some abandoned Arapaho kid. He was a good man, for a white man. He seemed to care about the people here. And he was intelligent, very intelligent. But he was a priest, and she suspected that everything he knew he had learned out of books. She was aware of an uneasiness crawling over her skin. John O'Malley didn't call her on Saturday afternoon with good news.

"You heard what happened?" he asked.

The uneasy feeling settled like chunks of granite in the pit of her stomach. "Tell me."

She could hear Father John draw in a deep breath on the other end of the line before he said, "Harvey Castle was murdered last night, Vicky. Someone stabbed him while he was sleeping in his tipi out at the powwow grounds."

Vicky sat bolt upright on the sofa. The gray carpet was dappled with yellow sunlight from the sliding doors that opened onto the patio out back. The whole living room seemed surreal, as if she had stumbled into a dream. The tribal chairman murdered!

"Who?" she managed. Questions jangled against one another in her mind. Who would do such a thing? Why? For what possible reason?

"Anthony's been arrested. The FBI agent, Jeff Miller, picked him up a little while ago. He and Banner took him to Lander."

"To the county jail!" Of course. That's where they took anybody arrested for murder. Vicky was on her feet now, carving out half circles in front of the sofa, moving in and out of the splotches of sunlight as far as the telephone cord would stretch. She felt slightly sick. Anthony was one of the most talented young people on the reservation. He was filled with possibilities, not just for himself but for Our People. Why was it that the most talented—the best and the brightest of the *Hinono eino*—self-destructed? Wrapped a pickup around the only tree in fifty miles. Drowned themselves in whiskey. Dropped out of school. Got mixed up in murder.

This couldn't be happening to Anthony, she thought. She had known him all his life, since the day he was born. He was almost the same age as her son, Lucas. But Anthony had a chance to make something of his life, and she knew how hard that was, how hard to catch and hold on to the slim, gossamer line that sometimes was tossed to you.

"Anthony didn't do it, I'm sure of it," Father John said. There was impatience in his voice, as if he were implying that somebody—Miller and Banner—had blundered onto the wrong track and were too pig-headed to do anything but continue down it. "Unfortunately Anthony and Harvey got into an argument last evening out at the powwow grounds."

Hearing Father John suck in another deep breath, Vicky sensed his reluctance to tell her more. She waited until he finally said, "They found what looks like the murder weapon, a hunting knife. Could be Anthony's."

So that was it. The murder weapon. A hunting knife that could be Anthony's. God, Anthony could be in deep shit. She felt as if a pit had opened and Anthony was falling into it. Trying to collect her thoughts, she was quiet a moment. He was no murderer, Father John was right about that. It was out of the question. He might fly off the handle, but he wasn't violent. She'd never known him to be violent. Harvey and Anthony . . . Harvey was like a father to Anthony.

There was little she wouldn't give for a cigarette right now, she thought, making another half circle in front of the sofa; but there wasn't one in her bag. Not one in the entire house, and there hadn't been for over a year. She glanced at the silver watch on her wrist—a gift from Larry. It was a few minutes before three. "I'll get over to the jail right away."

"I'll meet you there," Father John said.

Vicky set the receiver down firmly. She was standing in the dappled sunlight, but she felt cold.

She dropped down onto the sofa, trying to wrap her mind around the fact of the knife. The knife was a serious piece of evidence, like a wall of granite looming ahead. How could Anthony ever get around it?

∞ 7 ∞

VICKY WHEELED THE Bronco into the parking lot that butted up against the two-story, red-brick Fremont County jail and stopped in front of the doubleglass doors. She stepped out into waves of heat shooting up from the pavement like flames from a campfire. Sun gives himself for light and warmth, grandfather had told her when she was growing up. Well, sun was very generous today. But it always felt hotter in town than on the reservation. The asphalt and concrete and bricks captured the heat and stopped up the breeze.

The air conditioning in the waiting room sent a cold splash of air across her face and arms, causing her to shiver involuntarily. She had made a quick change out of the jeans and T-shirt she'd worn on the plane this afternoon into a dark skirt and pale silk blouse, complete with nylons and black pumps—an attorney uniform. She'd clipped her hair back with a barrette her grandmother had beaded for her years ago, and she wondered if she had remembered to touch up her lipstick. She was of the opinion she looked half dead without it.

The waiting room had all the personality of a meat locker,

with its floor swathed in white tile and walls washed in institutional green. There were two rows of molded blue plastic chairs backed against one another and bolted to the floor. At the ends of both rows, round platelike tables floated on narrow chrome tubes. Little puffs of smoke twirled out of an ashtray on one of the tables. She pursed her lips, trying not to breathe in the smoke, wanting to do just that.

At one end of the room was the glass-enclosed deputy's station. Vicky knew the two deputies, a man and a woman, their eyes glued on a couple of closed-circuit television monitors that scanned every inch of the jail, even the parking lot and the roof. Usually she'd stop and chat, get their views on whatever it was that was going on, but not this afternoon. She didn't want to hear any speculation that Anthony Castle might have murdered his uncle.

"Banner in the conference room?" Vicky called out as she walked past the station and down the hallway.

"You got it," a man's voice called after her. She held her fist in midair and took a deep breath before giving the conference room door a quick rap. Then she turned the knob and walked in.

Banner was standing in front of the window on the far side of the narrow room, a large, dark silhouette against the brightness outdoors. The new FBI agent was seated at the oak table that divided the room in half. He was writing in a small notebook that lay flat, a spiral spine of metal running between the lined, half-filled pages. He didn't look up.

Banner wheeled around as she shut the door, and she realized he had seen her drive up. The air conditioning hummed overhead.

"You know Jeff Miller, Vicky?"

"We've met," Vicky said, recalling a brief introduction

last week at the Lander Rotary club. It was as if she and the police chief were discussing someone who was not there.

"You here as Castle's attorney or friend?" Miller asked without looking up from his notebook.

Vicky pulled out a chair and sat across the table from him. Before she had decided whether to respond to this white man, Banner said, "Could be Anthony's gonna need both."

Miller laid his pen on the table and ran his hand carefully, almost caressingly, over the top of the opened notebook. Leaning back in his chair, he leveled his gaze at Vicky, as if expecting her to provide him with new material to consign to the pages.

"We got a murdered tribal chairman and a lot of evidence against one suspect," the FBI agent said. His voice was tinged with a Southwestern accent.

"What evidence?"

"Look, Vicky," Banner said, "I don't like this any better than you do. Anthony's a hell of a kid, but that temper of his just might've gotten him into real trouble this time."

"What evidence?" Vicky asked again. Any patience she had for the BIA chief was fading fast. Both Banner and this white FBI agent seemed to think they had everything figured out.

"Anthony and Harvey got into a hot argument last night out at the powwow grounds," Banner said.

"So?"

"So Anthony could've come back in the middle of the night and finished the argument." This from the agent.

"That's conjecture." Vicky kept her eyes on the white man across from her, his face red-blotched and creased from too much sun. She could see the sunburned scalp in the part of his hair.

"He took off when we went out to the ranch to pick him up for questioning," Miller said. "Ran out the back door like a coyote with its tail between its legs," the agent went on. This was the first Vicky had heard about Anthony running, and the fed seemed to sense this. He was enjoying himself. "Left us no choice but to arrest him on suspicion of murder."

"You had a warrant?"

"I imagine the magistrate's gonna oblige."

"On what grounds? Running out the back door?"

"Resisting arrest."

"You had informed Anthony he was under arrest?"

Banner gripped both sides of the table and leaned over the end. "No, Vicky. We just wanted to talk with him. We weren't fixing to arrest him." The chief shot a glance at the agent.

"So Anthony could hardly have been resisting arrest," Vicky said.

"Let's cut the crapola, counselor," Miller said. He placed his elbows on the table, made a tent over the notebook with his arms, and rested his chin on his knuckles. "Nobody runs unless he's got something to hide."

Vicky sensed the strength in the man, the determination. She forced herself to keep her eyes on his. "There is some explanation."

"How you gonna explain this?" Miller hoisted a large brown briefcase from the floor and set it on the table between them. Opening the lid, he pulled out a plastic zip-lock bag which he pushed toward her. A hunting knife lay inside. Leaning over, she could make out the initials AC on the silver band at the base of the handle.

"Behold the murder weapon," he said.

"Well, might be the murder weapon." Banner glanced again at the agent. "We won't know for sure 'til we get some lab tests done."

The entry compartment was the size of a small closet. Vicky felt wedged in between the BIA police chief she had known all her life and this white FBI agent who had suddenly appeared in these parts, like a strange prickly pear cactus. She could feel his breath on the back of her neck. They were standing still, but she had the sense of plunging downward in an elevator, of anticipating the inevitable hard stop.

How many times had she stepped into this compartment and waited for the electronic buzzer to swing open the door ahead and admit her to the inner sanctum of the Fremont County jail? On many of those occasions, John O'Malley had stood beside her, a tall presence looming over her, and she thought now what a calm and reassuring presence it was. She wished he were here now.

The buzzer rippled through the compartment like an electrical charge, and they filed through the opened door onto the gray concrete floor of the cell block. Directly across a narrow hallway stood another glass-enclosed station with three deputies watching other television screens.

One stood up, disappeared a moment, then reappeared outside the station. "This way," he said, leading them down the hallway between whitewashed cinderblock walls. He halted in front of a cream-colored metal door and slid a key into the lock. Pushing the door ajar, he said, "Knock when you're ready."

Anthony rushed toward them, and for a second Vicky feared he would make a break for the door. Instead he stopped abruptly, arms dangling at his sides, like a little kid who didn't know what to do next. She put both arms around him and hugged him. He was taller than Lucas and more muscular. It had been more than a year since she'd seen either Lucas or her daughter, Susan.

Swallowing back the tears, she said, "It's going to be okay, Anthony. Just tell Chief Banner and Agent Miller what you know."

"Have a seat," Miller said. Swinging the briefcase he had

brought from the conference room, he directed Anthony to the end of the oak table. The table covered most of the floor space in the narrow room. Miller and Banner settled in side by side while Vicky took a chair across from them. The agent plopped the briefcase onto the polished tabletop.

"I have the duty to remind you that you are a suspect in the murder of your uncle, Harvey Castle," the fed began.

"That's bull," Anthony said.

"Where were you last night after midnight?"

Anthony clasped his hands together and laid them on the table in front of him. Vicky saw the raw stubbornness and barely contained rage in the young man's eyes. It wouldn't have surprised her had he blurted out that it was none of their business.

"Just answer him," she said.

"I spent the night with a friend." Anthony's lips hardly moved.

Miller had pulled the little spiral notebook out of his inside jacket pocket and flattened it on top of the table. He was already busy filling in the first couple of lines on one page. "Name?" He didn't look up.

"I left the powwow about eight o'clock and didn't go back. So it doesn't matter who my friend is."

Miller glanced up sideways, locking eyes with the young Arapaho at the end of the table. "Not good enough. I need a name," he said. Anthony didn't flinch.

Vicky saw it all in a second's flash, as if a moving picture had fast-forwarded in front of her. Anthony had spent the night with a girlfriend, and the girlfriend was someone he wanted to protect. That meant she was from around here, and, more than likely, she was white. If Anthony didn't want to divulge her name, no power on the face of the earth was going to make him do so even if he had to sit out the rest of his life in Leavenworth for a murder he didn't commit. Vicky felt the muscles tightening in her throat.

"You've got your answer," she said to the agent. "My client has an alibi. He was with a friend at the time of his uncle's murder. Should you come up with any real evidence against him, backed up by scientific tests, which is doubtful in the extreme since he's innocent, we will supply the name."

She shifted in her chair toward Anthony and shot him a look meant to warn him against blurting out "the hell we will."

Miller bent over his notebook. "Refused to answer," he said, pen scratching the paper.

Banner leaned forward. "You and Harvey get into some kind of fight last night?"

"No fight. Argument."

"What kind of argument?"

"What kind?"

"Yeah. What was it about?" the chief persisted.

Anthony drew in a long breath, as if to pull in a string of thoughts. "About how, for no good reason, he changed his mind about buying the Cooley ranch, about how some oil company will probably buy the ranch now, and Arapahos will never get back what used to be ours. That's what it was about."

"You expect us to swallow some bull story that you and your uncle got into a violent argument over some land deal?" Miller had stopped writing, but kept his pen poised over the next empty line.

"That's your characterization," Vicky said, laying her forearms on the table. She felt more relaxed, more in control now that she knew Anthony had an alibi. "There's no evidence the argument was violent."

"You want violent arguments? Why don't you talk to

Ernest Oldman?" Anthony's words came like a blast from a shotgun.

"What are you talking about?" Banner asked.

Anthony shrugged. "Ernest got into a lot of arguments with Harvey this summer. They were all violent. Last week he came out to the ranch drunker'n a skunk. Stood out at the gate and shouted his head off 'til Harvey went out. I went out, too, case Harvey needed help. You never know about drunks." He shot a glance at Vicky, took a deep breath, then went on. "He was shouting something about his per capita being cut way back and Harvey not taking care of it. Like it was Harvey's responsibility."

Vicky pushed back against the hard wooden slats in the chair. She'd heard that several wells on the reservation had stopped pumping this summer. Ernest wasn't the only Arapaho to wake up one morning and feel the effects of even a few oil pumps standing mute as dead trees. When the oil companies decided to shut wells down, there wasn't much the business council could do. That didn't mean somebody like Ernest, who depended on the $200 or $300 per capita payment coming to his family every month, wouldn't be furious at the chairman of the council.

"Ernest hates Harvey," Anthony went on. "He might've gotten drunk and decided to do something real stupid, stupider than usual. Why aren't you questioning him? Why isn't he in this . . ." Anthony clenched his jaws. "Why isn't he in jail?"

Banner drew in a long breath and turned sideways, looking straight at the FBI agent's profile. "He's right about Ernest feuding with Harvey. Goes back to when Ernest fell out with his grandfather, Will Standing Bear. Will was real disappointed Ernest couldn't get his act together, with all his drinking. So he started taking an interest in Harvey. Harvey was his Sun Dance grandson, you know." Banner looked as if he was about to launch into an explanation of how the elder had become Harvey's grandfather in the Sun Dance years ago and how that created a spiritual bond, which lasted a lifetime, but thought better of it. "Will helped Harvey get elected to the business council. Ernest's been jealous of Harvey ever since," he said.

Vicky had forgotten about the falling out between Will and Ernest. It had happened at least ten years ago, about the time she had left the reservation to go back to school. The elders had enormous influence on who got elected to the business council. If things had been different, it might have been Ernest sitting on the council instead of Harvey.

"Do you really think Ernest could have . . ." Vicky stopped. It was hard to imagine someone she'd grown up with as a murderer.

"We're asking the questions here, counselor." Miller didn't look up, and his pen hadn't slowed down.

"That's what I was gonna find out," Anthony said, ignoring the agent.

"So that's why you ran out the back door? So you could talk to Ernest?" Banner looked as if he had just slapped the last piece of the puzzle in place.

"I was afraid you'd jump to conclusions and think I murdered Harvey. You'd throw me in jail, then you could go home, pop a few beers and watch the Red Sox while Ernest roams around free as a deer. Just what's happened." Anthony's words were crisp with sarcasm.

As if he hadn't heard, Miller opened the briefcase and pulled out the zip-lock bag. He pushed the bag down the table toward Anthony. "This look like Ernest Oldman's knife?"

"That's my knife," Anthony said. "Harvey gave it to me on my fourteenth birthday. He had my initials engraved on it."

"The lab will confirm that this knife was used to kill Harvey Castle," Miller said confidently. He placed the bag back in the briefcase and snapped the lid shut.

"I haven't seen my hunting knife since July fourth," Anthony said.

"You lost it?" Banner asked, hope tracing his face.

"It was stolen up at Washakie reservoir."

"Stolen?"

"Yeah. It was in my tackle box in the back of Harvey's pickup. Harvey and I were fishing at the reservoir. When we got back to where we'd parked, it was gone."

"The pickup?" the chief asked. Miller was pushing his pen across the notebook, his expression unchanged.

"Just the knife out of the tackle box."

"What did you do?"

"What could I do? There was nobody around. I was mad as hell it got ripped off. It was just a knife anybody could get in any sporting goods store in Wyoming. Only thing that made it special was my initials, and the fact Harvey gave it to me. That's all."

"You saying whoever took your knife intended to kill Harvey and make it look like you did it?" Banner asked.

"Damn right that's what I'm saying. Whoever took that knife must've recognized Harvey's pickup, saw the tackle box in the back, decided to have a look, and hit the jackpot. This is a setup, man. I've been set up."

Father John came toward them as Vicky led Anthony out of the compartment into the hallway. She saw the grin spreading slowly across the priest's face, but there was worry in his eyes.

"All right," he said, clapping Anthony on the back and winking at Vicky. "How'd you work this miracle?"

"Let's get out of here," she said, hurrying down the

hallway and past the deputy's station without acknowledging the two figures hunched in front of the monitors. She wanted Anthony out of the building before anybody had second thoughts.

Outside on the asphalt lot, she fumbled in her leather bag and pulled out the key to the Bronco before facing the tall priest with the tan cowboy hat pulled low over his forehead and the band of sunburn across the bridge of his nose like a warrior's paint.

"They don't have squat," she said, explaining how she had telephoned the federal magistrate and talked him into releasing Anthony on a personal recognizance bond. Of course Miller had objected, but it was for the record only. There wasn't enough evidence to keep Anthony locked up. He wasn't supposed to leave the reservation. What was new about that? The government had been trying to keep Indians on reservations for the last hundred years.

"Good work," Father John said. He was smiling at her, and she felt the warm sense of being appreciated by a man, not just appraised.

Ignoring the young Indian next to her, she said, "Somebody's gone to a lot of trouble to put this on Anthony. Stole his knife while he was fishing at Washakie reservoir, used it to murder his uncle, then hid it out on the powwow grounds under some sagebrush to make it look as if he'd tried to hide it, knowing, of course, that it would be found."

"Not somebody. Ernest," Anthony said.

"Ernest Oldman?" Father John looked surprised.

Anthony nodded toward the red-brick building behind them. "I told them inside how Ernest hated Harvey. That bastard killed him."

"Hold on," Vicky said, placing one hand on the young man's arm. "Right now you're the one under suspicion. That's what we have to worry about. If you want me to help you, Anthony, you've got to tell me everything you know, starting with the name of the friend you spent the night with."

Anthony stepped back, shaking his head. "There's no way I'm going to involve her in this."

So it was a girlfriend he was protecting. Vicky had guessed right. And from the expression on Father John's face, she knew he had guessed what they were talking about.

"You are in some serious trouble, Anthony," she said, trying to control her irritation at his calm stubbornness. He was so like Lucas, except that Anthony still had a chance to make something of his life while Lucas . . . It had been a long time since she'd even seen her son. The *Hinono eino* needed the young people like Anthony. They couldn't afford to lose one of the brightest, not for stubbornness.

"Vicky's right," Father John said, placing one hand on the Arapaho's shoulder as if to nudge him toward revealing the name.

"No way," Anthony said, shaking his head. "She doesn't have anything to do with this."

"In that case, get yourself another lawyer." Stepping toward the Bronco, Vicky shot a look at Father John that said, "Talk some sense into him." She flung open the front door and slid inside, slamming the door hard. She felt the heat of anger in her face as she caught sight of the two men in the rearview mirror, one white, the other Indian, standing in the parking lot, looking after her as the Bronco squealed onto the street.

∞ 8 ∞

VICKY GUIDED THE Bronco down the broad main street of Lander. Flat-faced, two-story buildings stood side by side, like ponies tethered together in a corral. Late-afternoon shadows floated down the buildings and out onto the sidewalks past wooden boxes of wilting petunias. An array of pickups, all different colors and sizes, lined the curbs.

She could still feel the warmth of anger in her face. She gripped the steering wheel as she swung the Bronco onto Highway 789 and held it steady all the way to Hudson. Anthony would have to level with her, tell her everything. There was no other way. This wasn't just his life, his future, for Christ's sake. This affected the people. Everything Anthony might be able to do someday for the people could be lost at this moment, torpedoed into oblivion.

It should be like it was in the Old Time, Vicky thought. In stories of the Old Time that grandfather had told her while she was growing up, the best people always stepped forward to help the others. Took their places, ran to their responsibilities, became leaders; chiefs looked out for the people. Now the best, like Anthony, wanted to look out for themselves, and that made her angry. Angry at him and angry at herself, because she'd come to care so much about such things, and there was so little she could do.

Slowing past the family restaurants and stores on Hudson's main street, Vicky made a left turn onto Rendezvous Road. The blacktop cut diagonally across the reservation's southeastern corner, slicing through fields of sagebrush and wild grasses and running parallel to the Popo Agie River. The river had been named by the Crow people. It meant "Beginning of Water."

At Little Wind River Bottom Road, Vicky took another left, then a right onto a narrow dirt road. The magistrate had also said that Anthony was not to contact Ernest Oldman, which, by implication, extended to her as Anthony's lawyer. But she was no longer Anthony's lawyer. She had just fired herself.

She made a sharp left into a driveway, and the Bronco veered sideways, spitting up clouds of dust. "Oldman" was etched on the lopsided wooden sign hanging on a rail fence. Ernest still had part of his great-grandfather's name.

Arapaho names were funny business. Vicky was always explaining to white people why some Arapahos had Indian names, others didn't. Grandfather had often told the story. Names belong to individuals, like fingerprints, the whorl of ears, the sheen of hair. They symbolize the person's spirit. And names can only be given away to someone who has the same kind of spirit. It is a special gift, when someone gives you his or her own name.

But Mathias Cooley, the first government man at Wind River, didn't like Indian names. It was too hard to keep track of his charges when people in the same family had different names. While her great-grandfather was alive, the agent couldn't do anything about it. But as soon as Chief Black Night had died, Mathias Cooley set about bestowing proper

English family names on Arapahos. The name of Ernest's grandfather was shortened from Old-Man-Who-Carries-Spears to Oldman. Harvey Castle's grandfather, White Eagle, got the name of a medieval dwelling place. Other Arapaho families received names of famous people, which accounted for the Franklins, Washingtons, Lincolns, and Roosevelts on the reservation. One family became Chaucer. Mathias Cooley must have been laughing up his sleeve at that one.

She had loved her first name, the name grandfather had given her, *Bi'h'ih Be'i'no*. It meant Singing Deer. On the night she was born grandfather had told her, he had gone into the foothills to pray for the new human being soon to come into the world, and as he prayed he had heard the deer singing. Her mother called her Vicky because school was easier for Indian kids if they had names like white kids. When she came back to the reservation, after she had been away all those years—seven years for her BA and law degree and three years in the Denver law firm—the elders gave her a new name, *Hi sei ci nihi*. Woman Alone.

Vicky stopped the Bronco behind a battered white pickup with a cracked windshield. Ernest's one-story house, with green paint peeling off the sides, squatted in the middle of a patch of dirt strewn with old tires, beer cans, scraps of paper, and torn cardboard boxes. A white propane tank stood on short metal legs alongside another pickup, rusted out and sagging to one side. Next to it lay a yellow refrigerator, a rope tied around the middle. Vicky could see Jenny Oldman pulling laundry from the clothesline that angled off a back corner of the house. Jenny must have heard the Bronco, but she didn't turn around.

Vicky slammed the Bronco door and walked down the driveway. The house looked like most houses on the reservation, some bi-levels, others tri-levels. How the houses came to be was one of grandfather's favorite stories. The warriors had come home from places like Normandy and Okinawa and Iwo Jima and had found the people still living in tipis and shacks. So they went to Washington and asked the Bureau of Indian Affairs people, "What were we fighting for?" After the warriors asked that, Arapahos got houses like other Americans. Her generation was the first to be born in houses. Her mother had been born in a shack. Her father, like her grandfather, had been born in a tipi.

Jenny kept her back toward Vicky, dropping clothespins into a bucket at her feet, adding to the stack of laundry piled over one arm.

"Jenny? How are you?" Vicky asked, walking up slowly behind her.

"Why'd you come here?" Jenny reached up and pulled another towel off the line, her cotton dress straining across thin shoulders. A thick black braid hung partway down her back.

"How are the kids?"

The pile of laundry started to slip from Jenny's arm, and Vicky reached out to help steady it. It was then she saw the angry purple bruise that spread from Jenny's right eye across her cheekbone.

"Oh, my God," Vicky blurted. She felt a knot tightening in her throat as she instinctively put an arm around the other woman's shoulders and pulled her close. The pile of laundry between them smelled like fresh, sweet sage.

Jenny started to cry. "Don't look at me," she said, pulling back and shaking her head. "He don't mean it. He ain't like this normally. He loves me and the kids, you know he does. It's just that things've been so bad since that job on the highway ended and the wells stopped pumping, so he got to drinkin' again."

Vicky took the clean towels and diapers and little shirts from Jenny's arm and laid them in a basket near the concrete stoop at the back of the house. Two small brown faces with wide eyes peered shyly around the top step, then quickly pulled back. Lucas and Susan had been like that, small and vulnerable. She felt herself trembling. Trying to swallow the knot still in her throat, she walked back to Jenny who was standing over the bucket single-mindedly plunking in clothespins like a child at a game.

"When did it happen?" Vicky asked.

"It don't matter." The last clothespin hit the ground. Jenny leaned over, scooped it up, and laid it in the bucket.

"Yes, it does. It matters, Jenny." Vicky heard her voice rising.

Jenny straightened up and looked straight at her. The white of her eye was the color of a raw beet. "It was my fault. I should've just let him alone. Only I was so worried, not knowin' where he was last night, so I started at him when he come in this mornin'."

"You need to get away for a while," Vicky said, glancing at the small red bruises going to blue on Jenny's arms. "Get the kids, and I'll take you to the shelter." Vicky knew it was impossible for Jenny to get away herself. There was no telephone in the house. Only one of the pickups was in running condition, and Ernest probably kept the keys.

That's how it was for many of the women on the reservation. The shelters were in Ethete—the Circle of Respect for women, the Circle of Love for children—but the women were miles away out on ranches, surrounded by open spaces. The old feelings of helplessness and rage flooded over Vicky.

Jenny was shaking her head again. "Soon's he stops drinkin', he'll be fine again, and I just won't cross him." Picking up the bucket, she walked over to the stoop. "You don't understand," she said.

"Yes, I do." Vicky followed her. "You know that. Ben

used to get drunk and beat on me, too, like I was some kind of kettle drum. I was scared like you. But I knew it had to stop, so I made it stop."

"You got divorced, Vicky." Jenny pivoted around, then slumped against the stoop. "I'm not strong like you. And I'm not smart like you, either. You think I can go off and go to college and become a big lawyer? How'd I get by, just me and the kids?" She started crying.

Vicky was staring at the other woman, but all she could see was her own life flashing across her mind like a grainy black-and-gray film. *She lifted the two kids into the pickup, jammed the key in the ignition, prayed the engine would turn over, held her breath, and stomped on the gas pedal. She was flying, flying out of the driveway, down the road. She drove ten miles before she knew where she was going, and then she turned around, retraced her route three miles, and followed the road that led to the house where she had grown up. Mama piled pillows and blankets on the living room sofa for her and spread blankets on the linoleum floor, the cold linoleum floor, for the kids, all the time saying, "A wife belongs with her husband. You stay here 'til it blows over." And she saying, "It won't blow over, Mama. It's never going to blow over."*

Vicky forced herself back into the present. She wasn't the one in danger now. She wondered where Ernest had been last night, but she checked herself before asking. Better not give Ernest any other excuse to hit his wife. She would find out herself. "Ernest inside?" she asked.

"He ain't gonna want to see you." Jenny pulled a tissue from her pocket and began blowing her nose.

"He's going to see me anyway," Vicky said.

Vicky walked up the stairs of the concrete stoop, stepping over the black space where part of the middle stair had been, and rapped on the screen door. Then she opened it and walked through the small kitchen into the darkened living room. Ernest slouched in a recliner with gray stuffing poking out of the sides. A stash of empty beer bottles lay on the linoleum floor. The white light from the television flickered across his face.

Slowly lifting his eyes from the television, Ernest turned toward her as if he were having difficulty comprehending her presence. His face was drawn, his eyes bloodshot. Shocks of black hair stood up on the top of his head. His shirt was unbuttoned, exposing rolls of brown flesh around his stomach, and bare feet splayed out of his blue jeans onto the floor. Balancing a half-empty beer bottle on the armrest, he said, "Why'd you come out here?"

Vicky sensed Jenny and the kids behind her in the doorway between the kitchen and the living room. One of the kids was whimpering, and the sound mixed in with the drone of television voices.

"Harvey's dead, Ernest," Vicky said. "He was murdered last night at the powwow grounds."

Ernest frowned, his eyebrows coming together in a bushy black line across his face. He seemed to consider this while he took a drink from the bottle. Then he belched and dropped the bottle on the floor. It clinked against the others.

"Were you at the powwow last night?"

Ernest rose halfway from the recliner before sitting back hard. The recliner skidded a couple of inches across the linoleum sending the beer bottles rattling against one another. "You made yourself chief detective? You tryin' to find Harvey's killer? Try lookin' someplace else."

"Where were you last night?" Vicky persisted.

"Who says I wasn't right here?" A glimmer of under-standing crossed his eyes. "Bitch," he said, looking back toward the kitchen. He tried again to push himself out of the chair. Then he sank down at an angle, one shoulder wedged into the back, his left hip climbing the armrest. Out of the corner of her eye, Vicky saw Jenny shrink behind the kitchen door. She was holding the little girl. The boy, who looked about five, hung on to her skirt, his eyes wide and wary.

"You've hurt Jenny enough," Vicky said. She made her voice as cold and sharp as an icicle.

"It ain't your business. Get outta here." Waving one arm, Ernest squirmed in the chair until he was facing the television again.

"The FBI agent will want to know where you were last night."

Ernest swept one hand over the floor and fingered the neck of a bottle. Nudging it toward the recliner, he picked it up and drained it with a loud sucking noise, as if he wanted to swallow the glass itself. Tossing it on the floor, he shouted, "Jenny! Where the hell are ya? Get me some more beer!"

Jenny set the little girl on the floor in the doorway before disappearing again into the kitchen. The refrigerator door opened and shut. Stepping around the child, she came toward Ernest and held out a brown bottle. He grabbed it with one hand while taking a sharp swipe at her stomach with the other. She jumped back, missing the blow, and ran into the kitchen, scooping up the child as she went. The child started wailing, but the little boy was silent, peering around the edge of the door.

Vicky had felt herself flinch, as if to ward off the blow. She wanted to run, but she forced herself to stand still. "Stop it, Ernest!"

He started out of the chair toward her, eyes blazing, beer sloshing out of the bottle. It was offensive to give an order to any Arapaho, but Vicky held her ground. "Look at yourself," she said. "What are you doing to your family?"

Ernest swiveled toward the kitchen. The boy, one fist in his mouth, backed slowly out of sight. The baby girl was gulping out loud sobs, and Jenny was trying to soothe her. "I told ya—keep those kids out of here today!" he hollered at Jenny.

Then, to Vicky, "I don't need this shit. Nobody needs it. And we sure as hell don't need no fancy white lawyer lady snoopin' round, givin' orders. Get out."

"I am not white," Vicky said, drawing out the words, making them as precise as possible. "I am Arapaho like you."

Vicky slammed out the front door and walked quickly to the Bronco. Fighting back the rage, she rammed into reverse and backed into the hard-packed dirt yard, crunching beer cans under the wheels. Out of the corner of her eye, she saw Jenny running around the house, dragging the boy with one arm and juggling the little girl and a pile of laundry in the other. Both kids were crying.

Vicky leaned over, opened the passenger door, and pulled the front seat forward. Jenny dropped the baby and laundry on the back seat. Then she swung the little boy in next to the baby and climbed onto the front seat herself, slamming the door. The Bronco filled up with the sweet smell of sage and cotton and the sound of the kids' sobbing. "I gotta do it for the kids," she said.

"You've got to do it for yourself," said Vicky. She gunned the Bronco down the driveway and out onto the road. She had seen a side of Ernest she despised. Drunk, he could be capable of anything, even murder.

∞ 9 ∞

THE SUN DROPPED behind the Wind River Mountains, shooting orange and magenta flames across the western sky. Long yellow shadows fell over the plains as Father John and Father Brad walked through the field turned into a temporary parking lot. Ranch hands ran along the rows of Cadillacs and Lincolns, directing the stream of incoming cars into available slots. The sounds of country music and laughter drifted from the Cooley ranch house where a large crowd had already gathered on the front lawn.

This was one party Father John was not looking forward to. After this morning, after Harvey's murder — well, he was in no mood for a party, but he'd gotten back to St. Francis by late afternoon and found his assistant all ready to go. They didn't need to stay long, Father Brad had said, just long enough for him to meet the next governor of Wyoming and a few people from Lander and Riverton.

Father John had said he wasn't going. Then he had slumped into the leather chair in his study, pushed the stacks of paper and books on his desk to one side, propped his feet on the desk, and thought about it. There was nothing he could do for Harvey's family tonight. Cousins and other family members would be dropping by the ranch all evening, coming from all directions, traveling I-25 from Denver and Cheyenne and Billings. Plains Indians moving across the plains, just like in the Old Time. No, they didn't need him tonight. And the party would be a chance to talk to Ned Cooley, maybe find out why Harvey had changed his mind about buying the ranch. Jasper Owens, who leased most of the oil wells on the reservation, would undoubtedly be there, and maybe he could explain why some of the wells had run dry all of a sudden. Finally Father John had swung his feet off the desk. "Okay," he'd said half-heartedly. "I'll go with you."

The guests clustered in groups across the wide expanse of lawn that wrapped around the house. On the west side, green-and-white-striped canopies stretched over rows of tables draped in white cloths that billowed in the breeze. Paper lanterns, like giant red cherries, hung from the cottonwood trees around the yard. Greasy smells of pork wafted through the air. Somewhere on the ranch a whole pig was roasting in a hole dug into the earth and lined with charcoal and mesquite. Several young white men wandered through the crowd, dressed in white waistcoats, carrying trays of beer and soft drinks. They looked about Anthony's age, college boys picking up an extra summer job.

The Cooley ranch dated from 1879, five years before the Jesuits had come to St. Francis. The house was built of reddish-brown bricks two stories high with pale yellow shutters and a cupola on the peaked roof. A wide L-shaped porch clung to the front and west side. In the corner, a cowboy band was strumming guitars and singing, "Mammas, don't let your babies grow up to be cowboys."

Father John took off his cowboy hat. Sticking one fist in the crown, he began spinning it around. Everybody looked alike: women in frilly blouses and skirts that billowed at their ankles, with silver and turquoise Indian jewelry around their necks and wrists. Men had on blue jeans, western shirts, and cowboy boots, all a good deal fancier than the clean, stiff blue jeans, faded green-plaid shirt, and scuffed cowboy boots Father John was wearing.

"Must be some rule around here everybody has to dress western." Father Brad let out a low whistle, like steam from a kettle. He had worn tan slacks, short-sleeved red shirt with a button-down collar, and Top-Siders, which had surprised Father John. He was just getting used to seeing his new assistant either in clericals or jogging suits.

"Hell, anything goes." The raspy voice came from behind, and Father John turned to face Ned Cooley. He stood about six feet tall, trim and athletic-looking in a pale-gray western suit with matching shirt and a bolo tie of woven black leather. He had pushed a gray Stetson back on his head in the manner of men who have worn cowboy hats all their lives and are totally accustomed to them. He took a long sip from a bottle of Coors, then stretched out his hand. His grip was strong, his hand as fleshy as a baseball glove. The rancher's eyes were almost the same light shade of gray as his Stetson. The smell of beer hung like a cloud between them, and Father John felt a part of himself yearning toward it. He stepped back.

"Meet the new assistant at St. Francis Mission, Father Brad Jansen," he said to Ned.

"Mighty pleased." The rancher extended his hand to the younger priest. Then he motioned to one of the women in a small group in the center of the lawn. "Come on over here, Dorothy."

As the woman came toward them, Father John noticed others turning to stare. She was at that indeterminate age some women—wealthy women, he thought—had the capacity of reaching. Probably somewhere in her forties, she

was slender and striking in a white dress with a ruffled top
that slanted off one shoulder. A silver Navajo Squash
Blossom lay around her neck. Curly blond hair framed her
face, which had a stretched look like a drum. She was
smiling, and bright red lipstick outlined a row of perfect
white teeth. Tiny lines fanned out from the corner of her
eyes like wisps of straw.

"We had to throw the last pig roast in the history of the
Cooley ranch to get Father John here. He's still got that
Boston accent thick as clam chowder," Ned said, directing
his comments to Dorothy, making a point to ignore the
priests.

"Welcome, welcome." Dorothy linked an arm through
Father John's. "Shame on you for staying away so long."
She glanced up at him sideways, as if to say that it was all
right to flirt a little. They both knew nothing would come of
it.

"This beautiful lady here's my sister, Dorothy Bennett,"
Ned said to Father Brad.

"You must be Father Bart, the new priest at St. Francis
we've heard so much about." Still clinging to Father John's
arm, Dorothy redirected her attention to the young priest.

"Brad. Brad Jansen," he said, a look of discomfort
crossing his face. Father John was starting to regret having
decided to come, and he wondered if his assistant would
regret it, too.

"You hear about Arapahos buyin' my ranch?" Ned took a
step toward Father John.

"I didn't know it was settled."

"A done deal. Business council's gonna put their John
Henrys on it next week."

"Oh? Everybody's for it, then?"

Ned leveled his gaze at Father John. "Everybody's been
for it except Harvey Castle. Harvey would've come around,

though. Those Indians like to make every vote unanimous," he said with the confidence of a man used to getting his own way. Obviously Ned understood the Arapaho custom. The business council always voted unanimously after thrashing out differences in private. It was a way of putting up a united front against whites, and it dated from the Old Time.

"Poor Harvey," Dorothy said. "Murdered by his own nephew! We were stunned when we heard."

"Anthony didn't murder his uncle," said Father John, taking his eyes from Ned and glancing down at the woman with her arm still linked in his.

Just then Melissa Bennett walked over, appearing from nowhere. Her dark blond hair fell in curls to her shoulders. Sunburn accentuated the freckles on her nose and cheeks and the green in her eyes. She had on a yellow dress with a long full skirt that swayed as she moved.

"Melissa. Good to see you." Freeing his arm, Father John grasped the young woman's hand. Her fingers felt slim and cool next to his palm. When he had first come to St. Francis, Ned Cooley's niece had been a long-legged teenager, home for the summer from boarding school, unsure of herself and a little too pretty. Now she was a young woman, beautiful in a casual, outdoors way. She was at the University of Wyoming. He hardly ever ran into her on the reservation; whether that was because she never came to St. Francis or because she seldom came home, he didn't know. Home for her and Dorothy was the little house about a mile down the road from the main ranch house. It was far from little, as Father John knew from the two or three times in the last six years that he and one of his assistants at St. Francis had accepted Dorothy's invitations to dinner.

"About to graduate?"

"Getting close," she said, smiling.

Father John introduced Father Brad, and she shook his hand. "I've heard about you. You're the runner."

"Well, I try to stay in shape." The younger priest seemed pleased with Melissa's attention.

"We were talking about last night's tragedy on the reservation," Dorothy said to her daughter.

"Does anybody know what really happened?" Melissa asked.

"Everybody knows Harvey Castle's nephew killed him. Except Father John here." Looking steadily at Father John, Ned asked, "Who do you think did it?"

Father John shook his head. "If I knew, the murderer wouldn't be walking around free."

Ned wheeled about and faced his niece. "Where's that young man of yours? Lots of pretty women here could be fixin' to run off with him."

Melissa exhaled a long breath. "If you mean Arthur, he's over there," she said, tossing her head toward the house. "He's not my young man."

"Well, he oughtta be." Looking back at Father John, Ned said, "Arthur Schwartz's family runs the biggest herd of Hereford in Wyoming on a ranch outside Thermopolis. With the Cooley ranch going to the Arapahos, it's only natural this little filly here should have another place to run on."

"Ned, you're incorrigible." Dorothy laughed. "Let's not be in a hurry to marry off Melissa."

"The way this conversation's going, I think I'll move along," Melissa said. The smile she flashed Father John as she walked away was warm and friendly, yet there was something uneasy about it, something sad. It surprised him.

"Have you heard the rest of our news?" Dorothy asked. "The polls say Ned is going to be the next governor. The other two candidates aren't even close. And the governor himself is coming tonight to endorse Ned. Isn't that exciting?" She beamed as she looked from her brother to the priests, and Father John noticed his assistant beaming back.

"About time a Cooley got to Cheyenne," Ned said. "Hell, we've been running Fremont County long enough. I spent twenty years as county commissioner here. Dad had the job for thirty." He took a step backward, folding his arms across his chest. "All the party bigwigs in the region support me. I was down in Denver this weekend meeting with some mighty important people. Gettin' my ducks in a row, you might say. Caught the flight back this afternoon just in time for the party here."

"It's hard to believe you're letting the ranch go," said Father John. "The Cooleys have been here even longer than the Jesuits."

"Hundred and fourteen years, to be exact. But running for governor is taking all my time. Hell, I've only gotten in a couple fishing trips so far this summer. Gonna take all my money, too, more'n likely." Ned threw his head back and laughed. "So I decided it's time to sell out. Those Indians are getting a hell of a deal. A hundred thousand acres and three oil wells for five million. And no tellin' how many oil wells might be sunk in the future. All you gotta do is poke a stick in the ground to get a gusher. Trouble is, oil business is kaput in this country for the time being. Indians can wait. I don't have the time. I mean to get on with my political career."

"Ned's also throwing the Cooley collection into the deal." Dorothy turned to Father Brad. "It's the best collection of Indian artifacts in the area."

The young priest looked more interested. "Where is it?"

"Turned the first floor into a museum just to show it off." Ned's head and shoulders pivoted toward the ranch house, and the cowboy band strumming a slow ballad seemed to grab his attention. "What the hell you boys playing now?"

he shouted. "Play something cheerful. This ain't a wake."
There was a burst of laughter from people milling about the
lawn.

"Come on," Ned said, looking pleased with himself. "I'm
gonna introduce Bart here to some important people. John
Frisco's over there, mayor of Lander. And that's Riverton's
finest, Mayor Paul Coulson, next to him. Jasper Owens is
around someplace."

"I think I already know most of those people," Father
John said as Ned began steering Father Brad toward the
center of the lawn.

One of the waiters happened by, and Father John helped
himself to a Coke from the tray the young man carried.
Sipping the Coke, glad to quench his thirst, he made his way
through the crowd to the long buffet table on the west side
of the house.

Darkness had begun to settle in, turning the sky a deep
lavender. The yellow light of candlelarias flickered on the
white-clothed tables, while circles of orange lights from the
cherry lanterns streamed across the lawn. Guests moved in
and out of the light and shadows.

"Hi, Father," another waiter said as Father John approached the buffet table. "You don't know me. I'm Tyler
Grant." The young man had been arranging fruit on a
platter. The table was laden with food. At the far end, the
roasted pig sprawled on a large silver platter, a red candied
apple in its mouth. Other platters and bowls were piled high
with corn on the cob, potato salad, steaming pots of baked
beans, bowls of grapes, strawberries and sliced cantaloupe,
and baskets of rolls.

"Is everything gonna be okay for Anthony?" the young
man asked.

"I hope so," Father John said.

"Anthony's in deep shit, ain't he?" Tyler's blue eyes

flashed with anger. He slapped his hand onto the table, and the platter of fruit jumped on the white cloth. "I go to the university with Anthony. He's a real good guy. There's no way he could've murdered his uncle with that knife. It got stolen about a month ago. And besides Anthony's no murderer."

The moccasin telegraph had been busy. It had even carried the latest news to this young white man. It always amazed Father John how quickly news traveled across the reservation, especially since only half the homes had telephones.

He decided to see what else Tyler might know. "Did you hear about the argument Anthony got into with his uncle at the powwow grounds? Strange, don't you think? I've never seen Arapaho families argue in public. Wonder why they didn't talk about the Cooley ranch deal at home?" He hoped he'd given the young man an opening.

"Cooley ranch deal?" A look of surprise stole across Tyler's face, even though he was making an obvious effort to keep himself unreadable. This young white man was definitely on Anthony's side.

"You know Ned Cooley's put this ranch up for sale," Father John said, gesturing toward the space around them. "That's what I heard the argument was about." Father John sensed that Tyler had heard otherwise, and he waited again for him to pick up the lead.

Instead Tyler said, "Anthony told you that?"

Father John shrugged. It didn't matter where the information came from.

"That must've been it, then," the young man said.

At that moment one of the musicians clanged a cowbell on the porch steps. Small groups began moving in the direction of the buffet table, then the entire crowd started rolling toward it, like tumbleweeds across the plains. "Nice to talk to ya, Father," Tyler called as he started toward the house, a sense of relief about him.

"John, jump in here." Father Brad was at the far end of the table waving a large paper plate. Other guests motioned Father John forward. Picking up a plate from a side table, he joined his assistant.

"Never expected to see a party like this out here in the middle of Wyoming." Father Brad grinned as he speared chunks of pork onto his plate. Father John followed his assistant down the table, absentmindedly helping himself to a small slice of meat, some potato salad, an ear of corn, and a bunch of red grapes. He was thinking about what Tyler hadn't said. The young man didn't believe Anthony and Harvey had argued over the ranch, and neither did he.

Father John slipped a brownie onto the edge of his plate between the slice of pork and the potato salad. He never got used to the way Westerners piled food together, but the brownie looked too good to pass up.

His mind was wandering down the relentless path of logic, and gradually the conclusion came into view. Last night had been a shouting match between Anthony and Harvey. Loud and emotional. Over what? Land? Father John had never completely bought that. What then? A girl? The same girl Anthony had spent the night with? The girl he didn't want involved? It was beginning to make sense. Anthony's cock-and-bull story about arguing with Harvey over land and his refusal to name his alibi were related.

But that raised other questions. Why had they argued over the girl? Was it because Harvey hadn't approved of her? Who was she? Why didn't she come forward and confirm Anthony's alibi? Still lost in his thoughts, Father John almost ran into the host.

"Got a place for you jebbies over here where the beer's nice and cold," Ned said, leading the way to a round table directly below the front porch. The musicians were strumming another Willie Nelson tune, and guitars wailed in the warm evening air. Open bottles of beer surrounded the candlelaria on the table. Father Brad was already seated between Dorothy and Melissa. Mayor Frisco, a beefy, red-faced man, made a show of seating his daughter and his wife before claiming the chair between them.

"Father O'Malley from the reservation, right?" Jasper Owens sat down next to Father John and stuck out his hand. He was barrel-chested with a fringe of black hair that wrapped horseshoe-like around a bald head. The candlelaria cast yellow stripes of light across his face. His smile revealed a mouthful of teeth as white and straight as tombstones. A young man, dark-haired and muscular, took the chair next to Melissa, and Jasper introduced him as his assistant, Luke. Luke gave a little half nod around the table.

Father John's path seldom crossed that of Jasper Owens. He knew the oilman mostly by reputation. Jasper Owens's oil company was headquartered in Pennsylvania, a family firm, and he'd been sent west to look out for the family's interests. A couple of years ago, he'd made a bid for Wyoming's sole seat in the U.S. Congress where, had he been successful, Father John was sure, Jasper Owens would have continued looking out for his family's interests. He was not someone Father John would have picked for a dinner companion, but neither was Ned Cooley, and here he was stuck between them. He tried to shrug off the growing wish to be back in his study at the mission. This was still an opportunity to get some insight into why Harvey had decided against buying the Cooley ranch and why, all of a sudden, some oil wells on the reservation had gone dry.

The conversation focused on Harvey's murder. Who found the body? What happened then? When was Anthony arrested? Father John ate silently while his assistant filled in the details. He even launched his hit-man theory, and Father John waited to see how he would handle the part about Harvey being killed over oil, with the oilman at the table. Father Brad finessed it brilliantly, calling the motive for the contract "Harvey's political decisions."

Jasper finally turned the conversation to the Cooley ranch. "This good man here's about to give this place away," the oilman said, pointing a fork at Ned. "Those Indians are gettin' the chance of a lifetime. I hope they're grateful."

As if the conversation had nothing to do with him, Ned tipped his chair back and motioned to one of the waiters. "Get me another chunk of pork," he ordered. "This here's tough as cowhide."

"I would think your company would want a ranch with oil wells on it," Father John said.

"We're in the oil business, not real estate," Jasper said, shoveling a fork full of potato salad into his mouth. He swallowed and went on. "What would we want with this enormous ranch? We're interested in pumping oil, that's it."

"I've heard there's more profit in owning wells than in leasing them. No royalties to pay out," Father John persisted. He remembered Anthony's concern that an oil company would buy the ranch and put an end to any possibility of Arapahos ever getting it.

Jasper laid his fork down and turned toward Father John. "More profit, more trouble," he said. "Best deal is to own the mineral rights. Of course, that's sometimes hard to get, especially around here. Oil companies can only lease wells on the reservation. Those Indians aren't selling any rights. And Ned here's makin' a package deal. Ranch and mineral rights together. Hell of a deal for those Indians, I say."

"Some wells on the reservation have been closed down, I hear," Father John went on, pushing the opportunity to find out as much as he could while the conversation was on oil wells.

The oilman was quiet a moment, as if arranging the words in his head before speaking. "Some wells just stop paying out. It happens. That's the oil game."

Jasper strung out the word "game" like a string of tobacco juice, and Father John felt a wave of disgust come over him. He fought the urge to push away from the table and head for the Toyota. This game determined whether some Arapaho families would have food this winter, or natural gas for heat, or coats for their kids. It wasn't a game to them.

Just then a light-gray sedan pulled into the driveway, followed by two state patrol cars and a truck with Channel 5 emblazoned on the side panels.

"The governor," Ned said, jumping out of his chair. He strode across the lawn toward the sedan.

The murmuring and laughter of the crowd died down as Ned ushered the governor past the tables and onto the porch. Two television cameramen stationed themselves below, right next to Father John, their cameras trained on the governor. Short and wiry in a dark, western-cut suit, he pumped Ned's hand up and down, grinning toward the cameras. The music ended in a loud crescendo.

Ned pulled the microphone over from the band. "Ladies and gents. We have with us here no other than the honorable governor of Wyoming. Let's give him a big welcome." The crowd stood up, clapping as Ned telescoped the microphone and pushed it toward the governor. Everyone sat down.

The governor gave a short speech about how happy he was to be at the annual Cooley pig roast. He spoke a few words about the great state of Wyoming, probably the same thing he said every place he went, before he got to the point. "You folks in central Wyoming have among you the best man to lead our state in the coming years," he said.

The guests were on their feet again, shouting and clapping, and the governor held up both hands to quiet them. "I'm going to do everything in my power to see that Ned Cooley is elected the next governor of our great state." The crowd whooped and hollered like cowboys at a rodeo.

Ned reached over and pulled the stem of the microphone back up to his level. Surveying his still-standing guests, he waited for the noise to die down. "As you all know," he began slowly. "Cooleys were the first people to come to these parts more than a hundred years ago. We settled this whole county. When my great-granddaddy Mathias Cooley brought his little wife across the plains and lit on this place, there wasn't anything here but buffalos and Indians."

Ned paused and waited for the laughter to die down.

"Ever since then, Cooleys have worked hard to make Fremont County a decent place for decent people. Now it's time to take all that Cooley experience to the statehouse. Friends, with your help, I aim to be the next governor of Wyoming."

In the midst of the cheers and clapping that erupted around them, Father John caught Melissa's eye. He'd been right earlier. There was sadness there.

∞ 10 ∞

FATHER JOHN OPENED the heavy, carved door and took a few steps into the front hall. His boots clumped on the hardwood floor. Father Brad followed. "I'll be darned if it isn't a museum," the young priest said, whistling between his teeth. Muffled voices and a slurry of footsteps came from the rooms that opened off both sides of the long hallway. A stairway ahead led to the upper level.

"Make yourselves at home." Ned appeared in a doorway, waving the two priests into what had been the front parlor. "Everything is authentic Plains Indian stuff, I guarantee. My great-granddaddy started this collection. He was always willing to help out those Indians by givin' 'em a few dollars for their trinkets. Family's kept up the tradition ever since."

Father John took in the room at a glance. Several guests were milling about. Large Plexiglas cases filled with Indian artifacts lined the walls. Heirlooms worth who-knew-how-much gotten from poor people for a few dollars. Well, at least the Cooleys had taken care of them. And now it looked as if they would go back to the Arapahos where they belonged, if the ranch deal went through. That was about the only good thing he could think about the Cooley collection.

Father John strolled around the room, waiting for other guests to finish examining the items in each case before he began. There were "possible bags," all-purpose storage bags the size of a woman's large purse, woven of horsehair and embroidered with delicate glass beads in traditional geometric patterns: stripes for the roads of life; triangles symbolizing tipis and home; circles for the camp and the people. The designs came in dreams to those who created them, and they served as ongoing prayers for the health and well-being of whoever used the bags. Ned was pointing to one of the cases. "These here are parfleches used for carrying belongings," he told Father Brad. The rawhide bags were large and beautiful, with geometric figures painted in the soft reds, blues, and greens distilled from clay, wild berries, and leaves. Next to one of the parfleches was a saddlebag, horseshoe-shaped rawhide that fit over the rump of a horse. It too was painted in intricate patterns and decorated in horsehair tassels.

Father John wandered through the large double doorway into the next room, with Ned and Brad following. Here several other guests bent over cases that held bows and arrows, spears and hatchets, plus rifles and knives Arapahos had gotten in trade with white men. One case displayed breastplates made of polished bones and rawhide shields that optimistic warriors in the Old Time had believed would deflect arrows and bullets.

"Best things are this way," Ned announced, striding across the hallway to another room. Father Brad and several other guests walked with him. After a while, Father John wandered over. Dorothy was there, pointing out something to a small group. The cases were filled with clothing: vests, gloves, moccasins, and leggings, all swathed in glass beads. White deer-skin dresses were pinned on the walls like giant butterflies.

"Imagine doing all that fine beadwork by campfire with chips of buffalo bone for needles." Dorothy glided across the room toward Father John, her skirt swaying. "Beading was almost a lost art, but I'm proud to say I've helped to reintroduce these crafts to Arapaho women. Beadwork groups meet every week at the Blue Sky Hall where I volunteer. I've gotten older women to come in and teach the younger ones."

Father John said nothing. He had often seen Maria and the other grandmothers in the meeting hall at St. Francis, fingers flying over their beadwork while younger women sat beside them, doing what they did. "Arapahos like to make the things we need in beautiful ways," Maria had once told him.

The other guests had already moved into the front room, and Father Brad poked his head through the doorway. "Ned's absolutely right," he called. "The best is in here."

Father John strolled through the doorway. All the cases displayed dance regalia: beaded aprons, bustles of eagle feathers, feathered headdresses. He stepped over to the narrow Plexiglas case at the far end of the room. Inside was a warbonnet, folded in half and pressed against the wall. Eagle feathers curved gracefully toward the floor.

"My pride and joy," Ned said, coming up behind Father John, boots clacking against the wood floor. "It belonged to old Chief Black Night. He let my great-granddaddy have it. Shows how grateful he was to granddaddy for all he did for the Indians."

Father John was thinking how each feather stood for a courageous or unselfish deed the chief had performed. Strange that he had given the headdress to a white man. After a moment he said, "It used to be on a stand in the center of the room."

"Had to put it behind glass so's it wouldn't dry out," Ned said.

The headdress was impressive, Father John thought, even flattened behind glass.

The Toyota's headlights bounced through the darkness ahead as Father John drove along Rendezvous Road back to St. Francis Mission. His assistant hadn't stopped talking about the party since they'd left. Father John nodded and uttered an occasional "uh huh," but he wasn't listening. Too many questions lodged in his mind, like little bones he could neither swallow nor spit out.

One thing seemed certain. Harvey had wanted to talk to him about the girl Anthony was seeing, the girl Anthony had spent the night with, the girl he was protecting. Father John had a pretty good idea who she was and why Harvey had sounded so worried when he'd called. Not that Father John could have been of any help. There was no stopping romance, once it started racing down the track.

Still, the Cooley ranch deal was hard to figure out. Nothing about it made sense. Why wouldn't Ned sell the mineral rights to some oil company? Jasper would be interested, that seemed certain. And Ned could still sell the land to the Arapahos, for a smaller price, of course. But a smaller price might make it easier for them to buy. Yet Ned seemed intent on keeping the two together—land and mineral rights—and offering the Arapahos a hell of a deal, as Jasper put it. Maybe that's what bothered him—all that generosity and altruism on the part of Ned Cooley. Even throwing in a collection for which any museum would pay a small fortune.

Well, maybe he was misjudging the man. It wouldn't be the first time he'd made that mistake—he'd never won any prizes in understanding why people did what they did. He had a hard enough time understanding himself. Maybe Ned had been pricked by conscience now that he was likely to become the governor of Wyoming and genuinely wanted to see the ranch and the artifacts go back to their original owners. But if that was so, why had Harvey opposed the deal? Even more puzzling, why had he changed his mind, jumped from one side to the other?

Father John pushed down on the accelerator, and the Toyota shot up a gradual incline, its headlights bathing the blacktop ahead. Father Brad's voice droned on, but Father John wasn't following, a fact the young priest didn't seem to notice.

What was it Rita had said? Harvey had changed his mind after talking to Will Standing Bear. And Charlie Taylor always went along with Harvey. Did that mean Charlie had also changed his mind? Father John decided to have a talk with the tribal councilman and the elder as soon as possible.

∾ 11 ∾

THE LAST PICKUP skidded around Circle Drive and out onto Seventeen-Mile Road as Father John turned back into St. Francis Church. Ten o'clock Mass had been packed. Even the vestibule was jammed. There were faces he'd seen only occasionally at Mass, and some faces he'd never seen, all drawn by the shock of Harvey's murder. The close, musty smell of the crowd lingered in the air.

Father John made his way down the side aisle, forcing the vent windows open as far as they would go. The warm breeze washed over him. He was comfortable in this church, a chapel really, built by Arapahos a hundred years ago. Above the entrance were the painted symbols of the Trinity: a thunderbird for God the Creator, a tipi, sacred pipe, and eagle feather for the Holy Spirit, and the figure of a warrior for the Risen Christ. Around the whitewashed stucco walls marched stick-figure drawings of the Stations of the Cross. And circles everywhere for all the natural things in the world that are round—Mother Earth, sun, moon. Chains of circles were linked together to symbolize that all living creatures are related.

A variety of geometric symbols covered the vaulted

ceiling: red lines for human beings; long blue lines for the roads humans must travel; yellow lines for the heavens; blue and yellow triangles for the morning star that connects heaven and earth. The floor was paved in light blue carpet, the color of the sky.

He crossed to the other side and pushed open those vents, drawing in a good cross breeze. Then he made his way down the center aisle checking for anything left in the pews. The kettle drum altar stood at the far end of the church. The people had insisted on the kettle drum. "Prayers will rise to the heavens, just like drumbeats," Will Standing Bear had told him. On the table to the left sat the tabernacle, a miniature white tipi the grandmothers had shaped out of soft deerskin. The arched ceiling over the sanctuary was trimmed with a yellow band that marked the space below as sacred.

Father John knelt down in the front pew and bent his head over his hands. He had offered Mass this morning for Harvey's soul, and now he prayed again, silently, for his friend and for Harvey's family. For a moment he felt at one with the peace at the center of himself, that place where the most important part of him lived, where he was a priest, a servant of the servants of God.

Exhaling a deep breath, Father John raised himself off his knees and walked over to the sacristy, the little room next to the altar. Then he removed his green chasuble and white mantle and hung them in the closet next to a row of vestments, different colors for the different Sundays of the church year. After checking to see that the altar boys had placed the missalology and sacramentary in the cabinet, he walked back through the church and out the front door.

The buildings of St. Francis formed a circle, like an Arapaho camp, like all sacred things. The front door of the white stucco church faced the mountains, but its altar faced east and the rising sun. Outside walls were also stenciled in the geometric symbols that reached back into the oldest of times.

To the south stood the mission's first building, the school. The two-story gray stone structure hadn't been used in thirty years. It stood empty and boarded up, but every time Father John suggested demolishing it, the old people raised an outcry. They had learned to read and write there. Their young breath still clung to the walls. Young voices echoed in the hallways. So the building remained, abandoned, sagging on its foundation. He tried his best to replace the broken windows and keep the doors on their hinges. If the truth were known, he had become as attached to the old building as the Arapahos were.

The administration offices, a white brick building, stood on the northern curve. His office was there, and Father Brad's.

Next to the building was the asphalt court where Arapaho kids played basketball. Behind it sat several squat white buildings for adult classes and meetings. On the western curve, next to the two-story red-brick house where the priests lived, stretched the open field where, six summers ago, Father John had marked off the pitcher's mound, home plate, first, second, and third bases. Then he had started the St. Francis Eagles. The Indian kids needed a baseball team to play on, he'd reasoned, but the truth was he needed a baseball team to coach. Beyond the field was the new St. Francis School, a one-story building with an entry that jutted forward. It was shaped like a tipi.

Cottonwoods, Russian olives, and evergreens cast long, cool shadows across the buildings and grounds, turning the mission into an oasis on the plains. Father John relished the quiet, and the soft sound of the wind rustling the leaves. A short distance to the southeast, on the banks of the Little Wind River, Chief Black Night and his people had camped when they first came to Wind River Reservation. It was Chief Black Night who had given the Jesuits enough land for a mission. "We would be glad of some good man to teach our people about the Great Spirit," he had said, according to one of the documents in the mission archives. *HeeniNouhu'*, Arapahos called the priests. It meant "long garments."

The sun crested overhead, and white fluffy clouds floated across the sky like cotton blowing off some giant cottonwood tree. On the western horizon, the Wind River Mountains shimmered in the iridescent yellow light. The breeze was steady, bending the wild grasses alongside Circle Drive. It never stopped blowing on Wind River Reservation, it seemed. He was used to it now.

Maybe he could catch thirty minutes of the Red Sox game. Television wasn't Fenway Park, but it was better than nothing. He intended to drop by Harvey's ranch later, have a few words with Anthony. With a little luck, he'd discover that the young man had calmed down and come to his senses by now. He had to learn to trust the people trying to help him, like Vicky. There was always hope.

Father John didn't recognize the white Miata in front of the house, but tourists often dropped by St. Francis. It was a historic site at the eastern edge of Wind River Reservation, a jumping-off point for a drive through Indian country. He'd get rid of whoever it was as quickly as possible. He wasn't in the mood for tourists today.

"Somebody's waitin' in the study," Elena said as he came up the front steps to the small porch. A sudden gust took the screen door and slapped it against the brick siding. The housekeeper followed the door out, propping herself against it. Somewhere in her sixties—even she wasn't sure of her age—Elena was part Arapaho, part Cheyenne, short and stocky with a smooth, round face and wavy gray hair cropped close to her head. She had on a pink housedress cinched around the middle with a white apron, its pockets bulging. The shoelaces from her black oxfords trailed onto the porch.

Elena had been the housekeeper at St. Francis for twenty-five years, outlasting numerous Jesuits in that time. She ran the house on her own schedule: breakfast at 7, lunch at noon, dinner at 6. There were days for cleaning, shopping, laundry. Father John did his best to stay in step, but it wasn't easy, not the way things popped up unexpectedly on the reservation.

"Father Brad know someone's here?" he asked, stepping into the front hallway. It was at least ten degrees cooler inside.

"Hmmmph. He's out runnin' round in blue shorts like some crazy man. He ain't got the sense God gave rattle-snakes. Least they know to stay out of the midday sun."

Elena laid a hand on his arm, as if to steer him toward the kitchen. "You come and eat your lunch first. You ain't had nothin' to eat this morning. She can wait."

"I better see what she wants. It'll only take a minute," he said, nodding toward the closed door of the study.

"Well, that's just fine." Elena padded past him and down the hallway, shoelaces flapping against the linoleum floor. "Poor Harvey's dead, that young priest's out runnin' himself to death, and now you're starvin' yourself to death. Lord only knows what's goin' on around here."

Melissa Bennett turned swiftly as Father John came into the study. She was standing in front of the wide window that framed a stretch of the Wind River Mountains. Sunlight shone through her blond hair, lacing the strands into intricate webs. She had on a light-blue T-shirt and white jeans that were so tight he wondered how she could breathe. He wasn't surprised to see her. He realized that at some level he had been expecting her.

The young woman bolted across the room. "Mind if I close the door?" she asked. Before she slammed it, he caught a glimpse of Elena running a dust cloth over the table in the hallway. She never dusted on Sundays.

"I've got to talk to you in private." Melissa leaned against the door, as if to make sure it stayed closed.

"Have a seat." He motioned her to the blue wing chair beside the desk.

"No, thanks." She started pacing the room. "I can't sit down. I can't eat. I can't think." She stopped and looked up at the ceiling a moment, then leveled her gaze at Father John. "Anthony was with me Friday night."

"I think I'll sit down, Melissa, even if you don't," Father John said, easing himself downward into the worn leather chair behind the desk. He was wondering where, within a hundred miles, this young white woman and an Arapaho man could spend the night together. Not on the reservation and not at some motel in Riverton or Lander. Not if they wanted to keep the romance a secret.

Melissa started pacing again and, as if reading his thoughts, said, "We stayed at the old cabin out on the ranch. Uncle Ned keeps it just like it was in his great-granddaddy Mathias's day. You know how Uncle Ned is about old things. It's full of all the original stuff—dishes, table, chair, the bed." Melissa cleared her throat, then hurried on. "The ranch hands use it sometimes when they're out calving. Anthony and I have been using it since last summer. Nobody knows, of course." She was carving out a circle around the wing chair. "I'm sorry if that shocks you," she said.

"Believe me, I'm not shocked," Father John said. After pushing aside the piles of paper on the desk to form a clear space, he clasped his hands on the brown blotter in front of him and waited for her to go on.

"Anthony and I love each other," she said. "We're going to be married. We had intended to tell our families this weekend." Finally, Melissa lighted on the arm of the wing chair. "Anthony told his uncle first. That's when everything fell apart. Harvey went ballistic. He said to forget it. There was no way his nephew was going to marry into the Cooley family." Melissa looked steadily at Father John. "He didn't even know me."

"Don't take it personally, Melissa."

"Don't take it personally? How am I supposed to take it? My uncle was the one supposed to say that no niece of his was going to marry an Indian. I was ready for that, but not for what Anthony's uncle said. They got into a big fight about it. First at the ranch. Then at the powwow."

"Did you tell your mother?"

Melissa shrugged. "Mom's just like Uncle Ned. Sure, she volunteers at the Blue Sky Hall. But she's a Cooley, and the Cooleys are like feudal lords. She's not going to be thrilled about her daughter marrying one of the serfs. Anyway, I never told her. I mean, if Harvey reacted the way he did, what would Mom and Uncle Ned do? What we decided was—well, we decided we'd just get married in Laramie and then tell everybody. They could accept it or not. It would be up to them." Melissa popped off the arm of the chair and, combing her fingers through her hair, started circling again.

Father John waited. Years of counseling had taught him that people needed time to sort their thoughts. Silence did not have to be filled with words.

"Yesterday, soon as I heard Harvey had been murdered, all I could think of was that Anthony had fought with him. Then I heard Anthony had been arrested. I was so scared. I jumped in my car and was halfway to Fort Washakie before I realized the minute I walk into Chief Banner's office, everybody's gonna know about Anthony and me. Then everybody's gonna think Anthony killed his uncle because he didn't want us to get married."

Father John pushed back on the leather chair, lifting the front legs off the carpet. "So you'd be handing Banner a motive for Anthony to kill his uncle."

"That's what scares me," Melissa said.

She walked over to the window and stood with her back to him, almost talking to herself. "I don't know what to do. Anthony will never tell anybody he was with me. He won't want me involved." Glancing back at Father John, she said, "He's the most stubborn Indian I ever met."

Father John smiled. "You got that right."

Melissa came back across the room. This time she flopped down onto the cushion of the wing chair. "It's so unfair," she said, shaking her head. "I mean, if Harvey hadn't blown up like that, there never would have been a fight, and Anthony wouldn't be a suspect."

Father John let his chair drop back on all four legs and leaned his elbows onto the desk. Obviously Melissa hadn't heard about Anthony's hunting knife.

"Don't get me wrong," Melissa went on. "I'm really sorry Harvey was murdered. I mean, it's so horrible. Who would do such a thing? Anthony loved his uncle, you know, 'cause he helped raise him. So it's going to be really hard for Anthony. Just the same, I wish—"

"You wish Harvey would have approved of you and Anthony," Father John finished her thought. Melissa nodded. There were tears in her eyes and she was obviously making an effort to hold them back.

"I've always loved Anthony," Melissa said quietly. "Ever since my folks got divorced and Mother brought me back to the ranch. Anthony and I became friends right away, even though we knew we were off limits to each other. I mean, we were only twelve and we knew." She brushed her fingers through her hair again.

"Anthony taught me to ride," she said, keeping her eyes fixed on a pile of papers on the desk. "All those white instructors Uncle Ned hired didn't know diddley about handling horses. Anthony knew everything." The shadow of a smile played at the edges of her lips as she talked.

"Then I went back east to boarding school and college, and I hardly ever saw Anthony. But when I transferred to the university, we started meeting for coffee. Just to talk. I was kind of uncomfortable about being at a big school. Anthony had been in Laramie three years, and he knew the ropes." She glanced up at Father John and took a deep breath before going on.

"Then about a year ago, we were able to get around that 'off limits' sign, and we admitted to each other how we really felt." Melissa broke into a smile for the first time since he'd walked into the study. "We've been together since. And we were together Friday night."

"Anthony was with you all night?" Father John wasn't sure why he'd asked, except it would be the first question the FBI agent would ask. Nothing added up about Harvey's murder. An air-tight alibi for Anthony was almost too much to hope for.

"What do you mean?" Melissa looked startled.

"You can testify that Anthony didn't leave the cabin all night?"

"He didn't leave," she said. "He went outdoors for a while, but he didn't leave."

Father John made a fist and blew into it. This was what he had been afraid of. As if she sensed this wasn't good news, Melissa hurried on. "We took a blanket outside and laid on the ground to watch the stars, that's all."

"Melissa, Superman couldn't have seen the stars that night."

"We were watching for them to come out. Anthony likes to do that. I stayed out with him for a while, but it got so cold I went back inside to bed."

"How long was he out alone?"

"I don't know." Melissa threw both hands in the air. "Thirty minutes or so. What does it matter? He didn't leave."

Father John blew into his fist again, calculating in his head the distance between the Cooley ranch and the Ethete powwow grounds. Not even Anthony could sprint up to Ethete and back in thirty minutes, but it could be done in a vehicle. "Did you hear the jeep's engine?"

"No. Anthony didn't leave." The look on Melissa's face took on a mixture of exasperation and fear.

"Is it possible you fell asleep?" Father John persisted. It was exactly the line of questioning Miller would take, and they had to be prepared.

The young woman burst into tears. "I thought you were Anthony's friend."

Father John got up, went around the desk, and patted her shoulder. "Melissa, I believe in Anthony as much as you do. But there's a hole in his alibi big enough to walk a buffalo through. He wasn't with you every minute. There's a chunk of time you can't account for."

"What are we going to do?" Melissa wiped at her eyes with two fingers as she looked up at him.

Father John leaned against the edge of the desk and stared out the window at the blue and white ridge of mountain peaks. This was going to make Miller's day. Sooner or later all this would come out. Melissa would blow an alibi and hand over a motive, all in one neat package.

Aware of the young woman's eyes on him, Father John turned toward her. "You and Anthony must tell Vicky everything. There can't be any surprises. She has to know what happened so she can be prepared to defend him."

"Defend him," Melissa said. "You think he'll be charged with murder?"

"I hope not. But it's possible."

Melissa seemed to sink into the chair. "You don't understand, Father. Vicky doesn't want to help Anthony."

"Wrong, Melissa."

The young woman looked up at him, eyes wide. "You mean . . ." She jumped up and walked over to the window. "Wait a minute. Are you saying what I think you're saying? Anthony wouldn't tell her about spending the night with me, right? So she doesn't know if he really has an alibi. Thanks, Father John," she said as she strolled back to the desk. "Now I know what I have to do."

He waited for her to explain what that might be. It wasn't the first time someone had come to him with a problem, figured out the solution, and thanked him for it.

"I'm going to tell Mother and Uncle Ned and everybody else. I might even put an ad in the *Gazette*. Anthony Castle and Melissa Bennett are in love and are going to be married. That should give the moccasin telegraph something to buzz about. Then that Arapaho warrior won't have to protect his woman. He can tell the truth, and maybe Vicky can clear him."

Father John stood on the front porch and watched the Miata curve around Circle Drive. As Melissa turned onto Seventeen-Mile Road, she stuck her arm out the window and waved. There was something light-hearted about the gesture, hopeful. He wished he could share her hope. The hot wind sighed through the cottonwoods and evergreens, but it seemed ominous, not calming. He could feel his heart thumping as he turned back into the house. A cold beer with a shot of whiskey—that always focused his thoughts. He shoved the idea away. Why did it always creep over him at unexpected moments?

The living room opened to the right, opposite the study, and he contemplated switching on the Red Sox game just to get the score, but there was no time. As soon as Miller heard about Melissa, everything would fast-forward. How long would it take—two days, three days, a week at most—before Anthony was indicted on first-degree murder? Unless . . . unless—God Almighty, he thought. He had to come up with some answers, connect some of the dots. And he had to do it fast. Meantime, there was Anthony out at the ranch, blithely refusing to name his alibi, protecting the girl he loves and unaware of how bad things could get for him.

∞ 12 ∞

FATHER JOHN NUDGED the Toyota close to the rear bumper of a gray pickup at the far end of the driveway that divided the barn from the white frame ranch house. He started walking out across the pasture. Gigantic white clouds drifted through a blue velvet sky, and the sun seared the back of his neck. Puffs of dirt rising off the hard-packed ground clung to the toes of his cowboy boots. Tumbleweeds skidded along in the hot breeze, stacking themselves against the barbed-wire fence where Charlie Taylor was tamping dirt around one of the posts with the handle of a shovel.

Flipping the shovel around, Charlie scooped up some dirt from the little mound next to the post, then began tamping it in the hole, seemingly engrossed in the task. As Father John approached, the Indian glanced up, a flicker of surprise in his eyes. Sweat ran from under his Stetson and down the sides of his cheeks.

"Hot day for setting a fence post," said Father John. It wasn't polite to get right down to business and say what was on his mind. A kind of dance had to be performed first, an exchange of pleasantries.

"One of my bulls don't like stayin' corralled," Charlie said, scarcely interrupting the rhythm of the tamping.

"This is the longest dry spell I've seen in these parts. No sign of rain," Father John said, glancing up at the mare's tail cloud swishing overhead.

Charlie set the shovel into the mound of dirt. "It'll rain when it gets to it," he said, bending into his shirtsleeve to wipe away the perspiration on his forehead. "You come out here to talk about the weather?"

"I'm worried about Anthony being caught up in Harvey's murder," Father John said.

"Maybe that hotshot kid had somethin' to do with it."

Father John took a deep breath, giving himself a moment to control the anger that flashed inside him. What Charlie had was a bad case of envies toward a younger man with more opportunities. But there was something else about this Arapaho, something hard to get a handle on. Maybe he seemed different because he was considered an outsider, born on the reservation but raised in Oklahoma. He'd only been back at Wind River a few years, but in that short time, he'd managed to get elected to the business council. He was an ambitious and determined man, this Arapaho.

"I thought you were Harvey's friend." Father John checked himself before adding that he must have thought wrong. He didn't want to stop the conversation.

Charlie pushed his cowboy hat back and dipped his forehead again to his sleeve in a continuous motion. "Sure, me and Harvey was friends."

"You think Harvey's work on the business council had anything to do with his murder?"

"Not a chance," the Indian said, grimacing, as if the suggestion were a bad joke. Folding his arms across his chest, he leaned back against the fence post. It held steady as a cottonwood.

"What about the oil wells that have been shut down?" Father John pressed on. The councilman shifted his position against the fence post and looked out across the plains. They were just two men talking about the weather, but Father John could feel the tension thick between them.

"Four wells on the south side is all. Just bad luck they belong to Arapahos. Hell, wells dry up all the time. 'Course, folks don't like it much. Ernest Oldman started raisin' a fuss so Harvey said he'd look into it. He asked the resources director for a report. It's due in a few days." Charlie stepped away from the post and turned around, examining it, as if to make sure it was still in place.

Father John was thinking about Father Brad's theory that somebody had put out a contract on Harvey's life. "What's more valuable around here than oil?" the young priest had wanted to know.

Pushing a little further, Father John asked, "You think there's a connection?"

The councilman pivoted around. "What?"

"Between the dry wells and Harvey's murder."

The Arapaho was quiet a moment. "Yeah, sure. Hell, anything's possible."

"But if oil wells dry up all the time, and that's the reason Harvey was murdered, why is it no councilman has been killed before now?"

Charlie squinted into the sun, as if he were having trouble following the logic. "Hell, it's your theory," he said finally. "You wanna shoot down your own theory, I ain't handing you the gun."

Father John laughed, and the councilman joined in. Some of the tension seemed to dissolve. "Odd about the Cooley ranch, though. I can't figure out why Harvey changed his mind about buying it. He was always anxious to buy back the old lands whenever they came on the market."

Charlie's eyes shut down as if a curtain had been drawn. The veins stood out in his neck. "You must've heard wrong. Business council's gonna vote unanimous for buying the Cooley ranch. That's a hundred thousand acres of good ranch land, plus oil wells, and all of it paid for in time by royalties. Soon as it's paid off, all Arapahos on the reservation are gonna share the royalties. It's a hell of a deal, and Harvey was riding the same horse as everybody else. End of story." The Indian whirled around, picked up the shovel, and started across the pasture.

Father John followed. He was struck by the councilman's words. They were almost the same that Jasper Owens had used. A hell of a deal.

When they reached the driveway, Charlie said, "I don't know what you been hearin' on the moccasin telegraph. Everybody around here's got an opinion on everything, mostly wrong. There's nothing unusual about this here Cooley deal. We buy back old lands every chance we get, that's the way it is. Next business council meeting, we're gonna do just what Harvey would've wanted."

Father John got into the Toyota and slammed the door. The councilman leaned down, his face framed in the opened window. "Take my advice. Don't go stirrin' up trouble and lookin' for things that ain't there. Could be dangerous."

Father John backed the pickup out of the driveway. By the time he pulled onto the road, the councilman had disappeared in the rearview mirror.

He flipped on the switch to the tape player and took a deep breath, drawing in the first notes of *Don Giovanni*. He'd misjudged Charlie Taylor. He'd assumed the councilman would be as eager to see Harvey's killer brought to justice as he was, but Charlie didn't seem fazed by Harvey's murder. He was lying, hiding something, Father John could feel it in his bones. And the idea lurking at the edge of his mind made him uncomfortable. Charlie Taylor was now the acting tribal chairman at Wind River Reservation. Did he have his sights set on being elected chairman? Had Harvey stood in the way of his ambition? Was that reason enough to murder a man?

∞ 13 ∞

FATHER JOHN DIDN'T intend to stay long. He paid his respects again to Maria ensconced in the rocker at the far end of the living room, the red sweater draped over her shoulders, as if she hadn't stirred since yesterday. People huddled in little groups across the room, in the kitchen, and down the hallway, their voices like the low, steady droning of bees. Will Standing Bear sat in one of the straight-backed kitchen chairs. Father John was tempted to ask him about the Cooley ranch deal, but decided against it. It would be impolite to ask for the gift of information before Harvey's funeral.

Rita was on the sofa talking with several Arapaho women. She seemed composed, relaxed even, with Anthony at home. He wished he could warn her that Anthony wasn't safe yet, not as long as the FBI agent considered him the main suspect. He worried how she would take Anthony's indictment, if it came.

Anthony and Vicky were huddled together on two kitchen chairs next to the sofa. Waving to Father John, the young man said, "I got a lawyer again." He was grinning, as if he hadn't grasped the extent to which he was going to need one.

As Father John got ready to leave, Vicky stood, scooped up a black leather bag that lay crumpled on the floor next to her chair, swung the bag over one shoulder, and led the way down the half flight of stairs. Father John grabbed his cowboy hat off the entryway bench and followed her outdoors. The sun was poised to drop behind the mountains at any moment, and the whole western sky was layered in pinks and reds and oranges. There was an orange cast to the air.

"Well, I'm the counsel of record again. You had something to do with that," Vicky said, daring him to deny it. She barely came to his shoulder, and he could see the sun glinting off her black hair, which was pulled straight back and fastened with a large beaded barrette. The ends curled just below the collar of her blouse. As she walked slowly down the driveway with Father John, she kept her hands in the pockets of her skirt which billowed out slightly in the breeze. Her high heels snapped against the gravel.

The strangeness of it struck him. He, a Boston Irishman, a priest, in cowboy boots and cowboy hat and blue jeans and plaid shirt, just like all the men on the reservation, dressed for the land, for the weather, for comfort. She, an Arapaho woman more interesting than beautiful, but attractive, stunning really, dressed for a stroll across Boston Commons.

"Well?" she asked, swaying slightly toward him.

"Melissa came to see me this morning," he said. "She decided to tell her family about Anthony. That lets him off the hook about protecting her."

"There's one sensible partner in that relationship. What do you think?" Vicky stopped and turned toward him, her head tilted upward.

"About what?" He was hedging. He knew what she was asking, and he suspected she knew that.

"An Arapaho man. A white woman," she said.

"I think they love each other a lot."

"Crazy, wild, and mad for each other, I'd say." She started walking again. "They're determined to overcome all the obstacles other people, Arapahos as well as whites, throw in their way."

"You think they'll succeed?"

"I'm a realist," Vicky said. "First things first. Anthony doesn't have any future at all with a murder indictment hanging over him." A strand of hair had come loose, and the breeze blew it across her cheek. She tucked it back behind her ear.

"Everything's coming together for Jeff Miller—weapon, motive, accessibility," Vicky continued. "And what do we have? An alibi as big as the sky and a gut feeling this kid didn't murder his uncle. No wonder the fed's not even looking for the real murderer. He thinks he's got him cold."

They turned into Little Wind River Bottom Road and started walking down the middle, past a line of parked pickups. Father John could see her Bronco ahead. He was aware of how much he was enjoying talking quietly with this woman and walking alongside her. He told her about his hunch that Harvey's murder had something to do with his work on the business council, that Charlie Taylor had scoffed at the idea, and that he was sure Charlie was lying. "How well do you know him?" he asked.

Vicky stopped and turned toward him, as if she were weighing the answer before offering it. "I don't think anybody really knows him. He's not from around here. But he convinced a lot of people that he knew how to deal with whites. That's what got him elected to the tribal council, and, as far as I know, he's done a good job. You don't think . . ."

Father John shrugged. "I don't know what to think.

Charlie admitted that Harvey had asked the resources director for a report on the oil wells that were shut down."

"Ernest Oldman is damned mad about that. Maybe Anthony's right. Maybe it was Ernest who killed Harvey," Vicky said, resuming the slow pace down the middle of Little Wind River Bottom Road. "He threatened Harvey last week, and Ernest can get violent, very violent."

In an orange flare of light, the sun was slowly dipping behind the Wind River Mountains, which were bathed in blue and violet shadows. Father John thought of Ernest as a seriously ill alcoholic. What Vicky said about the man's violence only confirmed what he'd suspected, the rumors he'd heard. He had no firsthand knowledge of Ernest's behavior, but he did have firsthand knowledge of the convoluted workings of the alcoholic mind.

"I suppose it's possible that in a drunken rage Ernest could pick up a knife and stab somebody," Father John said. "But Harvey's murder took some planning. Whoever did it made the most of an opportunity to steal Anthony's knife a month ago. That means a month ago the murderer had the intention of killing Harvey and making it look as if his nephew had done it. Then the murderer waited for the opportunity. What better opportunity than the powwow weekend? Harvey would be alone in his tipi, which he always set up in the same place. I can almost guarantee," he hurried on, "that if Ernest was drinking, his mind wouldn't have been clear enough to put it all together."

Vicky sighed. "You're right." Something in her voice made Father John wonder if she was speaking out of her own experience. She had never talked about herself or why she had divorced her husband and left the reservation ten years ago. He'd heard the grandmothers clucking over it, but they had never mentioned why she'd gone away. Maybe Vicky would tell him someday; that was up to her.

"Something else," Father John said. "Charlie insists everybody on the business council, including Harvey, wanted to buy back the Cooley ranch. But Rita told me Harvey had changed his mind after he talked to the elders. Will Standing Bear told him not to trust the agent."

Vicky looked out across the plains as if she were trying to remember, to pull something out of the far distances. After a moment, she looked back at Father John. "Grandfather used to say nobody could trust the agent, but he never explained why. It's part of the wisdom here even though Mathias Cooley's been dead a hundred years."

When they reached the Bronco, he opened the door for her. Vicky tossed the black bag over the front seat, then slipped inside. "I'm thinking about moving to L.A.," she said. She pulled the key out of the bag but made no effort to start the engine. "Larry's been offered a position with one of the big firms there. Token Indian and all that. He wants me to come with him."

"Will you go?" Father John rested his forearms on the window ledge and bent toward her. He felt the old wariness gathering inside him, preparing him for the answer. He knew she was involved with a Lakota lawyer in Lander, but he never thought about it, except once in a while. And then it was only to hope he was good to her.

"I don't know," she said, keeping her eyes straight ahead.

He wanted to say "I hope you won't go," but of course he couldn't. He was a priest, and she was a friend, that was all. He could never tell her how much he enjoyed having her at the edges of his life, working with her, walking into Blue Sky Hall and seeing her through the crowd of Arapahos, hearing her laughter break across the din of other voices.

"I like being here with my people," she said, turning toward him. "I flatter myself, I guess, by thinking I can help them. But I could practice Indian law in L.A. You know, help the Indigenous Peoples of North America." She laughed, but there was little mirth in her eyes.

He was aware of the wall blocking off the feelings inside him. This was how it always was. He was a traveler passing through the lives of others. He was always going away from the people he learned to care about, or they were going away from him. Maybe it was best. It kept things from getting complicated. But it seemed harder now. He felt as if he'd finally come home here at Wind River, yet people were still going away. Harvey was dead. Now Vicky was thinking about moving. Once he would have nursed a bottle of whiskey and waited for the pain to dull, but that wasn't an option now.

"You'll be leaving pretty soon yourself," Vicky said.

"I hope not. I've asked the Provincial to extend my stay. The six-year rule is for superiors, and I've only been the superior at St. Francis three years." This was surface talk, and the expression on her face told him that she knew it. What he wanted to say was: "I plan to stay on. You stay on, too. Let's both be here." But then he would have had to add: "And we can continue to be good friends." That was all he had to offer, and it wasn't enough.

Switching on the ignition, Vicky smiled, almost as if she knew the rest of it without his saying the words. The Bronco pulled out, and Father John watched it until it disappeared over the rise on Little Wind River Bottom Road.

Father John kept the steering wheel steady with one finger. Seventeen-Mile Road stretched ahead, awash in amber twilight. The hot, dry wind whistled through the cab, nearly drowning out the plaintive sounds of "Di Provenza il mar." The father imploring his son to return home made him think of how much Harvey had loved Anthony, and how hard it was going to be on the young man now that the only father he'd ever had was dead.

He thought of his own father and how he had worshipped him. With all his faults, he had worshipped him. His father had tended the steam furnaces at Boston College, and a lot of days he wasn't sober enough to finish the job. As a kid, Father John used to stop by after school and give his father a hand. He had learned his way through the labyrinthine tunnels under the college long before he ever set foot in the classrooms above. Often he wondered what his father would have thought, had he lived long enough to see the Great Fall. Whether he would have been ashamed, as his mother had been, or whether it was what his father had always expected.

Father John shifted in the seat and forced his mind back to Anthony. The young man's whole life was dangling from a thin string. How long would it be before the FBI agent got the results of the lab tests? Of course, Anthony's fingerprints would be on the knife. It was his knife. Whoever had used it to kill Harvey would have worn gloves and hoped some of Anthony's prints would still be detectable. It didn't take a genius to figure that out.

Father John glanced in the rearview mirror. A BIA police car, lights flashing, was coming up behind. He'd been lost in his own thoughts and hadn't heard the siren over the wind and the music. Easing on the brake, he pulled the Toyota over to the side of Seventeen-Mile Road. He'd probably been speeding. It wasn't the first time his foot had gotten heavy on the gas pedal.

He hit the stop button on the tape player and rolled the window all the way down, keeping his eyes on the side mirror. The short, heavyset Indian disengaging himself from the patrol car had been at the powwow grounds yesterday with Banner.

"We been lookin' all over the rez for you," the patrolman said, stooping slightly at the opened window. "All hell's broke loose with Ernest Oldman. He's gone crazy for sure. Chief Banner can use your help."

∞ 14 ∞

FOUR BIA PATROL cars were strung bumper to bumper out in the oil field on the southwestern edge of the reservation. Father John gunned the Toyota down a graveled road and across the field, bouncing over the packed earth. Banner and about a dozen BIA policemen huddled beside the patrol cars. Several hundred feet beyond, Ernest was circling an oil pump that rose out of the ground like the blackened frame of an ancient tipi. Suddenly Ernest faced the pump and raised a rifle to his shoulder. The sharp crack split the air like a sonic boom.

Father John flipped off the ignition and hopped from the Toyota while it was still coasting to a stop. Doubling over, as if to avoid the whirling rotors of an invisible helicopter, he ran toward the patrol cars. Banner motioned him on, and Father John hunkered down beside the chief.

"Ernest's been shooting at that pump for the last hour or so," Banner said. "He gets tired of that, he's likely to shoot himself. He's gone certifiable." The chief kept one hand over the mouth of a bullhorn. Another rifle shot sounded overhead.

"Got a team ready to crawl in behind him, but it's tricky

as hell. Ernest spots 'em, he'll turn around firing. Somebody might get killed. You think you could try talkin' him into layin' down that rifle?" Banner handed the bullhorn to Father John.

Dear Lord, thought Father John. Ernest was drunk, and Father John was an expert on drunks. There were the quiet ones—like himself—who sat in an easy chair wearing down a bottle of whiskey until they passed out. And there was the kind like Ernest that went to bars and picked fights with everybody there, stabbed people, shot people, and remembered nothing afterwards, insisted they couldn't have done anything so terrible—Father John had counseled them all, but the drunks like Ernest were usually in custody or in the hospital, the crisis over. He'd never had to talk a drunk out of destroying an oil pump—or killing himself—and he didn't want to do it now. But he had to try; there was no other way. Stretching himself slowly upward alongside the patrol car, he set the bullhorn on the roof and, shoulders hunched, knees bent, leaned into the mouthpiece.

"Be careful," the police chief said.

"Ernest, this is Father John O'Malley." His voice echoed across the open field. In the deepening dusk, Ernest and the black pump looked like two shadows plastered against the horizon.

Suddenly the Indian swung around in a half circle and pointed the rifle toward the patrol cars. "Get out of here," he shouted.

"I'm coming out to talk to you." To his own ears, he sounded as if he were shouting into a barrel. "I don't have a gun. I just want to talk. I'm coming now, Ernest." Father John straightened up and started around the patrol car.

"Hell you are," Banner said, gripping his leg.

"Let go." Father John didn't take his eyes off the shadow of the Indian in the field. He had to see Ernest face to face and look into his eyes. Banner's grip relaxed, and Father John wrenched his leg free. He started slowly across the open field, arms outstretched and palms up, hoping Ernest wasn't too drunk to recognize the Arapaho sign of peace.

"Be careful, Father," one of the BIA policemen called from behind.

"Go back," Ernest shouted. "I don't need no talkin'." He waved the rifle toward Father John, as if zeroing in on a target.

Father John walked on, his pace slow and steady. He kept his eyes on the shadow ahead. The wind moved the air gently around him, and sagebrush crackled under his boots. "Take it easy, Ernest." His voice was low, just loud enough for the Indian to hear. "It's a bad deal, these oil wells going dry. I know how much you need your share of the royalties for Jenny and the kids." He was taking a gamble, mentioning Ernest's family. It might calm the man, or set him off.

Father John was close enough now that the rifle barrel looked like a wide, black tunnel. "You hear what the business council's doing?"

Ernest stopped waving the rifle, and the barrel dropped a couple of inches. Father John kept coming. He was only a couple feet from Ernest now. He could see the metallic sheen of the rifle. It had a pink cast.

"The council ain't doing nothin'." Ernest brought the rifle up again.

Father John stopped. The sour smell of whiskey floated in the space between them, and for a moment Father John thought he was going to retch. He swallowed hard. Keeping his voice low, soothing, he said, "Harvey asked for a full report. The natural resource director's putting it together now. Business council will have it in a couple days."

"What good's that gonna do me?" Ernest raised the rifle

slightly, a reflex. Father John felt the metal barrel graze his arm. The Indian's eyes were outlined in red.

"As soon as the report's completed, the council can request the Bureau of Indian Affairs to conduct an investigation. It's a start."

Ernest exhaled a long breath. His shoulders sagged, his whole body seemed to relax, and Father John felt himself begin to relax. "Let me have the rifle," he said, taking a chance on the moment.

Keeping the barrel pointed down, Ernest held out the wooden stock, as if he were handing over a slab of beef. Father John took the gun. The wood felt cool and clammy. Tears were running down Ernest's cheeks, and he lowered his face into the palms of both hands. After a moment he looked up, his cheeks streaked with gray dust. "Jenny took the kids and went away. I ain't got nothin' left. No family. No job. No money." He swung around and kicked the metal oil pump.

"Where did she go?"

"Vicky took 'em to those shelters at Ethete, but they ain't there no more. Nobody'll tell me where they went. I didn't mean to hurt Jenny none," Ernest said. "I just had a little too much to drink was all." He started to sob.

Vicky hadn't said anything about taking Jenny and the kids to the shelters, but it didn't surprise Father John. "Come on," he said, putting enough pressure on the Indian's arm to nudge him forward. They started walking across the field, Ernest swaying side to side. Father John kept one hand on his arm to steady him.

Banner and the other BIA men had stepped out from the patrol cars and were coming slowly across the field toward them. Father John kept talking quietly to Ernest. "We're going to help you straighten everything out. Trouble is you've been tryin' to handle this alone. It's not easy alone. We all need help every once in a while. Have you talked to your grandfather?"

"He don't wanna talk to me," Ernest said.

"Maybe that's not true."

Ernest stopped and turned toward Father John. "Will you ask him?"

Father John nodded. He intended to talk to Will Standing Bear anyway, right after Harvey's funeral. Maybe the elder would be willing to meet with his grandson. God knows Ernest needed his grandfather now. Being a mediator in family disputes—that was something Father John was used to.

After handcuffing Ernest and reading him his rights, Banner ushered him into the back seat of one of the patrol cars. The Arapaho slumped against the car window, looking exhausted and, oddly enough, almost sober.

"You like givin' heart attacks?" the chief asked, taking the rifle from Father John.

Father John stuck both hands in the pockets of his blue jeans to keep them from shaking. He could feel the muscles in his legs twitching. "Not really."

Banner exhaled a deep breath. "Thanks," he said. Father John saw the mixture of relief and concern in the Indian's eyes.

"We could have Harvey's murderer here," Banner said, nodding toward the patrol car.

"Seems to me Ernest was shooting at all the forces that took Jenny and the kids away. He might've mistreated them, but he doesn't want to lose them. I don't think he'd commit murder. That would drive them away permanently."

"Maybe you're right," the chief said. He didn't look convinced.

Father John guessed he must have convinced himself.

Why else had he walked into the barrel of a rifle held by a drunk? The patrol cars and policemen looked like ghostly figures in the gathering darkness. The sky had turned violet, and the sigh of the wind sounded far away. Nothing made sense; it was as if balance and order and harmony had disappeared from the earth. It would not be restored, he knew, until Harvey's murderer was found.

The stars twinkled overhead like lights in some faraway city as Father John turned onto Circle Drive at St. Francis Mission. The evening air was warm with no hint of rain. All it had done this summer was threaten to rain, with gray clouds obscuring the sun and stars awhile before blowing over. He wondered how much longer before the hay dried up in the fields and scattered in the wind across the plains. He felt weary, bone weary. He wanted to hit the bed and sleep a long time and blot out all thoughts about Harvey and Anthony, about this woman at the edge of his mind, about the poor drunken slob he had just helped to get arrested.

In the headlights he saw Dorothy Bennett swing out of the front seat of the white Cadillac parked in front of the priests' residence. Father John pulled in alongside her. He took his time turning off the ignition, pushing the button on the tape player to stop *Don Giovanni* in the middle of "Il Mio Tesoro," and flipping off the headlights. Immediately Circle Drive, the Cadillac, and the house were swallowed in darkness.

"This is a surprise, Dorothy," he said, getting out of the pickup. It wasn't a surprise at all. He knew he'd hear from her eventually.

"Is it?" Dorothy's voice was cold. As his eyes adjusted in the light from the stars and the full moon, he saw she had stepped back against the side of the Cadillac, shoulders rigid, jaw thrust out. Her eyes were flashing.

"I can put on a pot of coffee," he said.

"This isn't a social call," she snapped. "I just want you to tell me one thing. What gives you the right to mix in people's lives?"

"Why don't you come inside and we can talk," he said soothingly, the same tone he had just used on Ernest.

"We'll talk here," she said. "How dare you encourage my daughter and some Indian in this preposterous romance. You just don't get how things are around here, do you?"

Father John swallowed hard, trying to keep his temper in check. It was so quick to flare, to interfere with the reasonable, logical way to handle a situation. "How are things around here?" he asked finally.

"Melissa Bennett will never marry an Arapaho, that's how things are. Anybody with any sense would know that. But you . . ."

Dorothy was spitting out the words, and Father John could feel the tiny stings of saliva on his face. "You encourage an Arapaho, and not just any Arapaho—a murderer—to think he can actually marry a girl like Melissa."

"Hold on," Father John said. He could feel the heat rising in his face. "Anthony Castle is no murderer. He's a fine young man. Any girl would be lucky to have him as a husband."

"Oh, my God," Dorothy said. She seemed to sink against the Cadillac, her whole body collapsing. "You really believe that, don't you? Your trouble is you've been here too long. You're nothing but an Indian masquerading as white."

Father John had to step back to keep from getting hit as she swung open the car door. She marched around and stood in the fold between the door and the seat. "Well, you've gone too far this time. You've taken sides against the wrong people. My brother can snap his fingers"—she put one hand over her head and snapped her fingers, like a flamenco dancer—"like that, and you'll be out of here. So pack your bags, Father O'Malley." She dropped into the seat and pulled the door after her. The heavy thud of metal filled the air.

Father John stepped aside as she raced the motor, backed up, and pulled onto Circle Drive. He could hear the gravel scattering under her wheels like bursts from a shotgun.

He let himself into the house, switched on the hall light, and set his cowboy hat on the little table. The hallway was cast in shadows, and the whole house had the stillness of evening about it. Elena would have gone home by now, but not before frying some chicken and leaving it in the fridge. Sunday was fried chicken day. The sharp odor of burning flesh lingered in the air. He wondered where Father Brad was, then remembered that someone at Cooley's pig roast had invited the priests at St. Francis to a barbecue tonight. He had declined, but Brad had probably gone.

He went into the study and slammed the door, more to confine the space for himself than to keep out anyone else. There was no one else here. He didn't bother to turn on any lights. Slivers of moonlight filtered through the window and lay across the carpet. Sinking into the old leather chair, he thought about Ned Cooley. He would call the Provincial; he wouldn't bother with a letter. And the Provincial would take a call from the next governor of Wyoming who would tell him how the superior at St. Francis Mission was causing problems. What kind of problems? Just problems that made it extremely difficult to work with him, and of course it's important to have a man on the reservation state officials can work with. When it comes to allocating funds for social programs and such, it's good to have someone on hand who is—trustworthy.

Then Ned Cooley would call all the important people he knew in Wyoming and all the bigwigs in Denver, including the archbishop, and ask them to call the Provincial. The

Provincial would say, well, your six years are up September first anyway, and we'll just stick to the rules on this one. Better to stay on the right side of the next governor. The Provincial expected superiors to run things smoothly. He didn't like having to step in, and when he did he moved people around.

Father John studied the way the moonlight flowed along the carpet and cast the faintest light over the blue wing chair, the draperies, the stacks of paper on his desk. The thought of leaving Wind River made him inexpressibly sad. He knew if there were any alcohol in the house, he would drink it now. He understood how Ernest must have felt.

～ 15 ～

Denise AND Homer Lone Wolf's baby was dying. The phone had jangled in the hallway at about six just as the sun had started to cast a red glow over the kitchen. Father John had already been up for more than an hour. He didn't remember sleeping, only mentally pacing off the night until light rimmed the curtains at the bedroom window. He'd already showered, shaved, and brewed a pot of coffee when the call came. It took him about twenty minutes to get to Riverton Memorial Hospital.

Three nurses and what looked like the entire Lone Wolf family were crowded in the tiny room off the nursery: grandparents, Denise's two sisters and their husbands, Homer's cousin and his wife. Denise sat in a wheelchair at the foot of a crib, looking like a child herself, bewildered by an incomprehensible adult world. Homer stood behind her, gripping the bar along the top of the wheelchair. The infant lay with eyes half closed in a wavy, dreamlike manner, tubes running from the tiny body to machines on a nearby roller.

"His heart don't know how to work," Homer said, slicing his index finger under one eye, then the other, to wipe away the moisture. "They're gonna fly him down to Children's

Hospital in Denver. I'm goin' with him." Father John caught the sharp odor of the Indian's breath, a distillation of morning and coffee and whiskey.

Slipping a folded white stole and the silver compact containing bottles of holy water and oil from the pocket of his windbreaker, Father John asked the baby's name. Denise answered so quietly he had to lean over and ask again. "George," she said.

Denise's grandfather, in his sixties with gray hair combed straight back from a pockmarked face, spoke up. "I was sickly, too, when I was born, and my grandfather gave me the name Little Wing. The name made me strong, so I give it now to my great-grandson."

Father John draped the stole around his neck and opened the compact. He handed the bottle of holy water to Homer. Then he placed a drop of oil on one finger and made the sign of the cross on the baby's forehead. The skin felt as soft as the silk stole that folded over the top of his hand. He took the bottle of holy water and, letting one or two drops fall on the forehead, said, "I baptize you, George Little Wing, in the name of the Father, the Son, and the Holy Spirit."

Afterward he and Homer walked down the hall of the hospital and out to the parking lot. Suddenly the Indian doubled over coughing. Father John winced at the thought of this alcoholic Arapaho, used to the open spaces of the reservation, surrounded by his own people, alone in a big city like Denver. How long before he wandered into the nearest bar and got himself rolled and beaten up?

Father John opened the door of the Toyota and fumbled among the opera tapes in the glove compartment for a tablet and ballpoint pen. He jotted down a name and telephone number, and, ripping off the page, handed it to the Arapaho who had just spit a ball of green phlegm onto the asphalt. "This is a Jesuit at Regis. You call him soon as you get to

Denver," he said. Watching Homer reverently fold the paper, as if he'd just received a sacred gift—a friend— Father John hoped that Father Dave Kelly would come through one more time. Homer wasn't the first Arapaho he'd asked Dave to keep an eye on in Denver. So far, the other Jesuit hadn't objected, even though he and Dave were no longer good friends. He couldn't say they were friends at all, not since the Great Fall. His, not Father Dave's.

Homer bent over again in the throes of another coughing spell. After a moment he straightened partway up and, clasping his chest, said, "Little Wing's gonna need me, and I'm gonna get myself together, don't you worry, Father. I wanna take the pledge."

Standing on the asphalt, with a cool breeze sighing through the evergreens at the edge of the parking lot and the sun climbing in the clear blue morning sky, Father John heard Homer pledge not to take a drink for thirty days. Taking the pledge was solemn and serious to Arapahos, almost a sacrament. Homer wouldn't take it unless he felt he had the spirit to honor it.

"I'm gonna do it this time," Homer said.

"You bet you are," Father John said as the Arapaho disappeared through the hospital's front door. He started up the Toyota and backed it out of the parking place. "Dear Lord," he prayed silently, "give Homer the grace he needs. Give us all the grace we need."

"Got a minute, John?" Father Brad poked his head around the door to the superior's office in the white brick administration building at St. Francis Mission. He looked as if he didn't know whether to come in or disappear down the hallway.

"Help yourself," Father John said, nodding to the small

metal table cluttered with a coffee pot, foam cups, creamer, and a box of sugar cubes.

Father John had just poured himself a cup of coffee and was about to tackle the papers on his desk: bills, letters, phone messages. The message on top read: "Lou Ann Red Cloud called. Can you find a family in Denver for her son to live with while he goes to Regis High School?" That wasn't going to be easy, he thought, shuffling through the stack. Many more requests for favors from Father Dave and he would tell him to get lost for sure.

"The Provincial called this morning. You just missed him," the younger priest said as he poured a cup of coffee and settled himself into the chair on the other side of the desk. He was methodically stirring a plastic spoon around the Styrofoam cup as if to create a design of some kind. "We had a chance to chat . . ."

"The Provincial?" Father John felt as if a yawning pit had opened beneath him. Ned Cooley had clout, but he hadn't expected him to exercise it this fast. Just then the phone rang, and Father John reached for the receiver. His hand was shaking. His assistant wouldn't miss it.

"We might have gotten us a break." It was Art Banner on the line. The chief sounded excited, his words spilling over one another. "I'm gonna need your help again. Can you get right over here?"

"Where are you?"

"Tribal headquarters. Harvey's office."

Father John was on his feet even before he'd replaced the receiver. Whatever Father Brad and the Provincial had talked about would have to wait. He didn't want to know anyway. He grabbed his cowboy hat from the rack behind the desk and was on his way out the door before he said, "Sorry, something's come up."

The young priest had turned partway around in his chair,

disbelief on his face. "Hey, no problem," he said. Father John could feel the wave of sarcasm at his back as he hurried down the hallway and out of the building.

He parked the Toyota outside the red-brick tribal offices at Ethete. The pickup had made good time on Seventeen-Mile Road, although after being pulled over yesterday, he had kept an eye on the speedometer. *La Bohème* poured from the tape player.

Banner was grinding a cigarette butt onto the sidewalk as Father John got out of the Toyota. Inside, the building was arranged in a V-shape with the lobby at the base and tribal offices down two hallways. The receptionist at the front desk, intent on a telephone conversation, was staring off into space. Two Arapaho women sat on metal chairs beneath a long window that captured a stretch of flat, open plains. They flipped through magazines, bored and impatient.

Banner led the way down the hall on the right. By the time they reached Harvey's office, the chief had pulled a small key ring out of his shirt pocket. It held two keys. "Wait 'til you see this," he said, jamming one key in the lock and pushing open the door.

Papers, file folders, and photographs spilled across one side of the tiled floor. Against the far wall was a metal file cabinet, its three drawers empty and tilting downward. Next to the cabinet sat a large oak desk with a swivel chair pushed against it. Nothing seemed out of place on the other side of the office where two file cabinets stood against the wall, drawers closed. Books were arranged on shelves in neat rows. Except for the filmy orange powder glazing everything in the room, half the office looked as if Harvey had just stepped away for a cup of coffee.

Father John picked up some papers by the toe of his boot. They were manuscript pages, each numbered in the top right-hand corner. He glanced down the top page: *That*

winter of 1878 was very hard. The children were crying with
hunger. Warriors rode great distances looking for food and
often returned to camp empty-handed. There was no place
on the plains anymore for Arapahos, so the government told
Chief Black Night to take the people to the Wind River
Reservation and stay with the Shoshones. Chief Black Night
went there first and said to Chief Washakie, "We want to
come under your robe."

"This is Harvey's history," Father John said, glancing up.

The police chief stepped across the office and drove a fist
against the top drawer of one of the undisturbed file
cabinets. "Over here's records on tribal business. Secretary
says nothin's been touched. You'd think anybody lookin' for
something important would go through these records, not
some history files. Who cares what went on a hundred years
ago? Nothin' anybody can do about it now."

"When did this happen?"

"Sometime between two and five Saturday afternoon,
near as we can tell. Custodian says he was here Saturday 'til
two tightenin' up some rattling windows. Before he left, he
checked the offices to make sure lights were off and doors
locked. A couple of my boys stopped in to check on
Harvey's office a little after five, and they found this mess.
Only thing we know for sure is that whoever did it had keys.
No sign of a break-in. Looks like he pulled out the files,
went through 'em fast, then tossed all the pages instead of
putting 'em back in the drawers. He was in one hell of a
hurry. Must've suspected we'd be checkin' on the office
after Harvey was murdered."

"He?" Father John asked. He'd heard enough confessions
to know women were also capable of nefarious deeds.

"Whoever killed Harvey," Banner said, leaning against
the closed drawers of the file cabinet and crossing his arms.
"Of course the fed thinks Anthony got released from

Fremont County Jail and hightailed it over here with Harvey's keys to get any evidence that might incriminate him."

"I drove Anthony back to the ranch myself," Father John said. "I'm sure Rita and Maria will vouch for the fact he stayed there."

The police chief shook his head. "Everybody vouching for that boy is on his side—his girl, his family. That's not gonna cut it with the fed. We had to notify Miller soon's we found the office ransacked. I hated callin' him in on my turf. My boys did the dustin', though. They went over this place lookin' for fingerprints, fibers, hair. The lab report might tell us somethin'. But it won't tell us what the burglar was lookin' for. If we knew that, maybe we could figure out who killed Harvey and why."

"You'd like me to put these files into some kind of order to see what's missing?" Father John asked. He stooped over and scooped up another pile of papers.

"Weren't you some kind of history professor?"

"I taught American history in high school."

"Well, since you were helping Harvey with this history project of his, I figure who better to put it into some kind of order. It could give us another angle to work on."

"It's not going to be easy," said Father John, flipping through the stack in his hands.

"What's not going to be easy?" Charlie Taylor leaned through the doorway. He had on gray velour warm-up pants and a dark-blue knit shirt. One hand gripped a blue athletic bag that looked crammed full. His black hair was slicked back into a ponytail.

"Gettin' this place back together," said Banner.

"I saw the BIA police dusting in here this morning." The councilman drew a long breath, coolly appraising the situation, as if Harvey's murder and ransacked office had happened on some other planet that had nothing to do with him.

"You got any ideas what the burglar was after?" Father John locked eyes with the tribal councilman.

"Not at the moment." Charlie leaned back and looked down the hall, as if he were expecting someone. "I got some guys I'm gonna shoot baskets with over at the school gym right now. But I'll give it some thought," he said, shifting the athletic bag into the other hand and backing out of the doorway.

Banner handed the key ring with its two silver keys to Father John. "This here's for the building, and this one's for the office," he said. "You can work here anytime's convenient. Sooner you get some answers, the better. We'll have the lab reports in a couple days, and the fed's gonna have his tail on fire to get an indictment. Unless we come up with some motive that somebody had for seein' Harvey dead, Anthony's gonna take the fall." There was concern that bordered on fear in the chief's eyes.

Father John slipped the keys into his jeans pocket. He couldn't stop thinking about Charlie Taylor. After years of counseling people, he knew when somebody was lying. Not just from what the person said or did, but from his own reactions, from the way the hair stood up on his arms like tiny antenna picking up invisible messages. The councilman knew something that might cast light on Harvey's murder, but he was covering it up, playing the role of the unaffected observer. Yet out at the ranch he'd warned Father John away. Away from what?

It didn't take long to figure out the system the burglar had used to rifle through Harvey's files. Whoever had done it had started at the front of the top drawer, pulled out the first file folder and probably looked through it before tossing it across the floor. Then he—or she—had pulled out the next folder and the next, tossing each one in turn so that they covered the floor in a haphazard yet obvious order.

Father John was on his hands and knees, sifting through the papers and pulling together bunches that looked as if they might have fallen out of the same folder. Since the pages were numbered, it was easy enough to order them within each folder, or shift them into other folders if it seemed that's where they belonged.

A definite pattern emerged. Harvey had gone about his work in a logical, organized fashion. Each folder contained a handwritten outline of the material in the chapter and notes on sources, a typed manuscript, and several photographs. The first chapter had landed clear across the room, almost at the door, while the last chapters lay in heaps at the foot of the file cabinet. Judging by the number of folders, Father John guessed there were about thirty or forty chapters. Pulling them together would be easy. Determining what was missing, if anything, would be hard.

It was past noon before he finished gathering all the pages and photos into folders and stacked them on top of Harvey's desk. He had just sat down in Harvey's chair and opened the folder containing the first chapter when the receptionist knocked at the opened door and crossed the tiled floor to deliver a sandwich, bag of chips, and can of Coke. "Chief Banner said to bring you this," she said, setting the lunch on the desk next to the folders.

"Thanks," he said. He hadn't realized how hungry he was until he saw the sandwich and chips. And how thirsty. He opened the Coke and took a long drink. The receptionist waited a moment, an expectant look about her as if she thought he'd talk about the burglary. Pretending he hadn't picked up the message, Father John bent over the page titled

"Chapter One Outline." She turned abruptly and marched out.

Harvey's handwriting was familiar and easy to read, the way he looped the i's and e's, cut off the last letters in words, as if he'd changed his mind, made little squiggly lines for "of" and "the." Father John ran one finger along the outline while simultaneously flipping through the manuscript, checking that every subject had been included, managing a bite of sandwich here and there as he worked.

He was struck by the wholeness of Harvey's work. Chapter One covered the earliest history of Arapahos, the oldest of times, when they left their mother tribe, the Algonquins, and moved west across the continent. It told how they settled in the Red River valley in Minnesota where they had lived as farmers for a thousand years, and how eastern tribes had eventually pushed them out of the valley and onto the Great Plains. There was nothing missing here that Father John could see.

The next several chapters covered the life of Arapahos on the Great Plains. He flipped through the photographs: warriors in deerskin shirts, beaded and fringed, with eagle-feathered headdresses; warriors astride ponies with buckskin saddles painted in geometric figures; warriors and ponies staring into the camera, stopped forever in time.

Harvey had titled Chapter Six "How Arapahos Earned Their Living." Glancing through it, Father John saw that it told how Arapahos had followed the buffalo, pitched villages in the lee of the mountains, ridden out like itinerant shopkeepers to trade buffalo robes and blankets with other Indian tribes. Intelligent, logical, peaceful, that was the Arapahos. "The businessmen of the plains," the first white traders had called them.

So far, everything in the chapters on the Old Time seemed intact. Father John knew he'd have to go back and give each one a closer reading, but first he wanted to move through as quickly as possible. He opened the next folder: "The War Years."

It was longer than the earlier chapters, and he made himself flip through it quickly, not wanting to get caught up in it. He knew the story. He and Harvey had often talked about how the chiefs had tried to make peace with white settlers on the plains, how the young warriors, impatient and angry, had attacked the wagon trains and ranches, how the soldiers had come and hunted the people across the plains, boxed them in until there was no place to go. Father John closed the folder, feeling the same sadness that came over him whenever he read about the struggles of his own people in Ireland and when they first came to America.

Chapter Ten was next: "Arapahos Find a Home." The afternoon sunlight streamed through the narrow window over the file cabinet. It was all he had time for. Harvey's wake was this evening, and he had to get ready. An eerie quiet engulfed the office—he was probably the only one left in the building.

He let himself out, locking both the office and front doors. The air was heavy with the day's heat, and he squinted in the sunlight skimming off the pavement. He'd found nothing unusual in the files, but he didn't feel discouraged. For no reason that he could explain, he had the kind of buoyant feeling of a gambler, sure this roll of the dice would pay off.

∞ 16 ∞

DARKNESS LAY OVER the reservation like a soft blanket, but orange traced the peaks of the Wind River Mountains, and the moon shone full in the eastern sky. A crowd was gathered on the pavement outside of Blue Sky Hall. The community center bore the name that other plains tribes had given to Arapahos—Blue Sky People. Vicky wound her way to the front door.

The inside of the hall resembled a gymnasium filled with rows of folding chairs. Most of the chairs were already taken, and people were staking out standing room along the back and side walls. Voices were hushed and respectful. There were more people here than she'd ever seen at a wake, even her mother's two years ago. Spotting her mother's sister in the middle row, Vicky walked down the center aisle to where the old woman was seated.

"You're lookin' tired," Rose whispered, lifting a stuffed woven bag from the chair next to her so that Vicky could sit down.

It was about 9 o'clock, an hour after the wake was supposed to start. Vicky knew that Father John would start the services on Indian time, when everyone had arrived and was ready. Indian time had nothing to do with clocks. Most whites never understood that.

An hour ago Vicky had been eating dinner with Larry at a Chinese place in Lander. Larry had gone back to the office to catch up on some work—he had never gotten to know Harvey or his family and he said he wouldn't feel right at the wake. She had taken Highway 789 to Hudson, then ridden Rendezvous Road across the reservation in the red-tinged dusk.

Vicky shifted in her chair, trying to see around the people in the rows ahead. The casket stood against the front wall. Harvey's head was propped at an angle, the dark mass of hair clearly visible. Anthony, Rita, and Maria sat in the first row, next to Father John and the new assistant at St. Francis Mission. Will Standing Bear and other Arapaho elders were also in the front row, heads high, shoulders squared. Behind them sat Charlie Taylor, Harvey's protégé, and four other tribal councilmen.

Harvey's murderer could be here—sitting in one of the folding chairs or standing against a wall, normal, mournful. A shiver ran across Vicky's shoulders, as if a cold wind had swept through the hall.

A group of women emerged through the door that opened onto the kitchen next to the hall. They walked down the aisle passing out plates of sandwiches and cookies. Vicky took a plate and handed it to the older woman, but she declined one for herself.

Rose took a bite of her sandwich. After a moment, she said, "You're not involved with this . . . this terrible thing, are you?"

Vicky knew that Rose worried about her defending people accused of crimes, as if they might commit some crime against her. "I want to see Anthony cleared, that's all."

"Can't the police do that?"

"Anthony's not guilty," Vicky said softly.

Rose sighed. "Nobody knows for sure what somebody might do."

Vicky moved her legs to one side to allow a young woman with a fussy baby to slip past toward a vacant chair at the far end of the row. What Rose said was true. She was seldom surprised anymore by the things people were capable of doing, but she didn't believe Anthony could commit murder. She didn't want to believe that.

Watching Father John step to the foot of the casket, she felt a prickly sense of surprise, as if the lens had gone out of focus just as she was about to snap the picture and she had to refocus. He wore black slacks and a black short-sleeved shirt with white Roman collar. She wasn't used to seeing him in clericals. She reminded herself again that he was a priest.

"Let us pray," Father John said, looking out over the crowded hall. The crowd fell silent. People set their empty plates on the floor, then straightened themselves in their chairs. Rose moved stiffly in her chair before seeming to settle herself, hands in her lap, rosary beads twined through her fingers. Vicky drew in a deep breath, waiting.

The Catholic ritual would come first, then the Arapaho. Just because her people had converted to Catholicism didn't mean they'd given up the old ways of believing. Those beliefs were still strong as a lodgepole pine, with the new way merely grafted on. Vicky thought of what her grandfather had told her once. "We pray with our ancestors, and we pray with the long robes. You can't pray enough."

"We ask Almighty God, our Creator and Savior, our Father and Brother, to be merciful and to show us, in His time, the place He has prepared for us," Father John said. Then he began the first decade of the Glorious Mysteries, the Resurrection. His voice sounded low and calm as he led the Hail Marys. Everyone joined in the last half of the prayers, sending a low buzz through the hall like bees in a field of wildflowers. Vicky stared at the red-haired priest, his head bowed, and thought how different he was from other men she had known. He asked nothing from her, seemed glad just that she walked the earth. It had taken awhile to accept that he was as he appeared, all of a piece, seamless as a fine buffalo robe.

She glanced around, half expecting to catch Ben's black eyes riveted upon her. Two of his cousins stood near the door, but she didn't spot her ex-husband. She'd heard he was working at the tribal ranch forty miles north, which meant he probably wouldn't get to the southern part of the reservation very often. She began to relax with the rhythm of the prayers.

Rose's voice was calm and distinct beside her. She was another mother to Vicky—there was no word for aunt in Arapaho. After Vicky had divorced Ben and left the reservation, Rose had helped Vicky's mother with the kids, Lucas and Susan. By the time Vicky had returned to the reservation, the kids were 18 and 20, off on their own in Los Angeles. Knowing her children would grow up in the Arapaho Way had made it possible to leave them. Still, it never left her mind that, to reclaim herself, she had lost her children.

The murmuring of prayers stopped, and Father John began reading the Psalm: "Out of the depths I have cried to Thee, O Lord." Then the Gospel of St. John about Lazarus's death and Martha's conviction her brother would not have died had Jesus been there, and Jesus' assurance that whoever believes in Him, even though he die, shall live. Vicky knew the story by heart. There had been too many wakes.

Father John stepped away from the casket and resumed his seat. A sense of anticipation filled the hall. Now the Arapaho ritual would begin with the cedar smudging.

One of the Arapaho men walked down the aisle carrying a pan filled with cottonwood coals and cedar chips, which, Vicky knew, were really a mixture of pulverized cedar and earth and pieces of animal bones, representing all created things. He removed the lid and offered the pan to Will Standing Bear who stood up, grasped the handle with both hands and raised it above his head. The black vest he had on stretched upward over his long-sleeved white shirt. As the sweet smell of smoldering cedar wafted across the hall, little clouds of smoke rose toward the ceiling and hung in the air, symbols of purification and forgiveness and respect for all life.

The elder's voice boomed through the hall. His Arapaho words beseeched Shining Man Above to allow cedar's smoke to mark Harvey's way to the spirit world. Then he said thank you to Mother Earth who gives herself for our home, to sun who gives himself for light and warmth, to four-leggeds and wingeds that share their lives with us. Vicky understood most of the words, even though she didn't speak Arapaho very well. Her parents had refused to speak Arapaho when she was growing up. They were not blanket Indians. They had been progressives.

Will came down the center aisle pointing the pan to one side, then the other. Everyone reached for the smoke that flumed along the rows of folding chairs. Vicky pulled the gray wisps toward her, breathing them in. Smudging made her feel connected to her people, to all living creatures.

The calmness that descends after a storm, when the wind begins to die down, settled over Blue Sky Hall as Will walked back to the front. He set the pan on the floor and replaced the lid, choking off the smoke. Head bowed, he prayed softly in Arapaho for a moment before taking his seat. The hall was submerged in quiet. Vicky glanced about, catching Banner's eye. The chief stood inside the front door. He motioned to her.

"Excuse me a moment," Vicky whispered to Rose, whose head was bowed in reflection. Wondering if Rose had even heard, Vicky got up and walked softly toward the police chief. Banner opened the door and stepped outside, as if he were confident she would follow.

"Hear about Ernest?"

Vicky nodded. There probably wasn't anybody alive on the reservation who hadn't heard about Ernest shooting up an oil pump. The news had blown through like tumbleweeds.

"What happened when you went out to see Ernest Saturday afternoon?" An official note sounded in the chief's voice.

"Is this an interrogation?"

Banner leaned against the wall and brushed one hand across his forehead. "Forget the lawyer stuff, Vicky. I just wanna know what set Ernest off."

"He was very drunk Saturday afternoon. Does that surprise you?"

Banner laughed. "The sun shines. Does it surprise me?"

"He'd already hit Jenny. He would have hit her again. Jenny didn't want to leave at first, but she ran out with the kids as I was about to drive off. It was a big step. I took them to the shelters."

Banner nodded. "Yeah, and soon's Ernest figured out Jenny and the kids were gone, he got in that old pickup of his. Went screaming down the road, probably doin' a hundred. Wonder he didn't kill somebody. We got three calls from folks yellin' at us to get him off the road."

Banner glanced around, as if looking for someone to corroborate the story. There was no one else outside. Then he leaned toward Vicky and said, "Showed up outside Circle of Respect hollerin' for Jenny to get her butt out. Would've tore the whole shelter apart if a couple of my men hadn't got there on the double quick. Arrested him for disturbin' the peace. We kept him overnight, but we let him go Sunday morning," the police chief said, a pleading note in his voice. "If we kept everybody locked up for drunkenness and disturbin' the peace, we wouldn't have any room at Fort Washakie jail."

"How about assault? You could've charged him," Vicky said. She felt her stomach begin to churn. Why was it that when a man hit his wife, it wasn't assault?

"You're soundin' like a prosecutor," Banner said, shifting his weight from one foot to the other. "Jenny refused to sign a complaint, as usual. She said she got a black eye by walkin' into a door. Anyway, we got a hold on Ernest now, after that oil pump business. He's at Riverton Memorial in detox."

Vicky drew in a long breath. "Father John could've been killed," she said. She would never have forgiven this police chief and his methods if that had happened.

"What about you?" Banner asked. "You shouldn't have gone out to Ernest's place alone, Vicky. You're gonna get yourself killed one of these days."

"I know. I know," she said, waving away his objections. She knew the unpredictability of drunks, but she had wanted to see for herself if there was anything to Anthony's suspicions about Ernest. "Did Jenny tell you Ernest didn't come home Friday night?"

Banner pushed away from the wall and drew in a deep breath. "You think he killed Harvey?"

Vicky took a moment before answering. "Ernest gets violent when he's drunk, but . . . Harvey's murder took more planning than Ernest may be capable of these days. Still, where was he Friday night?"

"Probably in a ditch somewhere too drunk to get home," Banner said, squaring his shoulders.

"Where was he Saturday afternoon?" Vicky persisted. "I heard about Harvey's office. Maybe Ernest broke into it."

"Lookin' for what?"

"Something about the oil wells that were shut down. Who knows?" She hadn't thought about it until now, but it made sense.

"The only thing the burglar was looking for was something in Harvey's history files. Father John's gonna put the files back together and try to figure out what's missing." Banner pulled in his lower lip and gazed across the open spaces. "Maybe Ernest was too drunk to find the tribal files, so he tore up the wrong files. It's a long shot, but all we got are long shots. We talked to everybody camped around Harvey's tipi Friday night. Nobody heard anything. Nobody saw anything. We got casts of a moccasin print and we got an eagle feather, but they don't tie up with anything. I don't wanna see Anthony go down for this any more than you do, Vicky. But I gotta tell you, chances are better'n good he's going to."

It was close to midnight when Will Standing Bear raised himself off his chair in the front row and faced the crowd again. The elder removed a buckskin pouch from somewhere inside his vest, close to his heart. Vicky knew the pouch contained the sacred red paint.

Moving toward the casket, Will Standing Bear uttered the Arapaho prayers said only by members of the Eagle Clan, those who had the power to apply the cleansing paint that prepared a corpse for the spirit world. He smeared the paint onto his thumb and forefinger, then touched Harvey's forehead and cheeks. Vicky knew he was painting the small red circles that would identify Harvey to his ancestors.

In a year Will Standing Bear would paint the same sacred circles on the foreheads and cheeks of Harvey's family to call them from the half-life, the mourning place spent half with the living, half with the dead. The sacred paint would give them strength to move forward into the new life, the life without Harvey. And tomorrow at the feast and the give-away, after the funeral, the elder would paint everyone else who wished it, so that Harvey's friends could move into the new life immediately.

As Will Standing Bear returned to his chair, the crowd let out a long breath, as if everyone had forgotten to breathe and had suddenly remembered. People were yawning and rubbing their eyes as they picked up bags and sweaters and prepared to leave. A few friends would keep watch through the night with Harvey's body. Anthony would stay, too.

After walking her mother's sister through the parking lot, Vicky waited as the old woman started the engine of her fin-tailed Chevy and turned on the headlights. Standing in the yellow glare of the other headlights switching on around her, Vicky watched the Chevy nose across the lot, up an incline and out onto Blue Sky Road. For an instant the headlights splashed across the white Cadillac parked on the other side of the road, silent and dark. Suddenly the Chevy squealed to a stop, and the Cadillac jumped forward and sped past, racing down the road, its red taillights fading in the darkness like the glow of fireflies.

"What was that?"

Vicky whirled around at the sound of Father John's voice. "A white Cadillac parked across the road just took off."

In the lights washing through the night, Vicky caught the puzzled look on the priest's face. "Only one person around here who drives a white Caddy," he said.

Vicky nodded. "What was Dorothy Bennett doing here?"

∞ 17 ∞

IT WAS THAT still time just before dawn when Vicky let herself in the front door of the rented bungalow in Lander. The town was shrouded in silence and the air cool with a faint hint of moisture. The day's heat seemed a dim memory. Maybe it would rain, she thought as she flipped on the lamp next to the sofa. They could use a cleansing rain.

Larry was stretched across the sofa cushions sound asleep, his blue tie unknotted at the opened neck of his crumpled white shirt. It startled her to see him. The idea flitted across her mind to let him sleep and go on to bed herself. Everything had gone out of focus. The murder of the tribal chairman, the almost certain indictment of one of the most promising young people on the reservation, the craziness of Ernest, the strange, complicated feelings she had for a man she had no right . . .

She closed the door on that thought. And now Larry was here. A good man, this Lakota. She was fond of him, but she wasn't certain of the direction in which she wanted her life to go. There were no signposts in bold letters to show the way.

She let herself down softly on the sofa next to the

sleeping Lakota. He opened his eyes halfway, stirred slightly, and slipped an arm around her waist. She studied his face in the lamplight. It was pleased, satisfied, a faint smile playing around his mouth. He had a strong hooked nose, eyes set so deep they seemed blacker than they were, and full lips. His hair was long and black, sleek as silk. He had pulled it back in a ponytail held with a red woven band. He was handsome, no doubt about it. She never imagined she would become involved with a Lakota. Lakotas were the enemies of her people in the Old Time.

He wanted more from her than she could give. He wanted a wife, a home, children. Why not? He hadn't had those things yet. He was six years younger than she was. He'd just turned thirty-six last month. When he'd asked her to marry him this past weekend in Denver, she had put him off, pleading for a little time. But he had kept asking. There was the job in L.A., a new life, and he wanted her in it. He would keep on asking, she knew. He was a stubborn warrior.

He pulled her toward him, and she felt herself relax against his chest. He wasn't Ben. The other time had nothing to do with Larry, but it existed, it was part of her. There were scenes that flashed in front of her at unexpected moments. Now she saw herself folding two dollars with a coupon from the back of a box of rice. She licked a stamp and plopped it on the envelope and dropped it into the mailbox at Ethete. The cookbook would arrive in six weeks. It was a guarantee that she would be alive in six weeks. She had to be alive because her cookbook was coming.

"What's wrong?" Larry asked. Vicky realized she was crying.

"Everything," she said, sweeping the tears across her cheeks with the palm of one hand.

She felt Larry kiss the top of her head, felt the warmth of his breath in her hair. "Why not let the fed find the murderer? That's his job. If Harvey's nephew gets indicted, you can do your job and defend him. It's simple."

"That's just it," she said, sitting up on the edge of the sofa away from him. "Jeff Miller thinks he's already found the murderer. He's not looking for anybody else."

Larry swung his legs down to the floor and slowly sat up. She knew by the way he pulled off his tie and tossed it onto the coffee table that he didn't like the drift of the conversation. Everything was simple to him, black and white.

"Who wanted the tribal chairman dead?" Vicky asked, letting her thoughts tumble out. "Why have some Arapaho wells suddenly gone dry? What had Harvey been working on? Why would anybody care enough about what he had written in that history of his to tear the files apart?"

"Why do you care so much?" Larry was looking steadily at her. There was silence between them. After a minute, Larry slumped back against the side of the sofa, his gaze still on her. "Now what?"

"John O'Malley . . ."

"Who?"

"Father John is going to put the history files back together. Maybe he can figure out what's so important in them. I intend to look at the oil angle. There has to be some reason for Harvey's murder." She heard the hope in her voice. What was she hoping for? That Larry would understand?

Larry put his arm around her and pulled her close. She liked the warmth and comfort of his body—it was easy to succumb. "You don't have to be so tough," he said. "Not with me." Brushing back her hair with his free hand, he removed her dangling silver earring and took the lobe of her ear between his lips. Then she felt the tip of his tongue in her ear. After a moment, he said, "No more talk."

*   *   *

Afterward, Vicky lay on her side and, in the golden light slanting through the half-closed blinds, watched Larry sleeping. His brown chest rose and fell with quiet rhythm above the top of the sheet crumpled around his waist. She would have to give him an answer, but not yet. She wanted to put it off a little longer.

∞ 18 ∞

FATHER JOHN TURNED the Toyota onto Seventeen-Mile Road, following the procession of pickups and old cars that had departed from Circle Drive as soon as Harvey's funeral Mass ended. The procession moved slowly down the middle of the blacktop, then veered right onto a narrow dirt path that led to St. Francis Mission cemetery. The cemetery sprawled across a brown bluff. Father Brad drummed his fingers against the metal frame around the passenger window. A black prayer book and a small container of holy water sat on the seat between them next to the tape player.

Easing the Toyota to the side of the path, Father John stopped behind the other trucks and cars. A white canopy fluttered in the hot wind over a casket and opened grave a short distance away. Already seated in metal chairs under the canopy were Harvey's family, Will Standing Bear, and several other tribal elders. The singers hovered over the drum, and Arapaho families crowded around, filling in the dusty, barren spaces between adjacent graves.

Grabbing the prayer book and holy water container, Father John swung out of the Toyota and made his way along the narrow dirt paths between the graves. Each grave was covered with brightly colored plastic flowers and crosses of weathered wood. Some had carved inscriptions: "Lovely Mother." "Here lies a Good Man that Cared for Children." "A Generous Man with a Good Heart." The white canopy over Harvey's casket snapped against its ropes, and the hushed whisperings of the crowd dissolved as the priests approached.

The young priest gasped, and Father John saw immediately what had caught his attention. On top of Harvey's casket sat a large brown saddle, stirrups and straps coiled against the polished wood. Father John shot a knowing glance at his assistant, meant to say he would explain later how Arapaho chiefs, in the Old Time, were always buried with some belongings so they would have what they needed in the spirit world. Harvey would be buried only with his saddle, the symbol of his worldly goods.

Opening the prayer book, Father John began reciting out loud the ancient Catholic prayers for the dead, asking God to bless the final resting place of His servant, Harvey Castle. Then he handed the container of holy water to Father Brad and, walking slowly around the casket, dipped the sprinkler into the water and flung it across the casket and the saddle. People in the front rows blinked as drops of water rained upon them.

When he had finished the blessing, Will Standing Bear stepped forward. *"Jevaneatha neshait hideniau hethehe vedaw nau neyesawathawid jethee hevedathu,"* the elder prayed, the words soft and lilting. Holding himself perfectly still, with head raised and shoulders thrust back, the old man gazed across the knoll to the plains that stretched endlessly away. White clouds sailed across a sky as blue as the sea, and the canopy billowed in the breeze. Then, the elder said: "No matter what has happened, we must keep God's commandments and walk in His road all our lives."

The singers stirred around the drum. Two men started turning the wheels attached to the wide belt under the casket. Slowly the casket descended into the earth as drumbeats punched holes in the air. Suddenly Anthony stepped forward and held up his hand. The wheels stopped turning, and the drumming stopped. Leaning over the grave, Anthony picked up the saddle. He held it out to Father John. "It is for you," he said.

Again the steady beat of the drums sounded across the knoll of the cemetery and drifted into the wind as the wheels began cranking. Father John watched the casket descend, the saddle heavy in his arms. He felt the moisture of tears on his cheeks at this double gift. He had the pleasure of receiving the saddle that had belonged to his friend, but since he didn't own a horse, he would have the additional pleasure someday of giving the saddle to someone who needed it.

The drumming continued several moments after the casket had been lowered. Harvey's family and the other mourners stood with heads bowed, and Father John let his gaze roam across the cemetery and onto the plains shining in the sun. Then he looked up. A golden eagle circled overhead. It swooped toward the group around the grave, then rose and glided west toward the foothills of the Wind River Mountains, wings outstretched. After a moment it circled back. Father John realized that everybody was looking up into the sky. Whenever the eagle came, it brought a blessing and the promise of harmony. It brought hope.

No one said anything, but the crowd, almost as one, had looked away from the sky and was watching a white Miata nudge its way along the dirt road past the line of parked vehicles and stop. Melissa Bennett got out and walked tentatively around the other graves toward Harvey's. Anthony had started through the crowd toward her, and as soon as she spotted him she ran into his arms.

It's no longer a buzz on the moccasin telegraph, Father John thought. It's out in the open now for all the world to see: Anthony's motive for committing murder.

∞ 19 ∞

"WHAT DOES MELISSA Bennett's family think about her and Anthony?" Father Brad's voice rose over the wind crashing through the cab of the Toyota.

"Just what you might guess." Father John flipped down the visor against the noonday sun dancing on the hood and washing across Seventeen-Mile Road. The idea of judging others by the color of their skin made his own skin crawl, which was why he'd usually turned down invitations to the Cooley ranch. But Melissa was different. There was hope for the young. Harvey's saddle shifted across the bed of the pickup, and thudded against the side.

As soon as they'd gotten into the cab, Father John had explained the double gift to his assistant who didn't say anything at first. Then, shifting in the seat and looking out the side window, he'd said, "You know, this isn't a bad place."

Father John had glanced sideways at the blond priest in the black wool suit who looked like a Wall Street banker and wondered if, maybe, he'd been too hasty. He was always quick to size up people, and lately he was turning out to be wrong more often than right. You could never tell about anybody. After all, he looked a little like a banker himself today, in his black shirt and slacks. Realizing Father Brad had said something about leaving, he pulled away from his own thoughts and gave the young priest his full attention.

"You weren't around yesterday when the Provincial called," Father Brad was saying, "so I grabbed the chance to talk to him about a job teaching in Chicago or maybe St. Louis. Wherever there's a prep school vacancy."

Father John felt his grip tightening on the steering wheel. The next governor of Wyoming was demanding his ouster from St. Francis at the same time his assistant of less than three weeks was asking for a transfer. The Provincial must wonder what in hell was going on.

"Nothing personal," the young priest added quickly, "but you've got to admit reservation work is pretty dull, except for when somebody gets murdered, of course, and I suppose that doesn't happen very often. It's too bad people like the Cooleys and Jasper Owens and some of the folks from Riverton and Lander aren't parishioners at St. Francis. It would make an assignment here more interesting."

Father John glanced at the speedometer and let up on the gas pedal. For a moment he'd thought this assistant was beginning to see beneath the surface of things. Why should he have expected that of Father Brad before his time? At least there was potential with this young priest, he was becoming convinced of that. He wished Father Brad had waited awhile before talking to the Provincial, that was all.

"When will you leave?"

"Depends on available jobs. By the way, the Provincial wants you to call him ASAP."

Message delivered, Father John thought. He had no intention of calling the Provincial any time soon to hear about his next assignment.

The parking lot in front of Blue Sky Hall was already

filled. It looked as if more people had come to the feast and the giveaway than had attended Harvey's funeral. Father John wheeled the Toyota into the vacant field across the road, and he and his soon-to-be-gone assistant walked in silence over the hard-packed ground past the old cars and pickups.

A couple of Arapaho men waited in front of the hall, doormen with John Deere caps pushed back on their heads. "Come on in," one said, pushing open the door. The hall looked much the same as at last night's wake—the same people milling about, except now there was the buzz of conversation. The table along one wall was covered with food: Hamburgers, potato salad, baked beans, steaming corn, and fry bread. The air was thick with the odors of fresh coffee, onions, hot oil, and dill pickles.

"What's over there?" Father Brad asked, nodding toward the end of the hall. He didn't point, and Father John felt a stab of pride. This assistant had figured out, in a short time, that Arapahos considered pointing rude.

Father John explained that the items Harvey's family would give away were stacked on the table—blankets, shawls, star quilts. "It's the family's way of thanking people for all they've done during the last couple days. In the Old Time . . ." He stopped, glancing at the young priest to see if this was a gift he wanted to receive. A hint of interest sparked in Father Brad's eyes, and Father John plunged on, explaining how Arapaho families used to give away the dead person's tipi and belongings, everything except for the things needed in the afterlife, which were buried with the corpse. Chances were that Maria and Rita had already quietly given away Harvey's personal items to people they knew could use them.

Father John spotted Maria seated in a circle of grandmothers not far from the table. Leaving Father Brad with a group of Arapahos who had come over to welcome them, he strolled over to the old woman. Maria held out a thin hand to him. Her other hand clutched the knitted shawl around her shoulders, even though the day's heat had settled over the hall like a shroud.

"Don't forget your promise about Anthony," Maria said, reaching for his hand. Her eyes, watery and clouded, locked on his.

Rita stepped away from the knot of people close by. Placing one hand on her mother's shoulder, she bent down, bringing her face close to the old woman's. "Anthony's gonna be fine. He's home now, isn't he?"

Maria ignored her daughter and kept her eyes on Father John. There was no mistaking the fear born out of memory, fear that the injustices of the past might be repeated in the present.

Anthony was talking to several young Arapahos in the center of the hall. He looked around, then started over. Anyone would know the young man had just buried someone he loved, by the sadness in which he moved.

Father John walked through the crowd to meet him. There were thousands of words he might say, all of them inadequate. Shaking Anthony's hand, he managed, "I can't tell you how much your gift means to me. I'm deeply touched."

Anthony nodded and said something about Harvey wanting him to have the saddle. Father John knew that wasn't quite true. Harvey hadn't planned to die.

"You see Melissa at the cemetery?"

"Didn't everybody?"

The young man shrugged. "I asked her not to come to the feast and giveaway. It's going to take some time for people to get used to us. She's been saying that all along."

"How about Dorothy and Ned? Will they get used to you?"

"I'm going out to the Cooley ranch tonight so Melissa and I can talk to them together. If they see how much we love each other, maybe they'll come around."

Father John doubted it. His heart went out to this young couple, burdened by the past.

"How about some fishing up at Washakie reservoir tomorrow, Father? I could really use somebody to talk to."

"Sure," Father John said. The magistrate's warning that Anthony should stay close at hand flitted to mind a moment, but he dismissed it. The young man wasn't running anywhere. He just wanted to go into the wilderness where he could think, and he wanted a sounding board to test his thinking on. Of course he wanted to go fishing at the Washakie. That was what he had done all his life with Harvey.

Nodding toward the elders in a far corner, Anthony said, "Grandfather wants me to be painted today."

Father John followed the young man's gaze. Several elders were standing in a circle, each holding a buckskin pouch. They would begin the painting soon. Everyone who wished it would receive circles of sacred red paint on their foreheads and cheeks. The paint symbolized the gift of life given by the sun and placed all who received it under the sun's care. It renewed the happiness of the mind.

Father John never ceased to marvel at the wisdom of Will Standing Bear. The rest of the family would not receive the paint until the first anniversary of Harvey's death. It would mark the end of the half-life and give them the strength to move into the new life without Harvey. But Anthony needed strength now to move into whatever the new life had in store for him.

~ 20 ~

FATHER JOHN DECIDED to turn in early, but the temptation was strong to see how the Red Sox were doing. He flipped on the television in the living room. The game was still on. He sank into the overstuffed easy chair, removed the black wing-tipped shoes, and parked his pinched, sock-enshrouded feet on the edge of the oak coffee table. It was the top of the ninth, the Red Sox leading the Mariners three-zip. With two strikes and a man on third, the pitcher wound up and sent a fastball across the plate. The batter laid a grounder out to left field as the runner pounded for home.

Now Father John's feet were planted flat on the floor. He was on the edge of the sofa, leaning forward, jabbing one fist like a boxer. He always watched baseball on the edge of his seat, the way he and his Dad used to watch it at Fenway Park. On the edge of the seat, leaning forward, punching the air. He was only dimly aware of the phone ringing in the front hall.

Slowly he backed out of the living room, keeping his eyes on the screen. The runner scored easily. The left fielder had the ball and was throwing to second as the hitter hurtled toward the base. The tag was good. Fenway erupted in cheers. The Sox would hold.

"St. Francis," Father John said, slightly out of breath. He always felt as if he were on the field himself when he watched the Red Sox.

A woman on the other end—he didn't recognize her voice—was talking about an emergency. It took a moment to focus on what she was saying. Something about an accident out on Seventeen-Mile Road and Charlie Taylor.

Fenway Park was still cheering as Father John slammed out the front door leaving the television blaring. The wind was calm, and a field of stars blinked in the dark sky. He slipped into the Toyota, turned the key and, ramming the gear into forward, shot out onto Circle Drive.

The compact of holy oil that he'd grabbed from the study rode light as a feather in his shirt pocket. Always carry your oils in an emergency—that was one of the first lessons he had learned at St. Francis. Steering the Toyota along Riverton's quiet main street, he thought about that summer six years ago when Old Man Wilson's daughter had asked him to come to the ranch because her father was feeling poorly. Feeling poorly! The old man had died in Father John's arms. It had taken a couple of hours to return to St. Francis, get his oils, and drive back to anoint the body.

A crowd of people hovered around Charlie's wife in the waiting area outside the emergency room at Riverton Memorial. Father John recognized a couple of parishioners. He could remember meeting Charlie's wife only once— about a year ago they'd come to Mass one Sunday. She had the look of a sleepwalker, dressed in a wrinkled pink pantsuit with long black hair bunched around her shoulders. She was weaving on her feet as one of the other women helped her to a metal chair.

"They're getting ready to take him into surgery, Father."

A nurse came around a counter and led the way into a maze of emergency treatment rooms. "Looks like the steering wheel crushed his chest when his pickup went off the road."

Charlie lay on a hospital gurney, a hose stretched upward from one brown arm to a bottle of fluid dangling overhead from a silver pole. A black blood pressure cuff was wrapped around the other arm, and another nurse was pressing a stethoscope into the crook of the elbow.

"You only have a few moments," the first nurse said. "The doctor is scrubbing now."

Father John slipped the compact from his pocket as the nurse with the stethoscope stepped back, motioning him forward.

"Can you hear me, Charlie? I'm going to give you the last sacrament," he said, leaning over the trolley. Charlie's eyes moved toward him, eyelids flickering as if he were making an effort to stay awake. There wasn't a mark on his face. His chest must have taken the full blow, Father John thought, as he made the sign of the cross on Charlie's forehead, touching it with the oil and softly repeating the prayers. "With this holy anointing, may the Lord in His love and mercy help you with the grace of the Holy Spirit. May the Lord who frees you from sin save you and raise you up."

"No," Charlie whispered.

Father John stopped. "Do you not wish the sacrament?"

Charlie's eyes were bright, desperate looking. He managed to nod his head slightly, and Father John continued the anointing.

"No." Charlie's voice was louder, rough as sandpaper. "Accident."

Suddenly the Indian stretched his fingers, clawing at the air, lips moving soundlessly. Father John bent over and placed one ear close to Charlie's mouth. "Three," Charlie whispered. Father John heard the rattle in the Indian's chest, the death rattle he'd heard other times in other emergency rooms. Then a burst of whispered words came from the Indian. "Three." "Three." "Three." "Ten."

Two orderlies came through the door. "Ready," they said, positioning themselves at both ends of the cart. Father John kept his hand on Charlie's shoulder as the gurney moved through the doorway and down the hall. The squish of rubber wheels on the tiled floor sounded like footsteps in soft mud. He watched the gurney disappear past two wide swinging doors.

"He gonna make it?" Charlie's wife asked. Her face pale, her eyes wide, as if she'd already guessed the answer.

"I hope so," Father John said, wondering if he shouldn't, instead, try to say something that would prepare her. There were no words that could prepare her for what was coming.

An Arapaho woman who looked enough like Charlie to be his sister got up from a metal chair across the room and said, "Charlie must've missed that big curve on Seventeen-Mile Road. He's always drivin' too fast." At this, Charlie's wife winced and drew in her breath. "Two kids came drivin' by and spotted the wreck. Happened maybe an hour ago," the other woman went on.

Father John was thinking that Charlie had been at the funeral Mass this morning and at the cemetery with the other council members. He was sure of it, but he didn't remember seeing Charlie at the feast and giveaway.

"Where was he going?" Father John asked.

Charlie's wife turned in the metal chair, pointedly ignoring the other woman. "He was out on council business. He works hard. He's always out takin' care of council business."

"He tried to tell me something," Father John said. "It was

hard to make out. He kept saying 'three.' Then what sounded like 'ten.'"

"It's about ten o'clock now," the Arapaho woman who looked like Charlie's sister said. "You think he was askin' the time?"

That idea hadn't entered his mind. Father John glanced around the waiting room at the other Arapahos, their eyes on him, obviously following the conversation and waiting for his response. "I don't know," he said finally.

In his mind, he was turning over the other words Charlie had uttered, but he decided against mentioning them. "No" and "accident." Charlie was in shock, but those words were clear. Was he in denial, saying that the accident hadn't happened? Or was he saying he didn't want it to have happened? Or—the idea hit Father John like a fastball in the stomach—was Charlie telling him it was no accident?

The minute the green-garbed doctor stepped into the waiting room, Father John knew Charlie was dead. "Mrs. Taylor?" the doctor said, moving toward the councilman's wife. From the look of terror on her face, she also knew what the doctor was about to say to her.

∾ 21 ∾

THERE WAS NO traffic on Seventeen-Mile Road. The morning was hazy and cool, but a blinding sun was climbing out of the east. Father John snapped down the Toyota's visor. Ahead the plains, brown and parched, lengthened into the gray-blue sky. It was a kind of miracle how, at certain times of day, in certain light, the earth and sky flowed together as if they were one. A couple of white clouds with dark edges drifted along in a promise of rain that would probably come to nothing. More than likely, it would be another hot day.

Father John slowed the Toyota a short distance beyond the intersection with Goes-In-Lodge Road, just before Seventeen-Mile Road angled north. It was the only bend for miles in the two-lane road that shot straight as an arrow across the reservation. Charlie's gray pickup lay on its side out in the field a good fifty feet. He wondered how fast Charlie had gone into the curve.

He'd passed the site last night on his way home from the hospital, but it had been too dark to see anything other than the shadowy hulk of the truck. He wanted to walk around in the daylight before Banner and his men and a phalanx from the state patrol converged for an investigation. Not until Father John eased the Toyota off the road and down into the barrow ditch did he notice the blue pickup parked in the scraggly bushes.

He wasn't the only one checking out the accident. Father John slowly got out of the Toyota, taking in everything: the wrecked truck, the bushes, and the yellow sunflowers in the ditch, the road a few feet above. Just then Ned Cooley stood up on the far side of the pickup and began walking around it, cowboy hat pushed back on his head, hands in the pockets of his tailored gray pants.

Meadowlarks trilled to one another through the morning quiet as Father John made his way across clumps of sagebrush, avoiding the prairie dog holes. He could feel his muscles tensing, the way they did when he was a kid in Boston walking through a strange neighborhood.

The rancher leaned against the tilted tailgate of Charlie's pickup, waiting. There was no trace of surprise on his face, nothing but the complacency of a man used to being in charge.

"Charlie Taylor a friend of yours?" Father John asked as he approached.

Ned lowered his eyes, folded his arms, and crossed one leg over the other. Gravel scraped under his boots. "All these Indians are friends of the Cooley family."

Father John walked slowly around the pickup. The sun flared off the tilted windshield. The hood and engine had been pushed back almost into the front seat. He wondered how they'd gotten Charlie out. "Think this was an accident?" he asked.

The other man guffawed. "Of course it was an accident."

"What brought you out here so early?" Father John

stopped next to the rancher, still leaning against the tailgate. Without answering, Ned squared his shoulders, dug his hands into his pockets, and began strolling along the pickup, his attention on the exposed axles and driveshaft. Finally he said, "Always hate to see something senseless like this." A speech. He was the candidate in a roomful of supporters. "Soon as I'm governor, I intend to do everything in my power to erase the scourge of alcohol from this reservation."

"Charlie didn't drink," Father John said, studying the tailgate where Ned had been leaning. It had a deep, rounded dent that pushed into the bed itself. It was hard to tell if the gray paint had been scraped off, or if those were flecks of dark paint.

Suddenly Ned whirled around and took a couple of steps forward. He was squinting in the sun which had already burned off most of the morning haze. White clouds drifted like snow over the Wind River Mountains, but everywhere else the sky was radiant blue. "That so? You seem to know everything on this reservation. You make everybody's business your own and go around interfering in people's lives. That doesn't work here, Father O'Malley. We got our own ways, and we don't like outsiders interfering. That's why your boss is gonna send you back to Boston or someplace else real soon."

"Maybe," Father John said, locking eyes with the rancher. There were no maybes, and Father John knew that the other man understood this. It was Ned Cooley who was interfering in his life, calling the Provincial, telling him God knows what to get Father John removed from St. Francis. If the Provincial ordered him to another assignment . . . Well, he had taken the vow of obedience. He would have to go. He swallowed back the anger rising in his throat like hot phlegm.

All of a sudden, Ned turned and started across the field. Father John watched him climb into the pickup. It wasn't long before it spun out of the barrow ditch onto Seventeen-Mile Road, doing fifty into the curve.

∾ 22 ∾

Banner and Jeff Miller were outside the red-brick tribal offices when Father John pulled into the parking lot. The morning sun burned with a white heat, and a hot wind sent tumbleweeds scuttling across the asphalt. The two officers of the law stopped talking as Father John got out of the pickup and walked over.

"Looks like we might have another murder. State patrol says Charlie's pickup was rammed from behind. He was pushed off the road." The fed looked as if he expected a denial from Father John. "It's time I got your boy into custody before somebody else gets killed."

"Are you saying Anthony killed Charlie Taylor?" Father John exchanged a quick glance with Banner. There was no mistaking the worried look in the chief's eyes.

"A sure bet," the agent said. "Evidence says he killed his uncle. Lab report came back yesterday. A couple hairs we picked up in Harvey's office came off Anthony's head. And guess whose fingerprints are on the knife?"

"How many times did Anthony visit Harvey's office? Probably every time he was back from school. And whose fingerprints would you expect to find on the knife if not the

owner's? If there weren't any other prints, it only proves the
murderer wore gloves," Father John said.

Exasperation flared in the agent's eyes. "I don't get you
two," he said, turning to the police chief. "You have to be hit
over the head with a baseball bat before you face facts? I'm
taking this case to the U.S. attorney today, soon as the state
patrol finishes its report on Taylor's accident which, I
suspect, wasn't an accident."

The fed stepped off the sidewalk and marched across the
asphalt lot to the tan jeep parked next to the Toyota.
Swinging open the jeep's door, he hollered, "Want to bet
your boy says he was with his girlfriend last night?"

Father John strode out after the agent and placed both
hands on the door just as the engine kicked over. Leaning
down so his face was only a few inches from the fed's, he
asked, "What possible motive would Anthony have for
killing Charlie Taylor?"

"As soon as I find out, you'll be the first to know," Miller
said, ramming the gear into first. Father John stepped back
as the jeep rolled past him.

Banner closed the door to Harvey's office the moment
they were inside and brushed the flat of one hand across his
forehead, wiping away little beads of perspiration. "Miller
could be right about Charlie's accident. First the tribal
chairman is murdered, and now a councilman has a very
suspicious accident. We could have some kind of conspiracy
going on."

The hit-man theory flashed through Father John's mind. It
was never far away, although he didn't like to admit it.
Settling into Harvey's chair, he told the police chief what
Charlie had whispered before he died.

"Why didn't you tell the fed?"

"I wanted to think about it first. Besides, he didn't ask
me."

Banner grinned. Then he said, "No accident. Charlie was right about that. But the numbers? What was he trying to tell you? That somebody forced him off the road by ramming his pickup three times, ten times? Jesus, there's nothin' but puzzles everywhere we turn. All except for the case Miller's building against Anthony."

"How long before the grand jury returns an indictment?" Father John asked.

"Two, three days. Miller talked to Anthony again. He knows about Melissa. Now he's got the motive, the weapon, and the fact Anthony could've driven to the powwow grounds and back to Cooley's old place without Melissa ever knowin' he was gone. Anthony's alibi has all the strength of a gnat." Heaving a deep sigh, the police chief hauled out a handkerchief and mopped his forehead.

Father John glanced at the stacks of file folders on Harvey's desk waiting for his attention. He was a third of the way through the manuscript and so far he had found nothing. It could be a waste of time, and time was what they didn't have. They were missing something here, some proposition in the syllogism, some path they should take. What was it? Why couldn't he see it?

"We tried talking to Ernest," Banner said. "He swears up and down it wasn't him that made this mess here. Hospital's got him pretty sedated, plus they got him on a twenty-four-hour watch."

"They think he's suicidal?"

Banner nodded. "You heard, didn't ya? Jenny took the kids and went down to Denver. She's got a sister there."

This was the first time Father John had heard of it. Usually he heard all the gossip, but he'd been so preoccupied the last couple days that he hadn't returned phone calls, and he hadn't been out talking to people. He hadn't even had the time to visit Ernest. Jesus, the poor bastard. He remembered how he'd felt those first few days at Grace House, sick as a dog, the earth dropping out from under him.

"One thing's for sure," Father John said. "Ernest didn't push Charlie off the road last night, and I don't think he's got it together enough to have planned Harvey's murder, no matter how upset he might've been over the dry wells."

"Another puzzle, those damn oil wells being shut down," Banner said, drawing his lips into a thin line. "We done some checkin'. Harvey asked for a report last week, but Marvin Antelope—he's that Crow the council hired on as resources director—says he's still workin' on it. The council don't have the report yet, and that means Harvey didn't know anything more about why those wells were shut down than the rest of us."

"Dead end," said Father John. "Just like this is turning into a dead end." He thumped the knuckles of his index finger against the folders.

The police chief picked up the top folder and began thumbing through the pages. "It would've been a great book all about Our People. Maybe, when all this is over, you could finish it for Harvey."

"I'd like to," Father John said. He didn't want to tell the police chief that, come September, he probably wouldn't be at Wind River Reservation, that the wheels were already turning to have him shipped elsewhere. Instead he launched into an explanation of Harvey's system, how each folder contained a separate chapter, and each chapter had an outline, a typed manuscript, research notes, and photographs. He was checking through everything in the folders, but so far nothing was missing.

Banner had pulled out a stack of black-and-white photographs and was flipping through them. "These look pretty recent," he said.

Father John glanced over the chief's shoulder. "They're

from one of the last chapters," he said. "Harvey had started at the beginning and was bringing the history up to the present."

The chief let out a low whistle. "Wonder how he ever got a hold of this," he said, holding one of the photos out at arm's length. "That was the first time anybody ever took my picture."

Father John leaned forward to get the photograph into focus. He recognized the canyon of the Washakie, the dirt road climbing upward, the jagged granite cliffs on both sides. A group of people—they looked like Arapahos, about seventeen or eighteen years old—posed alongside some pack horses, holding the reins, smiling into the camera. At the far left, one boy, thin and shy-looking, sat his horse. "That's me," Banner said, laying a pudgy brown finger against the image.

Father John's attention was drawn to the young man on the right, his arm around one of the girls as if he were pulling her close, claiming her. He looked like Anthony. The girl was slender, in blue jeans and a short-sleeved blouse. Light hair hung below her cowboy hat which partly shaded her face. Harvey and Dorothy Bennett were staring at him from the past, frozen in time.

So the rumor was true. Two or three times he'd heard the grandmothers clucking about Harvey and a white woman. One had even mentioned her name: Dorothy Cooley. But Harvey had never mentioned her, and Father John had dismissed the rumor as unlikely. Not everything the grandmothers gossiped about was rooted in fact.

"When was this taken?" Father John asked.

"Mid sixties, I guess. We took a pack trip up Washakie Creek, beyond the reservoir. My girlfriend just got a new camera, so she lined us up and took our picture. I haven't seen it in years." Banner's eyes remained fixed on the photo.

"Dorothy Bennett was one of your friends?"

"Dorothy Cooley then." The police chief looked up. "It was a long time ago. All us kids grew up together. Went to different schools, of course, but Dorothy always hung around with us Indian kids. Nobody else around here for her to associate with. She and Harvey . . ." He stopped, shaking his head. "It was sad, now you think of it. There was no way anything was ever gonna come of it. But that summer," Banner pointed to the photo again, "they were together all the time. Tried to keep it secret from their folks, and it's not easy keepin' secrets on the rez. If Anthony and Melissa hadn't been down in Laramie, their romance wouldn't have stayed secret long. Anyhow, the Cooleys found out about Dorothy and Harvey." Sighing, Banner laid the photograph back in the folder.

"What happened?"

"Old man Cooley was still alive then, so he and Ned sent her packin' off to school somewhere in the East. A couple years later we heard she got married. That's about when Harvey married that gal from Cheyenne. Didn't last long. They were like a team of oxen pulling in different directions. Then, about ten years ago, Dorothy got divorced and moved back to the ranch with her little girl."

"I'd heard the gossip about Dorothy and Harvey."

"Old news," the police chief said. "There was nothing between 'em when she got back. Oh, they were polite to each other whenever they met. I saw 'em talkin' over at Blue Sky Hall once. But, hell, there was nothin' going on. Everybody would've known if it was otherwise. Besides, Dorothy's a Cooley to the bone."

"She was parked outside during Harvey's wake," Father John said.

The chief's eyes widened into two black discs. "I heard that might've been her Caddy there, but it was gone by the time I got outside." He was silent a moment. Then, "Don't get your hopes up that it means anything, John. The girl in that photo couldn't murder anybody. She couldn't even spur her horse."

∞ 23 ∞

VICKY TOOK A step closer to the oak conference table and peered down at the large map of the Wind River Reservation.

"This what you wanted?" Marvin White Antelope leaned toward her, his Adam's apple bobbing up and down like a tetherball. His black hair, slicked back, brushed the collar of his light-blue shirt. Tapping the map with a pencil, he looked at her above wire-rimmed glasses. His breath smelled stale and sour like cigarettes and old bologna, and Vicky instinctively pulled back.

"Business council hasn't seen my report yet," he continued. "I shouldn't be showing you this."

"I appreciate it," Vicky said, running her index finger from one clump of black dots on the map to another. The dots marked the location of oil fields on the reservation.

"You owe me."

"Right." Vicky let her finger fall on a cluster of dots in the center.

"So have dinner with me tonight."

"I'm busy." Her finger moved to another cluster along the reservation's western boundary.

"Tomorrow night, then."

Vicky felt his eyes boring into her. She jerked her head upward and met his gaze. "No."

"You're a fine-lookin' woman, Vicky," he said, his smile curling into a smirk. "Woman Alone. That's your new name, right? You're too beautiful to be alone."

She looked back at the map, ignoring the comment. After a moment Marvin started to roll it up. "Nobody should see this before the council gets the complete report."

Vicky flattened her hand in the center, pinning the map to the table. "You might need some legal advice sometime."

"Can't think what about," he said, rolling the map tightly to the point where her hand lay. "Why do you care about the oil wells anyway?"

"The tribal chairman has been murdered, and now it looks like another councilman has been murdered. Several wells on the reservation suddenly stopped pumping for no reason anybody seems to know. Does all this strike you as strange?" She drew in a long breath, then went on. "Anthony Castle is a suspect in his uncle's murder, and I happen to be his lawyer. I can get a subpoena, or you can let me see this map."

The Crow Indian, who had found his way south from Montana and into the job of resources director, kept his eyes on her as he slowly uncurled the map. "I'm doin' this under protest."

Vicky took another breath. "Are these the wells that stopped pumping this summer?" She pointed to the black dots on the southwest.

"So far's we know." Marvin's words were terse, business-like.

"What about over here?" Vicky moved her finger to the cluster of black marks near Fort Washakie. "Or here," she said, lighting on another cluster further north.

"All pumpin', far as I know." Marvin tapped the pencil on

the table, as if he had better things to do than this dead-end meeting.

"So these are the only wells that have gone dry." Vicky's finger moved back to the dots on the southwest. "Odd," she said, partly to herself.

"No it's not." There was an edge to Marvin's voice. "Oil dries up in an area, it's gonna hurt the wells there."

"How long had they been pumping?"

"Twenty years or more on two of 'em. The others, about ten years."

"Who holds the leases?"

"Owens Oil Exploration," Marvin said, the pencil now rapping out an impatient rhythm. "We been doing business with the Owens family for years. They run a good company."

Vicky studied the little marks that Marvin's pencil had made around the lower edge of the map and thought of the oil pumps still moving up and down against the horizon, just across the line from the reservation. "Any wells stopped pumping here?" She ran one finger below the map.

"Not that I know of. Just bad luck Arapaho oil gives out. Not our business what happens to Fremont County wells."

"Does Owens hold the leases on those wells?" Vicky persisted.

The Crow took his time answering, letting his eyes roam over her. After a moment he said, "Nope. Several oil companies got 'em. I don't have all that information. I don't need it for the report."

"So your report will not explain why oil in part of the reservation suddenly ran out even though there's still oil just across the line?" She knew it wouldn't, that he had accepted the non-pumping wells as an act of God, finished.

The Crow took his eyes from her and set about rolling the map into a long, tight stick. This time Vicky didn't try to stop him. She had all the information he was about to give her without a subpoena. Everything else she wanted to know she would have to dig up herself in the records at the Fremont County courthouse. "Thanks," she said with effort as she opened the office door.

"Who is it?" the resource director called after her. "That Lakota or somebody else you're stuck on?"

It took all her willpower not to slam the door. Instead she kept on going, not shutting the door, not bothering to look back or acknowledge in any way that she had heard.

Vicky walked down the hallway of the tribal offices, past social services, finances, wildlife, and environmental protection, past the receptionist's desk at the foot of the V-shaped building. Then she turned down the other hallway where the councilmen's offices were located and rapped on Harvey's door.

"You missed him." The voice came from behind, and Vicky wheeled about. She hadn't been aware of anybody else in the hallway. "Father John left a few minutes ago," the receptionist said.

∾ 24 ∾

WILL STANDING BEAR was finishing lunch at a table in the far corner of the Ethete senior citizens center. Two other elders sat across from him fingering coffee mugs and chatting quietly. Except for a small group at another table, they were the only old people still there. It was almost two o'clock. Several middle-aged Arapaho women moved among the empty tables picking up dirty dishes.

"You eaten lunch yet?" Will Standing Bear asked as Father John walked over. Not waiting for an answer, the elder motioned to one of the women stacking dishes on a tray. When he had her attention, he nodded toward Father John.

Father John sat down across from Will, next to the other two elders, and tossed his cowboy hat on a vacant chair. He tried to stop at the center once in a while to have lunch with the old people, but he hadn't planned on eating today. What he wanted was advice from the elder who had given him an Arapaho name and had made him feel as if he belonged among the people.

The two other old men pushed their chairs back and rose quietly, as if sensing Will and the missionary priest wanted to talk in private. As they shuffled behind Father John, one patted him on the back. "Two of our councilmen dead now. We don't want no more. Thank you, Father, for what you're doin'."

The Arapaho woman sat a bowl of stew and a plate of fry bread on the table, and Will picked up a metal pitcher and poured Father John a mug of coffee. "Eat and drink," the elder said, pushing the mug toward him.

Politeness came before questions. Eating and drinking first, then discussion. The stew was hot and delicious. The broth was thin, filled with whole carrots, chunks of potatoes and beef so tender Father John could cut it with a spoon. Stew was an Arapaho specialty, he knew. In the Old Time, every family kept a pot of buffalo meat and wild vegetables simmering all day over the fire in the center of the tipi.

Father John pushed the empty bowl to one side and waited. It was not polite to speak before the elder indicated he was ready for the talk. After a moment Will Standing Bear said, "It's good Anthony's at his home now. But his trouble ain't over, *Teenenoo Hiinooni'it.*"

"I'm trying to help him," Father John said, "but I'm not getting anywhere. I wonder what I should do next?"

"To wonder is to begin to know," the elder said, his eyes watery but his gaze firm. "In the Oldest Time, Our People lived in the place where the sun rises, close to the waters that have no other side. At night they would go outside—all the men and women and children—and look up at the stars and moon. They wondered about the mystery of creation. And they wondered and wondered. One night in the Moon of the Drying Grass two stars streaked through the sky and fell near the village of Our People. Then two glowing shapes came into the village. They were the beautiful Star Men. Because Our People had wondered, the Star Men came to give them the precious gift of knowledge. They taught Our People all about the Star Nations, and the Milky Way and about all of creation. And they said not to be afraid, but Our People were still afraid. Knowledge is a hard gift."

The senior citizens center was quiet except for the gentle clatter of dishes and the soft swishing of a wet cloth as one of the women wiped a nearby table. Father John found them reassuring, this old man's stories that he had heard from his grandfather who had heard them from his grandfather—stories emanating through time, like a faraway light in a dark tunnel.

After a moment Father John said, "Harvey was working on at least two things that could have led to his murder. He'd asked Marvin Antelope for a report on the oil wells that stopped pumping in the southwest. Ernest was angry with Harvey for not doing something about it. Maybe somebody else was angry. Oil's worth enough to kill for, I guess." He was thinking of Father Brad's hit-man theory, even though it still seemed preposterous.

"Lots of things more important than oil," Will Standing Bear said. "Our Arapaho Way, our religion, our elders and our children, our brothers and sisters, all the creatures that make our life rich—the four-leggeds and the wingeds—Sun that shines every day, Mother Earth that gives us all we need to live. Lots of things."

Father John realized he'd been looking at things through his own eyes, the eyes of a white man. Oil means money, which places it high on the white man's scale of values. Oil is important to Arapahos, too, but in the whole scheme of things, its importance is minor. That didn't mean Harvey hadn't died for it, however.

"There's something else, Grandfather," he said. "The Cooley ranch deal."

A long silence seeped into the space between them.

Finally the elder said, "I told my grandson what my grandfather told me soon as I was this high." He flattened one hand and brushed it over the table. "Our People don't trust the agent."

"But government agents don't run things on the reservation anymore," Father John said. "The people do. Why is it important today that Arapahos didn't trust old Mathias Cooley a hundred years ago?"

"My grandfather would not speak of it. None of the elders would speak of it. They said some things must not become words until the time is ready."

"What does that mean, Grandfather?" Father John persisted.

"This is our place on the earth. The Cooley ranch is next to our place. So we must live side by side, and the Cooley family is very powerful. I think that's why my grandfather said it is best not to speak of these things."

"But what made Harvey change his mind about buying the ranch?"

"My grandson told me he believed the time was now ready to make many things known."

Father John sank against the padded back of the folding chair and drew in a long breath. So Harvey had discovered something while researching Arapaho history. Chances are that's what he had wanted to talk to him about the morning of the powwow. "Do you have any idea what Harvey had found?"

The elder shook his head slowly. "My grandson was always finding secrets buried by white men."

Buried was the right word, thought Father John, taking the first sip of the coffee the elder had poured. It had turned cool. Harvey had often complained about how the records of government dealings with Arapahos were hidden in other government records, making it difficult to locate information. To find out about some Indian battles on the plains, he'd had to slog through records of the entire Civil War.

"*Niatha*'s too clever for himself," Will said. The Arapaho word for white man was also the word for spider, a mysterious, clever creature. "*Niatha* tries hard to bury his shameful deeds. Trouble is, he wants to write everything down. So pretty soon somebody like Harvey finds what *Niatha* wrote down. *Niatha* gets tangled up in his own web."

Father John was thinking of some of the events Harvey had talked to him about—events that whites, especially those involved—would want to hide. What cavalry man wanted his family and friends to know he had ridden into an Arapaho village of women and children and killed everyone there? Yet somebody had written it down. It was somewhere in the records, all the horror. On the other hand, what difference did it make if such things became known today? Everybody involved was dead.

He finished off the coffee and set the mug on the table. Will Standing Bear kept his eyes on him, as if prodding him on. The elder didn't have the answers—he would tell him if he did. He expected Father John to connect the parts. He was counting on him to do so.

Father John began stumbling out loud down the relentless path of logic. "Harvey was always pushing to find out what happened on the plains in the Old Time. He discovered something new, something no one had ever known before, something in the past that someone did not want uncovered. It had to do with something Arapahos consider important." He took a deep breath, turning over in his mind what Will had told him. Arapahos value many things more than oil. All living things. Sun. Mother Earth.

"Of course," Father John said, pushing back his chair and jumping up. The chair squealed against the tiled floor. Why hadn't he seen it? It was as obvious as the whole outdoors.

"Land," he said. "Harvey stumbled onto something that had to do with Arapaho land, something about the Cooley ranch."

Will Standing Bear got to his feet and leaned against the back of his chair. "When you find what it is, *Teenenoo Hiinooni'it*, you'll know who took my grandson's life from him."

"Thank you for all you have given me, Grandfather," Father John said, picking up his cowboy hat.

"Something else." Will Standing Bear pushed his chair against the table. "My grandfather said that when the murderer tries to eat, all the food's gonna taste bad."

Father John walked out to the parking lot with the elder and helped him into his Chevy pickup. The old man pulled himself upright over the steering wheel before turning on the ignition. Remembering his promise to Ernest, Father John held up his hand and leaned toward the opened window. "One more thing, Grandfather. Ernest wants very much to see you."

The Indian stared out across the steering wheel. "Yes," he said, after a moment. "Ernest is ready now. I will go to see my grandson."

The dry wind blew little eddies of dust across Seventeen-Mile Road. The heat inside the Toyota was stifling, even though the sky was as gray as the strip of asphalt ahead, and steel-colored clouds rose over the rim of the Wind River Mountains. He kept one finger on the hot steering wheel, aware of perspiration soaking the back of his shirt. For the first time since Harvey's murder, he felt as if he had finally found the right path. Now he knew what to look for in Harvey's history files.

～25～

BEFORE FATHER JOHN could return to Harvey's office, he had to put in a little time in his own office. The stack of messages and bills and other mail, the unreturned phone calls all needed attention. St. Francis Mission seemed to be running itself these days, although Father John had to admit his assistant was doing a good job of holding things together. As soon as he got back, he stuck his head in Father Brad's office and told him he appreciated his efforts.

The young priest grinned, then mentioned he'd just finished counseling a couple with marital problems. Father John had married them last May. He thanked his assistant again, feeling guilty for not having been here. Then Father Brad said the Riverton coach had called. His team would be at St. Francis tomorrow morning ready to go against the Eagles. Father John had forgotten about the game, but he knew the kids wouldn't forget.

"I won't be leaving anytime soon," Father Brad said, shoving his swivel chair back from the small oak desk in his office. The desk was clear as a blank sheet of paper, except for the yellow tablet the young priest had been writing on.

"The Provincial called again?" It seemed a minor annoyance now, a mosquito buzzing around.

"He wants me to stay on awhile." Father Brad smoothed the top of his hair, which already lay like mown hay against his head. "I was hoping for a teaching post this fall, but . . . well, if I have to stay on, it won't be too bad, I guess."

Father John got the picture. The Provincial wasn't about to move the assistant, not when he intended to move the superior. Somebody had to stay, and this young priest, even though he didn't know it yet, was about to be in charge of St. Francis Mission.

"The Provincial's bent out of shape you haven't returned his calls," Father Brad went on. "I told him you've been pretty busy."

Great. Busy investigating a murder. Just what he wanted the Provincial to hear. Father John felt irritated, then he realized his assistant had stalled for him, tried to give him an excuse. "Thanks," he said again.

As he sat down at the desk in his own office, Father John's eyes fixed on the blue message sheet on top of a stack of paper. "A.M. Thursday. Provincial. Call back. Important." He crumpled it up and tossed it in the wastebasket.

The next message: Homer Lone Wolf called from Denver—reversed charges. Baby okay after operation. Homer keeping pledge.

At least there was some good news, Father John thought as he flipped through the rest of the stack, pulling out obvious bills. He opened each envelope and made a new stack with the contents. There was no way he could pay all the bills this month, any more than he had paid them last month. St. Francis Mission was always short on funds. He slit open a plain envelope with no return address. A five-dollar bill fell out. A donation. Donations came from unexpected places. Last month out of the blue, a large check had arrived from a lawyer in Baltimore, someone he'd never heard of. And before he'd come to St. Francis, some anonymous donor had willed the Toyota to the mission. It was a kind of miracle, the way St. Francis kept going.

Father John called Elena and asked her to put up some bologna sandwiches for later. Then he paid bills until the balance in the Mission checkbook hovered around zero and, at five o'clock, he locked up the office. Father Brad had already left, probably to get in his afternoon run down Seventeen-Mile Road, which had begun to make Father John feel a little guilty. He knew he ought to get in more exercise than an occasional run around the ball field with the Eagles.

Over at the priests' residence, he picked up the cooler with the sandwiches and cans of Coke and stashed it in the back of the Toyota. Next to it he laid his fishing pole, tackle box, and waders. Driving out to Harvey's ranch, he listened to *La Traviata* and thought about Anthony's loss. He felt a sense of unworthiness that the young man had asked him along on his first fishing trip without Harvey. He would do his best to be a good friend, even after he left Wind River, but he knew that no one would ever fill the empty space Harvey's death had left in his nephew's life.

Cool mist sprayed upward as Father John moved with his neoprene waders into the water. A few feet from the shore of Washakie reservoir, he planted both feet on a bed of pebbles that promised to be stable. Steep, rocky slopes of Washakie canyon rose all around. The sky was blue-gray, but the clouds bunched overhead were laced in black.

Father John flipped the line back, then snapped the pole forward to cast further out into the dark blue water. The number 14 Adams fly that Anthony had suggested he try skimmed across the surface before catching on a boulder that jutted out of the water. He had no illusions about being a great fisherman, not like people from these parts. The first time he'd ever tried fishing had been with Harvey six years ago. He'd come here every summer since, sometimes with Harvey and Anthony, sometimes with other friends from the reservation. Ned Cooley had invited him on a couple of fishing trips. Those invitations he'd turned down.

Anthony was along the shore a hundred yards away. He had reeled in a three- or four-pound trout thirty minutes ago. Father John had watched him dip his net and scoop up the flailing fish. Holding it upside down, he'd removed the hook before putting the trout back into the water. That was the last strike for either of them.

Father John was about to back cast again when he saw Anthony coming along the shore toward him. Picking his way wherever he could get a sure footing in the water, Father John walked toward the Indian.

"That's enough for me," Anthony said as Father John scrambled out of the water. "Trout ought to be biting in this weather, but they're not. Maybe it's not going to rain after all," he said, glancing at the darkening clouds overhead.

"They're not biting anywhere if not here." Father John pulled down the tailgate of the Toyota and laid his rod on the ridged bed. This was the best place on the reservoir. All the good fishermen came here. It was where Harvey had always fished.

Balancing against the tailgate, Father John removed the long neoprene waders. Then he pulled on his cowboy boots. Through a clearing in the thick stand of ponderosas alongside the road, he could see down Washakie canyon to where it spilled out onto the flat, open plains. It looked like a perfectly framed picture postcard—golden plains under a sea-blue sky dotted with clouds.

"How'd things go between you and Melissa's family last night?" he asked.

Anthony was lacing up his sneakers. "Can't you guess? They refused to see me. Cooley ordered me off the ranch. It's bad enough I'm Arapaho, but now I'm also suspected of killing my own uncle." His chest rose and fell, as if the words took his breath away.

Father John was sorry he hadn't tried to warn the young man. The fact he was suspected of murder made little difference. The Cooleys would never accept an Indian for Melissa any more than the family had accepted an Indian for Dorothy. He wished, with all of his heart, there was some way to spare Anthony from ever knowing that fact, but sooner or later, he would know. Father John pulled the bologna sandwiches out of the cooler and handed one to the Arapaho. Then he grabbed two Cokes. "Now what?" he asked.

Pushing back the plastic bag, Anthony bit off a chunk of white bread and pinkish bologna. After a moment he said, "We're gonna cool it for a while. Melissa thinks her family will come round soon as I'm in the clear. She wants to wait and not push them."

Father John popped the tab on a Coke and drank almost all of it, letting the cold syrupy liquid quench his thirst before opening his sandwich bag. Anthony had stopped eating and was staring down the canyon at the plains shimmering in the last light of the sun. "Chief Banner and that FBI agent are taking their sweet time about finding Harvey's murderer, and meanwhile my life's falling apart."

This was how the young warriors were in the Old Time, thought Father John, biting into his sandwich. Impatient to right the wrongs. Anxious to settle matters fast, while the chiefs signed treaties and believed promises. They had brought a lot of trouble on themselves and on their people, those young warriors.

"I heard Ernest went before the tribal judge today for being drunk and disorderly," Anthony went on. "They let him out on bond. Can you believe it? A crazy guy like that. He's supposed to stay in the rehab program at the hospital. I figure I'll go over and pay him a visit."

"Look, Anthony," Father John began, choosing his words carefully. "Ernest didn't murder Harvey any more than he could've forced Charlie Taylor's pickup off the road from his hospital bed. Whoever killed two tribal councilmen is playing for a lot bigger stakes than the royalties from some oil wells."

Anthony shifted toward him on the tailgate, his expression wary and curious. Father John hurried on. "I think Charlie had an idea of what was going on. He might have known who killed Harvey. When I talked to him, he was either covering up what he knew or he was flat-out lying."

"What makes you think so?" Anthony asked.

"Charlie said he wanted to see the Cooley ranch deal go through. Then he tried to tell me that Harvey had intended to vote for it."

Anthony looked puzzled. "He said that? Harvey planned to do everything he could to get the council to vote against the deal. That's what we were arguing about. That and Melissa, of course. You know what's odd, Father?" he said. "Harvey was absolutely sure that Charlie was with him all the way."

Father John finished off the sandwich. "Could be that Charlie changed his mind about buying the ranch after Harvey was murdered. But why would he do that?" He wished he had asked Charlie's wife that question before she'd left Wind River Reservation today to take her husband's body to Oklahoma for burial.

"Who knows," Anthony said. "Nothing's making sense anymore. Everything stinks." He threw the empty Coke cans back into the cooler and slammed the lid. "I'm gonna take a run up the mountain. You wanna come?"

Father John glanced at the sky fading into shades of gray and lavender. It would be dark before long, but he understood the Indian's need to work off some anger and frustration. Anthony needed to feel himself moving across the earth like the wind. "Sure," Father John said, wishing he were in a little better shape for a run to the top of a mountain.

The young Arapaho sprinted across the dirt road, and Father John followed. There was nobody around. Not more than three or four other fishermen had been at the reservoir in the couple of hours they'd been there. Anthony attacked the mountain like a young bighorn sheep. Three steps right, three steps left, he zigzagged upward through the scrub brush and around the boulders, ducking under the thick branches of ponderosa trees. Father John had to push just to keep the young man in view. He wished he had on sneakers instead of cowboy boots that slipped with every step.

Halfway up, Anthony stopped and waited, but as soon as Father John caught up, he started off again, slicing away the mountain at short angles. Father John had to wait a minute to catch his breath before starting out again. He wondered how this modern-day warrior had ever sat still long enough to be within a few weeks of a college degree.

The Arapaho scrambled up a clump of boulders near the summit and stood on the top, outlined against a sky of deepening shades of blue. The wind flattened his shirt against his back. Father John climbed the boulders, hand over hand, bracing against one in order to leap to the next, trying to keep from slipping back, hearing his heart pounding in his ears. Finally he reached the Indian. On the other side were sheer cliffs of granite that dropped straight into the valley of the next canyon.

Father John let his eyes range across the distant views. Most of the plains lay in shadow, except for a slim golden strip on the east that still caught the setting sun. The ranches were marked off in squares, like patterns in a quilt. Lander huddled close to the foothills while Wind River Reservation spread northward and wrapped around Riverton on the east. So much space, so few people.

Neither he nor Anthony spoke for a moment. Finally the young man said, "Harvey used to bring me here when I was little. He'd tell me to look out there, 'That's your place on earth,' he'd say. 'That's where you belong.'" Anthony stretched out one arm. "The beautiful prairie lands, that's what Chief Black Night called this place."

Suddenly Anthony jumped down and edged his way along the ridge below the boulders. "Come on," he called. "I'll show you something else." Father John started after him, but by the time he reached the ridge, Anthony had disappeared. He looked down the mountain expecting to see the Indian zigzagging through the brush and trees, but no one was there. "Where'd you go?" he hollered. The wind sighed through the ponderosas, and the last of the daylight played across the bushes and rocks.

"Here I am." Anthony sprang upward, as if he'd been propelled out of the pile of boulders a few feet above Father John.

"How'd you get up there?"

"I'm in the eagle catch," Anthony said. "Only way in is down below." He nodded toward two boulders, close to where Father John stood, then slid down out of sight. After a moment he appeared several feet down the mountainside. Father John picked his way down. He couldn't make out where Anthony had come from. The boulders were wedged together without enough space for anyone to squeeze through.

"Harvey showed me the eagle catch when I was little," the Arapaho said. "Only eagle clan people know how to catch the eagles and take their feathers. Harvey was the last to catch the eagles when he was still a boy. He'd gather brush and pile it on top of the catch like a nest. Then he'd lay a dead rabbit on it and slip into the catch below. Sometimes he'd wait there two or three days. Soon's the eagle swooped down for the rabbit, he'd grab it by the legs and hold it while he plucked out a few tail feathers. Then he'd let it go. He always left some sage in the catch to thank the eagle for his feathers."

Pushing back thick scrub brush, Anthony exposed a narrow opening between the boulders. "Want to go in?"

Father John bent down and looked into the narrow tunnel running under the boulders. If he got inside, he might not get out. "No thanks," he said. "I'm not a member of the eagle clan."

"I would've been an eagle catcher like Harvey if the government hadn't outlawed it. Just as well, I guess. It was a lonely job. Now we get our feathers from the forest rangers. Whenever they find a dead eagle, they freeze it and send it to us." Anthony let the brush fall slowly back into place. There was no trace of the tunnel. "When the eagle catcher dies," he went on, "he turns into an eagle and flies straight to God."

The last of the daylight shimmered through the trees under a sky that had turned purple. "Hadn't we better get down?" Father John suggested. "While I can still see where I'm going?"

∾26∾

MOONLIGHT WASHED ACROSS the red bricks of the tribal office building as Father John turned off the ignition and pressed the stop button on the tape player. *The Magic Flute* snapped off, leaving the last notes to fade in the air. Grabbing the handle of the player, he stepped out of the Toyota. The parking lot was deserted. With no interruptions—just Mozart for company—he could put in a couple hours on the history files. The answers were there, he was certain. He had to find them.

Using the keys Banner had given him, he let himself in the front door and groped along the wall for the light switch. Moonlight poured like rain through the window, but most of the lobby was shrouded in darkness. He thought he saw something move in the shadows of the hallway. "Who's there?" he called.

From somewhere came the soft gurgling of water pipes. He inched along the wall keeping his eyes on the hallway until his fingers touched the light switch. Before he could flip the switch, someone lunged out of the darkness, across the shaft of moonlight, and slammed against him, jamming his right shoulder into the wall. Pain shot down his arm all the way to his fingertips. He swung the tape player, but it flew out of his hand and thudded against something. There was the clack of boots on the tile floor, and then the sound of a door slamming shut.

Father John sank down against the wall, trying to catch his breath, which finally came out of some deep well inside him. Grasping his shoulder, he lifted himself up along the wall and moved toward the door. It took all the effort he could muster to let go of his shoulder long enough to yank open the door and slip outside. The parking lot was bathed in moonlight. The only vehicle there was the Toyota.

Leaning against the brick, he edged to the corner of the building and looked toward the back. Suddenly headlights were beaming down on him. He jumped back just as a jeep sped by, its wheels shooting out gravel. It swerved up a knoll and onto the highway.

Holding on to his shoulder and biting his lower lip against the pain, Father John made his way back into the building and flipped on the light. The little tape player lay against the wall, its top cracked, the *Magic Flute* tape hanging out. He bent over slowly to pick it up, then looked around for the keys.

Spotting them against one leg of the receptionist's desk, he set down the player, fingered the key ring, then wedged player and keys together in one hand. Pain pulsated down his right arm as he walked along the hall to Harvey's office.

The door was locked, and he had to go through the whole rigmarole again: Set the player on the floor, grapple with the keys, unlock the door, push it open, pick up the player. It made him slightly dizzy, and he had to lean against the jamb a moment to steady himself. The office looked the same as when he had left this morning. Whoever had attacked him hadn't gotten in, although Father John had no doubt that had been the goal. He had arrived just in time—just in time to get his shoulder dislocated. Perfect, he thought.

Grunting with pain, he sat in Harvey's chair and placed the tape player on the desk. Then he picked up the phone and punched in 911. "This is Father John O'Malley," he told the operator. "Get me Chief Banner."

The chief wasn't in, he was told, but the operator would put out a call for him. There was no sense of hurry in her voice, and Father John heard himself shouting into the phone that this was an emergency and that the chief should call him immediately at Harvey Castle's office.

He slammed down the phone and forced himself to take long, deep breaths and try to relax his shoulder and arm muscles. He didn't think anything was broken, but his shoulder was definitely separated. He'd separated it a couple of times before, pitching fastballs. His throat felt dry and scratchy, and every cell in his body was crying for something to drink. He forced himself to think of something else.

He had to get to emergency at Riverton Memorial, a good thirty-minute drive away, and that wasn't going to be easy with his right side convulsed in pain. Whoever had attacked him would be miles gone by now. "Where the hell are you, Banner?" he said out loud. "Come on, call."

∽ 27 ∽

THE EMERGENCY ROOM whirled around as Father John sat up, swung his legs off the examining table, and willed the room to stop moving. His right arm rested against his chest in some kind of high-tech combination of buckles and bandages. They had wanted to give him a general anesthetic, but he'd said no, thank you, no general. That would be the beginning.

The doctor had seemed eager to talk him into it, explaining how much better it would be—relaxed muscles, less pain. Then he'd stepped behind the table. Suddenly he'd gripped Father John around the shoulder, and his dislocated arm had shot into its socket. A fireball had hit him, every muscle in his body had twitched, and little lights had flashed everywhere.

He'd rested on the table awhile as the nurse hummed around. At one point she came at him with a needle—"it'll feel better"—and he'd rolled to the side, nearly falling off the edge. "Okay, okay," she'd said. "Have it your way. But you're gonna want something to get you through the night."

Now he wanted out of here. He struggled off the table. The nurse grabbed his left elbow and, with surprising strength for a woman who barely reached his chest, steered him out the door. The waiting room looked like another Arapaho funeral, it was so full of brown faces: Anthony, Rita, some parishioners, Banner, and three or four BIA policemen. And Vicky. She took his arm from the nurse. "You okay?" she asked. Everybody was asking the same question.

The Toyota moved down Riverton's main street and slowed for the blinking yellow lights at the wide intersections. A couple of oncoming cars passed. Anthony was driving Vicky's Bronco right behind them, then Banner in his patrol car, then two other patrol cars and a couple of pickups. They were their own parade through town.

The Toyota's windows were rolled partway down, and a cool night breeze stirred through the cab. Father John shifted slightly to keep his right shoulder from touching the passenger seat—it'd been a long time since he'd been a passenger in the Toyota. Not since that first year at St. Francis when old Father Peter pulled rank as superior and insisted upon driving. It's a wonder they'd survived. He smiled thinking about it, and pain lit up his shoulder. He heard himself grunt.

"You're not going to take those painkillers, are you?" Vicky asked, her eyes straight ahead. He could see the moonlight in her hair as she smoothed back a few strands that had blown across her face.

"Nope, I'm not going to take those painkillers."

She glanced at him, then turned her eyes back on the street. They were moving through moonlight and the dark shadows of Riverton's flat-roofed stores, motels, and gas stations. "Fact is, there's probably nothing you'd like more right now."

"Actually I prefer my painkillers in liquid form."

"You are one stubborn Irishman, John O'Malley."

They were on Highway 789 now, heading south of town, and the Toyota speeded up. "Who hit you?"

"A four-hundred-pound Sumo wrestler." Father John squirmed in the seat. There was no place to hide from the pain. "How'd you hear?"

"Moccasin telegraph." She glanced at him, smiling. "If you must know, the police dispatcher is a friend of Rita's. She called Rita, who told Anthony, who called me. We thought you'd need somebody to drive you home. They usually put you under for these things."

"It's nice to have a chauffeur anyway," Father John said. He found that if he leaned his head against the window frame, his right shoulder floated in space, which relieved the pain a little.

"I was there twice, the emergency room," Vicky said. "Courtesy of my husband." She seemed lost in thought, and Father John waited for her to go on. "So I got a divorce, left my kids here with my mother, and moved to Denver."

This was what she'd never told him, but for some reason she was telling him now. The tone in her voice was one he was accustomed to hearing in confessionals from penitents needing forgiveness.

"The thing was, Ben loved the kids. He was good to them, he really was. But in the divorce, well, I paid him back for what he'd done to me. I made sure he didn't get the kids. It just about destroyed him, although I hear he's getting on his feet now. But the kids . . . well, they lost both of us." She stopped, glancing quickly at Father John before turning her eyes back to the highway. "I don't know why I'm telling you this. It's over now. It's in the past, and the past is over."

"Except," Father John said, "it has a way of hanging around, demanding we understand it and weave it into ourselves so that we can go on." He watched the Toyota's headlights dance over the asphalt ahead, illuminating the stands of cottonwoods along the highway, and thought of the hell she had broken out of, and the cost.

Vicky shifted behind the wheel, as if forcing her consciousness, her whole being, into another position. After a moment, she said, "Did you hear that Miller had Anthony in for more questions today? He's trying to pin Charlie's murder on him. That fed's not going to give up."

Anthony hadn't said anything about that, but Father John wasn't surprised. Up at Washakie reservoir, the young man's mind had been on Melissa.

"Whoever trashed Harvey's office last Saturday didn't find what he was looking for. So he came back tonight," Vicky continued, drumming her fingernails against the steering wheel. "I don't think it has anything to do with the oil on the reservation."

"No?" Father John sensed they were closing in on the same path. He thought of what Will Standing Bear had told him about Mother Earth being more important than all of her gifts, but decided against telling Vicky right now. His shoulder hurt less if he didn't talk, and trying to follow her train of thought helped to take his mind off the pain.

"I did a little research this afternoon," Vicky said. "I drove out on the county roads south of the reservation. All the wells on the Fremont County side are pumping, but right over the line on the reservation, several wells have supposedly gone dry. The storage tank for one of the county wells was being emptied, so I stopped and talked to the guy doing the work. He empties all the tanks in that area and hauls the oil to the refinery in Cheyenne. He said business has picked up this summer. He's been hauling out more oil than ever before."

"Who holds the leases?" Father John asked. The pain in his shoulder was sharp and steady, and he tried rubbing lightly on the sling. He had to work to focus on what she was saying.

"Not leases," she glanced at him. "Rights. I also spent some time at the courthouse. Last May, Western Resources, Buffalo Oil and Gas, and Intercontinental Oil bought the mineral rights from ranchers in the area. Mineral rights don't come cheap, but now those companies don't have to pay any royalties. They're pumping a lot more oil and raking in all the profits."

"So the companies are doglegging," Father John said. Vicky shot him a quick glance, and he saw the surprise in her eyes.

"You know about that?"

"I've heard about it. Oil companies drill slantwise into the oil basin under the reservation and help themselves to Arapaho oil. It's happened around here before. What I don't get is why Jasper Owens stands still for it. He holds the leases on the reservation wells. Wouldn't he suspect right away what was going on?"

"I did a little more digging," she said, slowing for the right turn onto Seventeen-Mile Road. "Western Resources, Buffalo Oil and Gas, and Intercontinental Oil are all subsidiaries of Owens Oil Exploration Company. One big, happy family."

Father John let out a long breath. "Jesus. I've misjudged Jasper Owens. I didn't think he was stupid. How long before somebody figured this out? Marvin Antelope . . ."

"Forget him," Vicky said. "My money says he's collecting a small percentage not to figure it out, which is why he's dawdled over getting out the report Harvey requested."

"Harvey would've figured it out," Father John said, thinking how thorough and organized and logical Harvey had been in researching Arapaho history.

"Of course," Vicky said. "He would have gotten the

business council to request a Bureau of Indian Affairs investigation, and Jasper would've been stopped, eventually."

"So you think Jasper Owens stopped Harvey?" Father John tried the idea out loud, feeling his way around it. Parts made sense, but other parts didn't. Suppose Jasper had decided to preempt Harvey, kill him before he could take action? Had he also killed Charlie for the same reason? What was his plan? Murder the entire Arapaho business council?

"Why would he have to kill anybody?" Vicky asked. "That's the real question. Sure the doglegging would've been stopped, and Jasper wouldn't have made as much money this year or maybe next. But the penalties are zilch. All he'd have to pay the tribes would've been triple royalties for the time he was doglegging." The Toyota had turned off Seventeen-Mile Road and was slowing around Circle Drive at St. Francis Mission.

"And get this." Vicky was shaking her head. "The BIA lets the oil companies estimate the royalties they would've paid if they hadn't been doglegging. So there's a lot of number-juggling to prove the wells wouldn't have paid out much anyway. They triple that and, bingo, they're home free. It's large-scale fraud, and everybody blinks at it."

"I thought fraud was still a crime," Father John said. He had caught her anger, and his shoulder tensed with pain.

"I called a law school friend of mine. She's with a firm in Chicago that represents some major oil companies. She said that the government usually makes a deal with the companies, so criminal charges are seldom brought. Deals are common, according to my friend. Welcome to the oil world."

Vicky stopped the Toyota in front of the priests' residence, and Anthony pulled the Bronco in alongside. It looked as if they'd lost Banner and the other BIA patrol cars and the pickups somewhere on Seventeen-Mile Road. She flipped off the ignition and leaned against the door into the moonlight. "If Jasper Owens got caught doglegging—worst-case scenario— all he would've had to do was cough up a little money and continue on his merry way. Why would he commit murder, two murders?"

Father John smiled at her. "So how come the Sumo wrestler was outside Harvey's office tonight?"

"I don't have all the answers," Vicky said. She jumped out, marched around the Toyota, and flung open the passenger door. Anthony was right behind her. They both looked ready to grab him if he stumbled getting out of the pickup. Dear Lord, he felt like some kind of invalid.

∾ 28 ∾

Having only one useful arm would not stop Father John. He would coach the Eagles' game this morning and then drive the Toyota over to the tribal offices where he'd find out what Harvey had discovered and what had gotten him killed.

Father John had drowsed off a few times during the night, only to be jerked awake by pain tearing down his shoulder and arm like a race car skidding across the pavement. The bottle of painkillers stood on the dresser and, about three o'clock, he'd flushed them down the toilet. They would've been like whiskey, numbing, calming, and he would've wanted more.

After watching the little pink tablets disappear in a swirl of water, he'd brewed a pot of coffee and sat at the kitchen table most of an hour. The strong bitter coffee eased him a little. If Homer Lone Wolf could keep his pledge, he would keep his, too. *God help me to keep it*, he prayed.

Father Brad had offered to stand in as the Eagles coach this morning, and Father John had considered it. His assistant was trying, he had to give him that, but this was likely to be the last summer Father John would have with the Eagles, and he wanted all of it.

The Eagles were on their feet hollering for Jonathan Little Bear to keep running, and Father John was yelling, too. The boy had hit a grounder to left field, made it to first base, and was looking around, satisfied, while the Riverton Buffalos scrambled for the ball. Finally the boy looked over at the bench and got the message. He put his head down and took off just as the left fielder gloved the ball and threw it in to second base. The kid on second base stepped out, caught it, dropped it, scooped it up and darted for the sandbag, but not before Jonathan slid in. "Safe," called the umpire, one of the Buffalo fathers.

The Indian kids were jumping up and down, shouting. The Eagles had their first chance to score, and it was the bottom of the sixth. Father John glanced over at Jonathan's dad behind the bench. "All right," the Arapaho said, shoving a fist over his head.

"You're up." Father John motioned to the next batter. The kid grabbed the bat and ran for home plate. He was good when he was on. He could bring Jonathan in.

Keeping his eyes on the pitcher, Father John hunched over his right arm, instinctively protecting it. For the most part, his shoulder and arm were numb, except for occasional shocks of pain when it felt as if his muscles had contacted hot wires.

The batter swung wide at the ball, missing it by a foot. "Come on," Father John said under his breath.

Another pitch. Another swing, closer this time. Jonathan, halfway to third, darted back. On the next pitch, the batter connected and sent the ball arching over the field. The right fielder pedaled backwards and leapt into the air, but the ball flew past, hit the ground, and spun out, the kid after it.

Jonathan fast-tracked around third and into home with the batter on his tail. Jonathan's dad had both fists in the air and was jumping up and down. All the kids were shouting. A couple were even rolling on the ground in glee.

The Eagles were still behind by one run, but it was clear the momentum had changed. Father John patted both kids on the back and motioned up the next batter. He was glad the morning was cool, the sky overcast. Except for an occasional gust of wind, it was calm, but the clouds over the mountains looked ominous. And the air felt heavy, like a magnet that might attract rain. The plains stretched away into the far distances, and the great expanse of quiet swallowed up the shouting voices, the whack of the ball.

It was good here. He would miss it more than he could say. St. Francis Mission, the people—his friends, the Eagles. There was a connection between the kid on the Boston sandlot thirty years ago and the Arapaho kids up at bat in the middle of Wyoming. Baseball had taught him some useful lessons: play by the rules, be part of the team, do your best, learn from errors, enjoy the rewards. But his world was white. He wondered what useful lessons baseball had for these Indian kids in their world.

The next batter struck out, but the momentum was still strong. Then he saw Elena walking stiffly across the back field, an apron tied over her dress. Only an emergency would send the housekeeper outdoors in midmorning. He hurried down the sideline, his hand grasping his bad arm to hold it steady. It hurt to walk.

"Two white guys come to the house," Elena said when he reached her. She was out of breath. "They don't wanna see Father Brad. They said they was gonna wait for you over in the church."

Father John could see the dark Lincoln parked on Circle Drive. He had to walk all the way back to the bench, gripping his arm, to ask Jonathan's dad to take over as coach.

Jasper Owens sat in the last pew of St. Francis Church, just inside the wide double doors. The fronts of his suit coat bunched up against the polished wood of the pew, and his feet were planted squarely on the kneeler. The burly young man who had accompanied him to the Cooley pig roast lounged against the side wall under a window.

Father John took his time genuflecting. He was used to Arapahos gravitating to the church when they wanted to talk to him. It never surprised him to step inside at any time in the day or evening and find someone waiting for him, as if he had been expected. This was the heart of St. Francis Mission, the sacred space where Arapahos came to look at their lives, to unburden themselves, to pray for grace. But he wondered why Jasper Owens and his sidekick had come to the church.

"What can I do for you?" Father John whispered, slipping into the end of the pew. He kept his voice low and reverent. They were in the Presence of the Blessed Sacrament. His shoulder and arm were throbbing, and he worked his fingers gently past the buckles and into the thick fabric of the sling.

Jasper squared his shoulders and crossed one leg over the other. "You remember my assistant, Luke." He nodded sideways at the dark-haired, muscular man. Father John didn't say anything.

"This is a real pretty church," Jasper went on. "I been sitting here thinking it's been thirty years since I went to confession."

Father John waited. An interesting opening. Maybe this oilman had a conscience after all. Maybe that's why he'd come here, to unburden himself.

"It's too late for me now." Jasper smiled and shook his head.

"You think so?" Father John leaned his good shoulder into the hard wood corner of the pew, keeping his eyes on the bald, perspiring man a few feet away.

"Yeah. I didn't come here for confession. You know that, don't you?" The oilman hoisted himself to his feet. "Is there someplace private we can talk business?"

Father John realized he'd been hoping Jasper might take a different turn, and he felt a slight sense of regret as he gripped the knob of the pew in front and pulled himself upright. The kneeler clanked against the floor as Luke scrambled across the pew and followed them outdoors. The sky was hazy, and the breeze sweeping through the cottonwoods around Circle Drive felt cool, refreshing. The sounds of the Eagles' game floated over from the field.

"This is as private as it gets," Father John said, gesturing to the sky. They had stopped on the sidewalk in front of the church. The oilman folded his arms across his chest and rocked back heavily on his heels, looking upward. "I'm a businessman," he began. "In business you've got to make hard decisions and do what's best for the company, you understand? My grandfather founded Owens Oil and Gas Exploration almost seventy years ago, and Dad's run it for forty years. Soon as he retires, I'm gonna take over. Our company comes first. Maybe in your way of thinking that might not be right, but it's what I know. 'Do your best for the company.' Yeah. I can still hear Granddad saying that."

A faraway look came into the oilman's eyes, then he seemed to shake off the memory. "You know oil's been down the last few years. In the toilet, unless you're some damn Arab. All of us American companies are struggling to stay alive. We gotta watch the bottom line all the time. Can't stop, not for a minute."

"Where are we going, Jasper?" Father John asked. He had a pretty good idea, and he hoped the oilman would get to the point before he reconsidered what he was about to divulge.

"You know, don't you?" Jasper said, locking eyes with Father John. "Soon's I heard you were working on Harvey Castle's history files, I figured you'd put it all together. They don't let dimwits into the Jesuits, last I heard."

Luke shifted from one foot to the other, a mixture of impatience and boredom on his face.

Jasper went on. "Next thing I hear, that Indian lawyer lady's poking around Marvin Antelope's office wanting to see his report on the reservation's oil wells. So I figure the jig's up, as they say in the movies."

"Did you kill Harvey and Charlie?" Father John asked.

Jasper laughed out loud. Turning to his assistant, he said, "See, what did I tell you? The minute they figure out I've been draining off reservation oil, they're gonna jump to the conclusion I killed off two tribal councilmen to keep 'em from blowing the whistle."

Redirecting his attention to Father John, he said, "I've gotta do whatever's best for my company, but murder would be stupid. We lease the rights to oil on reservations in six states. What d'ya think the headlines would do to business? 'Oil executive murders tribal chairman and tribal councilman.' "

Father John studied the bald puffy-faced man in front of him. It was fascinating, in a strange way, that his only problem with murder was that it would be bad for business. After a moment Father John said, "I suppose you have alibis for the night Harvey was killed and the night somebody saw to it that Charlie didn't make the only curve on Seventeen-Mile Road."

"Sure. Saturday night Luke and I went over to Hudson for

steak dinner. You know the place where those big, juicy steaks hang over the plate. Then we hit a bar in Lander."

"Harvey was killed in the early morning hours," Father John said.

Jasper exhaled a long breath. "Well, I was home asleep by then."

"An airtight alibi."

"What can I say? I was alone. My wife's been out of town all month." He threw both hands in the air. "Okay, the truth. She left me this spring."

Father John was almost more surprised to hear Jasper had a wife than that she had left him. "What about you?" he said to the younger man waiting impatiently next to his boss. "I suppose you were home in bed too."

"Yeah, but not alone." Luke looked at the oilman and grinned.

"You gotta be kidding," Jasper said. "Not that bimbo from the bar."

"Hey, I wasn't alone." Luke seemed to have started enjoying himself.

Jasper swung his shoulder around, dismissing the younger man. "I was playing cards over at the Elks the night Charlie Taylor had his accident. Anyway, why would I kill him? I figured Harvey Castle was the one who might've caught on to what I was doing. I got nervous that whoever broke into his office might have found some evidence and would come after me. Blackmail." Jasper threw out both hands. "Geez, I need that like I need cancer. So I waited for a phone call or letter. Nothing. Then I decided it must've been something else the burglar was after, and I start breathing easier. Next thing I hear, you're going through the files. I get nervous again, so I told Luke, 'Get over to Harvey Castle's office and see what the hell he knew.'"

Father John felt his face going red with anger. He sucked

in his breath and dug his fingers into the contraption holding his arm to his chest. He had a strong urge to smash a fist into the face of the young man who was now grinning at him, to settle matters the way they were settled in the streets of Boston when he was a kid. Luke kept his eyes steady, daring him. Even with both arms, Father John knew he was no match for this young thug. He forced himself to take a deep breath. "So it's you I've got to thank for this." He raised his shoulder slightly. A bolt of pain shot through his arm.

Luke seemed to relax, but his eyes were wary. "I had to get outta there before you saw me."

Father John turned toward Jasper. "You owe me a tape player and a visit to the emergency room."

"Fair enough." Jasper fumbled inside his suit coat, pulled out a wallet, and removed a stack of bills. He peeled off a couple and held them out. Father John took them and stuffed them into the back pocket of his blue jeans. There were people who could use some cash right now. Ernest, for one. Homer in Denver with his sick baby boy.

"Why are you telling me all this, Jasper?"

"I'm glad you asked," the oilman said, replacing the wallet in the inside pocket of his jacket, then adjusting the cuffs over those of his white shirt. "I want to know whatever Harvey found out about the drilling I'm doing into the southwestern part of the reservation. Any records he might've come across, I want them. All you gotta do, soon as you find 'em, is make sure I get 'em. Nobody else is ever gonna know."

"Don't, Jasper," Father John said, holding up the palm of his only usable hand, but the oilman was plunging on. "Fact is, you and I both know the financial situation at St. Francis Mission is pretty sad. It's a real joke among us businessmen around here. You could do a lot for these Indians if you had, shall we say, a regular source of income."

Father John was shaking his head. A few minutes ago he

had been willing to give Jasper Owens the benefit of the doubt, to believe the oilman might actually regret what he'd done. He'd missed the measure of this man by a mile.

"Let me get this straight," Father John said. "If I give the information to the FBI, it could prove you had a strong motive to murder two Arapaho councilmen. On the other hand, if I give the information to you, you can continue stealing oil from the reservation."

"I wouldn't put it that way," Jasper said.

"And as soon as the Arapahos buy the Cooley ranch, you can lease those wells, close them down, and draw out even more oil through your wells in Fremont County."

"The way I see it, we'd be helping each other here. It's just business. I'm a businessman. I'm not a murderer," Jasper said.

"I believe you," Father John said. "The stakes weren't high enough for murder. Even if Harvey had found out about the fraud you're up to, he couldn't have hurt you much."

The oilman drew in a long breath, as if he were trying to process the words he'd just heard. Then the color began to drain from his face. "You telling me Harvey didn't know? He didn't have any evidence? I just spilled my guts for nothing?"

Father John was quiet, but Luke snickered and looked away.

Jasper had pulled out a white handkerchief and was mopping the perspiration from the top of his head. "You going to bring the police in on this?"

"They're already in. I intend to help them all I can," Father John said.

"Let's get out of here," Jasper said to his assistant. Turning on his heels, he started for the dark Lincoln nudged against the curb.

Father John watched the car swerve around Circle Drive

and careen out onto Seventeen-Mile Road as a roar went up from the ball field. He was anxious to get back to the game, but he stepped inside the church first. Kneeling down in the same pew where he had found the two men, he prayed silently for a few moments for all the brokenness in the world.

∞ 29 ∞

FATHER JOHN KEPT the Toyota at fifty-five heading west through the empty spaces. He wondered where the Provincial would send him. Another prep school? A university assignment? Funny, he would have jumped at the chance not long ago. Now it was the last thing he wanted. Maybe he'd take a vacation before he started a new assignment. Go back to Boston and see his brother, Mike. He hadn't seen much of Mike and Eileen and the kids since he'd been at Wind River Reservation. Visiting them was always a little uncomfortable.

"Some rival I've got," Eileen had said, when he'd told her he had decided to become a priest. "God Almighty. How can I compete with God Almighty?" She was crying then, but he usually remembered her laughing, and how blue her eyes were, and soft her hair, and all the colors brown hair could be, and how smooth her skin was. He'd been at the Jesuit seminary about three months when he'd heard she had married Mike.

He forced himself back to the present. *Dear God*, he prayed, *let me find some way to help Anthony before I have to go away.* He had no intention of calling the Provincial to hear about a new assignment, but he wondered how long he could stall before the Provincial caught up with him. The Provincial wasn't a man easily put off.

The sky was uniformly gray except for the black-rimmed clouds descending over the mountains. Moisture hung in the air, and a few drops of rain spattered the hood and windshield. Not enough to turn on the wipers. Rain was coming, though, and judging by the clouds, it would be a downpour. That's how it was on the plains. No rain for weeks. The earth parched and brown. Then a downpour and all the precious water cascading through the arroyos and gullies out to Nebraska.

He had to reach across the steering wheel to turn off the ignition and ram the gear into park when he pulled up in front of the tribal offices. He longed to rip off the contraption that kept his right arm against his chest, but that would prolong things. He'd been through this before. At least the pain had subsided into a mild roar.

He didn't expect to see Vicky, but there she was, dressed in blue jeans and a T-shirt, a black bag slung over her shoulder, chatting with the receptionist.

"I'm sorry about the Eagles," she said as they walked down the hallway. "Maybe next time."

"We can always hope." Father John didn't like to lose— for his team to lose.

"How's the shoulder?"

"Almost completely healed. It feels really great, better than ever."

"Right," she said. After unlocking the office door, he pushed it open and followed her inside. There was a grayish tint to the daylight filtering through the window.

Vicky strode across the room and dropped her bag on the floor next to Harvey's desk. Turning around, she said, "When I called your office, your new assistant said you were on your way over here, so I thought I could lend you a hand—no pun intended." She smiled and hurried on. "We don't have much time to find out what's in these files, or not in them as the case may be. The fed will have an indictment against Anthony before the day's over."

He pulled out the desk chair for her. After sliding a corner chair across the tile floor for himself, he said, "You were right about Jasper Owens." Then he told her about the visit he'd had a couple hours ago from the oilman and his side-kick.

"*Niathas* are very clever creatures," she said, settling into Harvey's chair. "We have to watch them every minute." Father John smiled at the fact she had said "we," as if she'd forgotten he was a *Niatha*.

"I spent the morning in the Lander offices of the state oil and gas commission," Vicky continued. "The records indicate a tremendous oil volume in the southwestern part of the reservation. There's a lot of oil under this land. Owens has probably been pumping out oil as fast as possible, getting as much as he could before he's forced to stop. A real windfall for him, I'd say. I've asked to be put on the agenda for next week's business council meeting. I intend to present everything we know about what Jasper Owens has been up to. I'm sure the council will ask the BIA to investigate. Eventually Owens will be ordered to pay back royalties."

"You'll have his undying gratitude," Father John said, picking up a folder from the stack on the desk. "Somewhere in this manuscript is the information that got Harvey killed. And so far, all we know is that it wasn't about oil fraud." Opening the folder, he began flipping through the pages. It was awkward with one hand.

He realized this was the chapter on the early years at Wind River Reservation. He pulled out the photos and spread them across the desk. Both he and Vicky leaned over for a closer view of the fading black-and-white images.

Several photos showed groups of Arapahos, blankets wrapped around their shoulders, standing outside tipis. "Black Night's camp on Little Wind River," Vicky said, her fingers resting on one of the photos.

Another showed several Arapahos outside a log cabin. A man in a white shirt with thick black suspenders and dark pants, a cigar dangling from his mouth, stood on the porch, like a king surveying his subjects. "Mathias Cooley," Father John said, touching the image. On the porch next to the agent were two piles of what looked like blankets. A couple of cows were grazing to the side of the cabin. Across the bottom of the photo someone had written, "Annuity distribution day, 1878."

Staring into the black-and-white image, Father John felt transported in time as if he were standing below the porch with the Arapahos, listening to the strange words that the white man spoke. Vicky was also staring at the photo as if she, too, were there, with her grandparents, her great-grandparents. "We were a pitiful lot," she said after a moment. "Only nine hundred of us made it to Wind River Reservation, freezing and starving. But we were alive."

Father John opened the folder again and glanced down the outline for something about annuity distributions. It was there, halfway down. Awkwardly he flipped through the manuscript to that section, then skimmed the paragraphs, aware of Vicky watching him and of her quiet breathing.

"No wonder the elders said don't trust the agent. Here it is." He handed the page to her. "The government delivered the food, blankets, tools, cloth, utensils, cattle—all the things promised in the treaties in exchange for Arapaho lands. But instead of distributing the goods, Mathias Cooley sold them for whatever the Arapahos had of value."

"We didn't have much," Vicky said. "A few warbonnets, saddles, parfleches, bows and arrows, deerskin shirts and dresses. What is it that Ned Cooley calls them? Indian trinkets?"

Father John picked up the photos and slipped them back into his folder. He was thinking of what Will Standing Bear had told him: Mother Earth gives us all we need to live. Mother Earth—the basis for all life. The logic was beautiful. All you had to do was set up the correct propositions in the syllogism, and the conclusion became obvious. After a moment he said quietly, "Mathias Cooley didn't buy a hundred thousand acres of reservation land from the Arapahos. He took it in exchange for their own annuities. He stole the land."

Vicky leaned back in her chair, eyes wide. "My God. After he'd taken everything else we owned, he came after our land. Now his great-grandson wants us to give him five million dollars for our own land."

"And Ned has sweetened the pot by throwing in the artifacts, hoping Arapahos won't be able to refuse the deal."

"Or hoping we wouldn't take a close look at how his ancestor got the ranch in the first place," Vicky added.

They were both quiet, trying to absorb the enormity of it. Finally Father John said, "Harvey must have found some old records that prove what happened. That's why he changed his mind about buying the ranch. Ned Cooley killed him to keep the secret hidden."

"What about Charlie Taylor?" Vicky asked.

Father John was turning over an idea, looking for the logical path, the correct propositions. "Harvey must've told Charlie. My guess is that Charlie came here Saturday afternoon. As a councilman, he had the keys. He knew what to look for, and he knew he didn't have much time. He tore through the history files until he found what he wanted. Then he went to Ned Cooley with a deal. Charlie would give Ned the records and would get the business council to purchase the ranch, probably by claiming that Harvey had approved of it. And Ned would pay Charlie a percentage of the five million dollars."

Vicky was shaking her head. "Blackmail. So Ned saw to it that Charlie didn't make the curve on Seventeen-Mile Road. That Indian forgot about *Niatha*'s trick."

"It all fits except for one thing," Father John said. "Ned couldn't have killed Harvey himself. He must've hired somebody to do it. A hit man." That had been his new assistant's theory from the first, and now here he was entertaining the idea.

"What makes you think so?" Vicky had taken the folder from him and was skimming rapidly through the other pages.

"He spent part of the weekend meeting with politicians, financial supporters in Denver," Father John said. "He told me he caught the flight back Saturday afternoon."

Vicky looked up, surprise flashing in her eyes.

"John, there is only one flight from Denver to Riverton each day. It's a little cigar plane with sixteen seats, you know the type. Last Saturday Larry and I were on it. It was half empty. Ned Cooley was not on that plane."

A mixture of anger and revulsion rose in Father John's throat like thick smoke. It was one thing to believe that a hit man, someone he couldn't imagine, someone inhuman, had plunged a knife into his friend's chest. It was something else altogether to recall the human face, the voice, the fleshy feel of the hand—the murderer's hand. Then another thought hit him and made him shudder. Did Ned Cooley hate Harvey because Dorothy had once loved him? Perhaps still loved him? Had Ned Cooley enjoyed his terrible deed?

Vicky tossed the folder on the desk. "There's no mention of the Cooley ranch or how the agent got his hands on it in this chapter."

"It's got to be here," Father John said, pulling out the

outline and running his eyes down the typed lines. About an inch from the bottom, something had been penciled in. It was Harvey's handwriting, a note to himself. Father John had to bring the page up close to make out the faint words: "Add insert here." Then, "MA 2250 MA 2274."

"Look for something marked 'insert,'" he said. Vicky stood up, leaned over the desk and began leafing through the pages again. Father John picked up the next folder in the stack and started through it. Maybe he'd stuffed a section marked "insert" into the wrong folder. He checked another folder, and another. "It's not here," he said.

Vicky was waiting. "No sections on the ranch. No records. Nothing. We've found what's missing."

Father John sank back into his chair and rubbed his shoulder in an effort to loosen the muscles that felt as if they were clamped in a vise. "It looks like Harvey wrote this chapter before he came across the evidence about the Cooley ranch. He intended to insert the information later, so he made a note on the outline. It would have been a humdinger of a chapter. This was probably what he had wanted to talk to me about the morning of the powwow. This, and the fact his nephew had fallen in love with Cooley's niece, of all the white girls in the world. Harvey had a lot on his mind when he died."

"So how do we prove this? We don't have the evidence."

"Maybe we can reconstruct it," Father John said. "You know what this means?" He pointed to the penciled words on the outline.

"Mission Archives. Files 2250 and 2274."

Vicky was out of the chair again, scooping her bag off the floor. "There has to be something on the Cooley ranch in the Fremont County records. I'll check on it while you check the mission records, which you are going to do, of course. I'll meet you back here in an hour, two max."

Father John got to his feet. "How do you know what I'm going to do? Did I say anything?"

"Volumes," she said, leading the way out of the office and down the hallway.

∾ 30 ∾

FATHER JOHN TOOK the stairs at the administration building two at a time. The wind whipped across the grounds of St. Francis Mission, bowing the trees and flattening the wild grasses. Blue-black clouds rolled through a sky of mossy gray. He slammed the front door and ran down the hallway past his office to the mission archives, the heels of his boots clumping against the wooden floor.

He flipped on the light switch in a room about as big as an oversized closet. The saucerlike globe suspended from the ceiling cast a circle of light over a small oak table. Wind whistled around the edges of the window on the opposite wall, and cottonwood branches scratched against the pane. Father John had to turn sideways to get around the table to the shelves. Cardboard boxes stood upright on each shelf, like fat, gray books. He ran the fingers of his good hand along the numbers on the spines until he came to 2200–2300.

He almost dropped the box pulling it off the shelf one-handed. Plopping it onto the table, he shook out the contents, as if he were shaking rocks out of a sack. Two leather notebooks skidded across the table, and he pulled one toward him and opened the cover. "Father Jaime Stanislau, S.J. Letters. 1886–1888." It was the letter book with copies of letters written by the first Jesuit missionary at St. Francis. Each letter was numbered, beginning with 2200.

Nudging a wooden chair away from the table, he squeezed himself downward onto the hard seat. Thunder shattered the air and rattled the window as he thumbed through the loose letters looking for 2250. When he came to where it should have been, his heart stopped. The letter was missing. In its place was a small sheet of white paper with Harvey's signature, sprawling and confident, and the date, two weeks before his death. He and Harvey had made an agreement. Harvey could borrow whatever he wanted to copy. All he had to do was leave a note in place of the missing page.

With a sinking feeling, Father John picked up the second leather notebook. "Day-by-Day Accounts of My Mission to the Arapaho People on the Wind River Reservation of Wyoming." It was Father Stanislau's diary. The pages were loose, and each page was numbered. He flipped quickly through. Page 2274 was missing, replaced by another note. He brought his left fist down hard on the tabletop, sending a shock of pain across his shoulders and into his sore arm. Ned Cooley had gotten the original records that told exactly how his great-grandfather had defrauded the Arapahos of their land. Father John was close. Close. But Cooley was a step ahead.

He had to struggle to line up the pages so the edges didn't hang outside the notebooks, then to get the notebooks back into the box. A sudden swoosh of air preceded another rumble of thunder and sent a small tremor through the old building. Suddenly Anthony was in the doorway, breathing hard, rain splotches darkening his T-shirt and gray sweatpants. "God, I'm glad you're here," he said.

At the sight of the Indian, Father John jumped up, sending the chair crashing against the shelves. Charlie Taylor had worn that—a dark T-shirt and gray sweatpants—the day he was headed over to the high school gym to shoot baskets. And as he was dying, Charlie had tried to tell him something. He'd whispered four numbers. The combination for a locker. Charlie hadn't given the records to Ned Cooley—he had stashed them in his gym locker."

"My God," Father John said under his breath. Ned Cooley was still looking for the records. That's why he was out at the accident site yesterday morning, hoping they might be in Charlie's pickup, or thrown in the field nearby. "Something's going on, Father," Anthony was shouting, and Father John had to force himself to focus on what the Indian was saying.

"Melissa's gone. I've been calling her all day. I finally got a hold of her uncle. He tried to tell me Melissa and her mother left for France. No way she'd take off for France without calling me. And two weeks before she's supposed to graduate? So I went out to the Cooley ranch. The little house is all boarded up as if they really did leave. I ran into one of the ranch hands, and he said Melissa and her mother flew out of Riverton yesterday."

Anthony took a deep breath before going on. "I called the airport right away. They said they couldn't give me any information. So I drove out there, and one of the women at the counter was Arapaho. I said, you gotta tell me if Melissa Cooley was on any flights yesterday or today. She said, ask me a question I can answer. So I said, should I get a new girlfriend? And she says no. No! Melissa didn't fly out of here. So where is she?"

Father John felt his jaw clenching, his muscles tensing down his neck and across his shoulders. His whole right arm screamed with pain. What if Melissa and Dorothy had suspected something and had challenged Ned? He didn't want to think the man would harm his own sister and niece, but if he felt desperate . . . He'd already killed twice to keep his secret. The women could be in danger. But he had to get the proof—the missing records—before he could convince Banner, or the Fremont County sheriff, or the FBI agent or whoever the hell had jurisdiction at the Cooley ranch to get out there.

"If Ned Cooley wanted his niece and sister out of the way for a while, where would he take them?"

"Why would he want them out of the way?" In an instant, the look of comprehension crossed the Arapaho's face. "You think Melissa's uncle . . . you think he killed Harvey?"

"Where would he take them?" Father John heard himself shouting.

Anthony wheeled around as if he'd been shot out of a cannon. "The old cabin," he hollered from the hallway. "They're in the old cabin."

"Wait, Anthony," Father John shouted again as he came around the table. By the time he reached the hallway, the Indian was already out the front door, and Father John ran after him. He flung open the door and hurried outside. Rain was falling in great white sheets, and the sky erupted in thunder as Anthony jumped into his jeep.

"Wait," Father John hollered again, running out to Circle Drive and grabbing the door handle as the jeep lurched forward. "Be careful," he yelled into the rain as he let go of the moving vehicle.

∞ 31 ∞

Rain plopped onto the hood of the Toyota and washed over the asphalt moving toward him like a conveyor belt. Thunder roared overhead, coming out of the west—the place of the Thunder Beings—and lightning flashed through the air like neon lights blinking on and off. The old pickup shuddered and protested as Father John floorboarded the gas pedal. Before he'd left the mission, he'd dialed Banner's office only to be told the chief was out. Of course he was out. He was always out. Father John told the operator to get a couple of cars—BIA, sheriff, somebody—out to the Cooley ranch fast.

It was nearly five o'clock as he swung past the tribal offices. Vicky's Bronco wasn't in the parking lot. A short way down the road, he pulled up in front of Indian High School. Let it be open, he prayed, hitting the brake. He sprinted up the sidewalk, water sloshing over his boots and running off the brim of his cowboy hat, and yanked on the knob of the large metal door at the entrance. The door didn't budge.

"Damn," he said under his breath as he ran around the building to the back door, each step sending shock waves into his dislocated shoulder. An old Chevy was parked out back. Good. Somebody was here, he thought, grabbing the knob of a smaller metal door. It inched slowly forward, and he slipped inside, clipping his arm on the door's edge. The pain made him groan. The rhythm of a bouncing basketball floated out of the gym and into the hallway, which was banked with lockers. One of them was Charlie's. But which one? There were at least fifty on each side of the hall.

Father John burst into the gym and strode out onto the floor interrupting a scrimmage. Three Arapaho high school boys stopped in place, startled. "Anybody know Councilman Taylor's locker?" he demanded.

"Nah, Father," said the kid palming the basketball, a baffled look in his eye. The other two kids were shaking their heads. "I know it." The voice came from behind, and Father John whirled toward the bench against the far wall where a younger boy was lacing up one of his hightops.

"He don't know nothin'," one of the older kids muttered.

"Show me," Father John said. The boy jumped off the bench and marched into the hallway, and Father John followed.

"I saw him put his stuff in here." The kid stopped in front of one of the lockers. "I don't know the combination."

I do, Father John thought. There were only two possibilities. He held the lock tight against the metal door with his left palm and twirled the knob. 3-33-10. The lock held. He swirled the knob a full circle, then tried again. 33-3-10. The shaft slipped free. "All right," the kid said.

Father John opened the locker door. The inside was crammed with sweats, T-shirts, sneakers, towels, a deflated basketball. A pump tilted forward, about to fall out, and he jammed it back. He held his breath, scarcely believing his luck was holding. Charlie's wife hadn't cleaned out the locker. With one hand he pushed aside folds of terry cloth,

T-shirts stiff with dried sweat, and plastic shampoo bottles. Then he gripped something flat and hard.

Father John pulled the plastic file box toward him. It came free, trailing the leg of gray sweatpants. He sank onto the shiny, waxed floor and set the box upright against the wall. The kid had gone back into the gym, and Father John was alone. Slowly he lifted the lid. The pages inside were thin and yellow with the musty smell of archives. He pulled out the first page. Page 2274 of Father Stanislau's diary, handwritten in precise, carefully formed, easy-to-read, yet tiny, script, the work of a precise, careful, logical man.

"January 17, 1887. This morning at 10 o'clock, Chief Black Night brought the leading men of the Arapaho to the mission. They said they wished to tell the Great White Father how the agent had falsely claimed part of their lands. They believe that as soon as the Father in Washington is told of the fraud committed against them, he will require the agent to return their lands. They said it has caused much hardship to lose these lands, which are the most desirable on the reservation because of clear streams and stands of good timber and nutritious grasses. They need the water and the grasses to preserve the last of their pony herd.

"I agreed to take their depositions and to forward them to officials in Washington. Accordingly, each of the leading men recounted how, in 1878, Agent Cooley held their annuities for many months. It was winter, and there was nothing to eat. The warriors hunted deer and small game, and so the people were able to stay alive. But the children were crying with hunger and many were sick in the freezing cold. Finally the leading men said they had no choice but to allow Agent Cooley to carve off a large part of their lands. They said he made them sign some papers. He would not give them the food and blankets that Washington had sent them until they signed the papers. They feared the papers meant their lands were gone forever, but it was never their intention to give over the lands. They had signed because they were afraid the people would die if they did not.

"I wrote all of it down exactly as the leading men told it to me, and they signed the depositions with their X's. Afterwards my two assistants and I also signed to prove to the government that three white men were witnesses. I immediately dispatched the depositions to Washington with little hope that anything will be done. The great bulk of their lands has been taken from these Indians, and this additional outrage will not, I fear, make any difference to the government. Nevertheless, these leading men have told the truth. My hope is that the future will know the truth."

Father John returned the page to the file box feeling as if he had heard the words, not read them, as if the voice of a long-ago Jesuit priest had spoken to him. The thumping of the basketball reverberated down the empty hallway as he leafed through the other pages. It was all there. A copy of the actual letter Father Stanislau had sent to Washington. At the top of the page was the number 2250. And ten depositions, carefully written copies of the originals, each signed with an X. Under the signatures were the names of the leading Arapaho men. Black Night's name was on the first deposition.

There was more. Several typed pages stapled together and titled "insert." It was the section Harvey had intended to include in the chapter on the early days of the reservation. And there was a letter from the Commissioner of Indian Affairs to Father Stanislau, acknowledging receipt of the depositions and promising prompt redress.

Not so prompt redress, Father John thought, lifting himself stiffly off the floor. He had to get these records to Banner. This and whatever forged records it was likely that

Vicky had found in the Fremont County courthouse. That they would be forged he was certain.

There was no sign of Vicky's Bronco at the tribal offices. Inside the receptionist was on the phone staring off into space, absorbed. "Any messages for me?" Father John waved to get her attention. She looked away. After a couple seconds, he realized she was talking to a friend, and he hit the disconnect button. She looked up, startled. "Father John!" Her voice was a whine.

He repeated his question.

"Chief Banner called." A note of pained reluctance crept into her voice now. "Something about jurisdiction problems at the Cooley ranch. He said to call him. Vicky Holden called you. She said, and I quote, 'He's gonna like what I found.' She said to meet her at the Cooley ranch."

"What?"

The receptionist flinched, pedaling backward a couple inches on her chair, an automatic reflex.

"I'm just telling you what she said." The whine was back.

"Listen to me," Father John said. He was leaning over the desk. "Call Chief Banner right now and tell him . . ." The woman looked as if she might burst into tears.

"Never mind," he said, picking up the receiver and pushing in Banner's numbers. "Be there," he said under his breath. Then Art Banner's familiar voice came on the line. "Get some cars out to the Cooley ranch right away. BIA, sheriff's deputies—don't tell me about jurisdiction."

"Wait a minute," the chief yelled. "I can't ask the sheriff for cars at the Cooley ranch without a damn good reason. Ned Cooley'll have the sheriff's ass in a sling and mine, too. What the hell's this all about?"

"About stopping a murderer," Father John shouted as he slammed down the receiver.

～32～

FATHER JOHN CLAMPED the gas pedal to the floor and willed the Toyota faster down Highway 287. The file box with its precious records lay on the seat beside him. A clap of thunder drew an instant flash of lightning. White sheets of rain washed over the windshield and hood and spread into miniature lakes on the asphalt ahead. He had to hunch over the steering wheel to keep the center line in view between swipes of the windshield wipers. He swore out loud, a string of words he'd forgotten he knew. What was she thinking of? People could be so damn impetuous. She was impetuous. Going by herself to see Ernest Oldman, a crazy drunk who tried to shoot up an oil pump. Coming out here alone to confront Ned Cooley. What would that get her? Dead?

The Toyota skidded on the rain-soaked pavement as he wheeled onto Rendezvous Road. Another sharp turn and he was heading down the long driveway to the Cooley ranch, its front lawn gray with rain. Vicky's Bronco was parked at the end of the driveway where the food tables had been set up last Saturday night. There was no sign of Banner or the sheriff or anybody else, for that matter.

Father John left the engine running and, nearly doubled over, dashed across the soggy lawn. Rain pelted the back of his shirt and spilled off his hat. He mounted the stairs to the porch two at a time and slammed his left fist into the door before turning the knob. The door swung open.

"Vicky!" he shouted. The sounds of the rain diminished as he stepped inside and closed the door. He felt as if he'd stepped into the eternal quiet of a museum. The hallway stretched toward the carved wooden banister on the stairway ahead. Starting toward it, he shouted again. "Vicky! Ned! Anybody here?"

Rooms filled with Arapaho belongings opened off either side of the hall, and, as he glanced through the doorway on the left, his eyes fell on Chief Black Night's warbonnet. He stepped into the room, drawn to the warbonnet draped against the wall, eagle feathers graceful and elegant behind Plexiglas. The warbonnet of a great man. How much food, how many blankets and bolts of cloth had it purchased for Chief Black Night's people?

And Ned Cooley had worn it the night he murdered Harvey. Father John could feel the truth of it, as if he had seen with his own eyes the white man darting past the tipis, in and out of the shadows of flickering campfires, dressed in buckskin shirt, beaded apron, angora leggings, moccasins, warbonnet with eagle feathers trailing down his back. Ned Cooley had his choice of regalia, all authentic. He was one of the powwow dancers walking through camp. No one would have noticed him. And then, as he did his terrible deed, one of the eagle feathers had fallen from the warbonnet. It lay on the dirt floor of the tipi, a fact Ned Cooley hadn't realized until he got home and draped the warbonnet back on its stand in the center of the room. The empty woven shaft that had held the feather was obvious. He had arranged the warbonnet behind Plexiglas so no one would notice.

"Help you, Father O'Malley?" Father John swung around and faced one of the ranch hands in the doorway.

"Where's Ned?"

"Gone fishin' up at Washakie reservoir. Says nothin' like rain to get those trout bitin'.".

"Where's Vicky Holden?"

"That Indian lawyer lady?" The ranch hand shrugged. "So that's the lady he had in the pickup with him. You ask me, she's a darn fool just like Mr. Cooley if she likes fishin' in this weather."

"He took her up to the reservoir?" As Father John gasped the words, he realized Ned intended to kill her. Not on the ranch. In the steep, rock-studded canyon of the Washakie. Jesus, she would never be found.

"Listen to me," he said. "The police are on their way here. Send them up to the Washakie fast. Do you understand?"

The ranch hand looked startled, perplexed.

"Do you understand?" Father John shouted.

"Yeah. Yeah," the ranch hand said as Father John yanked open the front door and dodged into the rain.

Washakie reservoir washed over its banks in places, spilling across the road, and Father John had to fight with all the strength in his one good arm to keep the Toyota on track. He hit a dip, and, suddenly, he was hydroplaning out of control. He took his foot off the gas, but as soon as the wheels touched the ground, he jammed down the pedal again. Thunder rolled above the canyon and lightning danced through the rain-filled air. Just as he came out of a long curve, he spotted the blue pickup nudged into the scrub brush along the side of the road, across from where he and

Anthony had been fishing last evening. The Toyota slid in the wet dirt, and, pumping the brakes, Father John pulled in behind the pickup. Then he saw them.

In the stand of aspens about fifty feet up the mountain, Ned Cooley was gripping Vicky's arm, and the force of his grip propelled her uphill. In the man's other hand was a rifle. Father John laid on the horn with all the strength in his left arm. Ned turned, swinging Vicky around with him as if they were doing the do-si-do in a western bar. After a moment, they started down. Father John had to twist around in the seat to grab the file box before he got out of the cab. The rain crushed his shirt against his back and shoulders and beat on the sling that held his arm to his chest.

Slowly Father John made his way alongside the bed of the pickup. Ned and Vicky were still about fifteen feet up the slope. Vicky's hair was matted against her head, and water streamed down her face. Her T-shirt looked as if it had dissolved into her skin. Ned had on a hooded, full-length brown slicker, the rain pinging against it like pebbles on a lake. Still gripping Vicky's arm, he pointed the rifle at Father John.

"You got the records?" Ned hollered.

"Here," Father John shouted, lifting the box into the rain.

Pushing Vicky ahead, Ned came toward him. "I figured you'd find them. All I had to do was wait. Then I'd get 'em from you. Of course, you'd have to have yourself a tragic accident afterwards. I wasn't countin' on this lawyer lady showing up waving copies of county records at me. That was perfect. I knew you'd come after her and bring the mission records right to me."

"You didn't have to kill Harvey," Father John said. "The Arapahos would've worked out a fair price for all the years your family's taken care of the ranch. Harvey was a fair man. He would've seen to it. Isn't that the deal he offered you? Why didn't you take it? Was it the five million dollars? Is that what you wanted?"

The rancher's head was shaking inside the hood of the slicker. "Ned Cooley's gonna be the next governor of this state, and nobody's gonna say the governor's family cheated a bunch of damn Indians out of anything."

"So you killed Harvey to protect your reputation?" *Keep him talking,* Father John thought. Stall until Banner and the sheriff get here.

"The Cooley name, you fool. We been here more than a hundred years. We built this place. We are Wind River Reservation."

Lightning struck the boulders up above and sent a charge of electricity through the air. Rain fell in waves between Father John and the man and woman, who, like Siamese twins, were still inching downslope toward him. He could see the defiance on Vicky's face, her lips drawn into a tight line.

"Nobody would've been the wiser if you hadn't come pokin' around here." Ned waved the rifle, and Father John felt the muscles tighten in his chest. "Fremont County records show who's got title to the Cooley ranch. There are sworn statements from a lot of Indians that my great-granddaddy bought the land fair and square. Without those old mission records, nobody's ever gonna know any different."

"How many years were you and your father county commissioner? Fifty? Did you change the records so they showed exactly what you wanted?" *Keep him talking,* Father John was thinking.

"They outdid themselves," Vicky shouted.

Ned jerked her arm, nearly lifting her off her feet as

lightning danced through the canyon, bouncing off the ground. It had moved in close, striking all around them.

"There are sworn statements in the records that Mathias Cooley bought a lot of ranches on the reservation," Vicky shouted into the storm. "My great-grandfather's. Ernest's. Harvey's. A lot of others." She snapped sideways, momentarily breaking the rancher's grip, but he grabbed her arm and pulled her back.

Father John held his breath. Stay calm. Stay calm. He tried to send her a silent message. This was a waiting game.

"Forgeries," Vicky yelled, her voice still defiant. "So many forgeries it's a joke. Mathias Cooley was planning to take over the whole reservation." She faced her captor again. "What happened? Didn't your great-granddaddy live long enough to see his plans through? Why leave those forgeries in the county files? Did you really think someday the Cooleys could claim all that land?"

The rancher flinched, jerking the nose of the rifle upward. Water ran like black oil along the metal barrel. "This is our place," he shouted. "Indians don't belong here."

Father John took another step along the pickup. Thunder cracked overhead, and another flash of lightning lit up the grove of aspens upslope. Rain splashed against the file box, rolled over it. It felt heavy in his hand. "I'm going to set the records on the seat," he shouted as he reached through the opened window. "Let her go and I'll drop the box. The records are yours."

Ned flung Vicky out to one side, and Father John lowered the box onto the seat. Then he heard the snap of the bolt, muffled in the rain. He looked up into the barrel of the rifle. Just then Vicky whirled around and flung herself against the rancher. The rifle flew out of his hands as he stumbled sideways, slipping in the mud, fighting for balance before pitching forward.

"Run," Father John shouted. Vicky started up the mountain and into the clump of aspen trees. Father John was close behind as thunder shook the ground, muffling the crack of the rifle.

They sprinted sideways, left, then right, up the slope in the rain, slipping backwards in patches of mud, pushing through mushy mounds of wet twigs and pine needles. Thunder shattered the air again, and he didn't hear the shot that whizzed past his ear. "Stay low, stay low," he shouted, digging his boots into the mud that oozed over the packed earth. God, they were going to be struck by lightning, if they didn't get shot first.

Another shot, and Vicky went down. "No!" Father John shouted. He threw himself on top of her, pain ripping through him as his shoulder snapped out of its joint.

"I'm okay, I'm okay!" she yelled, scrambling uphill, pulling on shrubbery for support. She got to her feet and started running again, but he had to wait. He couldn't catch his breath—his shoulder was on fire. He forced himself to his feet. Cooley would be close. He could be in the rifle sights. Taking off his cowboy hat, he aimed it sideways at a clearing between the trees and tossed it with all the strength he could muster. The gunshot erupted. Staying low, he zigzagged uphill after Vicky. He could see the soles of her sneakers kicking back little clumps of mud.

Vicky reached the ridge and started up the stand of boulders where he and Anthony had climbed last night. "Wait!" he hollered, stooping between two boulders. It was here somewhere, hidden behind the bushes, but he couldn't spot it. He couldn't get his bearings in the rain. "I see you!" Ned shouted from below. He couldn't see them, Father John knew, or he would shoot them.

Vicky inched her way back down to him just as lightning

lit up the ridge where she had been standing. "Oh, God," she said. "We're going to die." Rain was running down her face and arms in little rivers, and she was shaking. Her T-shirt and jeans were covered in mud.

Father John pulled her down. "Stay low," he ordered. Where was the boulder Anthony had climbed last night to survey his world? If he could spot it, he could find the bushes below it.

"He's coming," Vicky shouted just as Father John saw what he was looking for.

"This way," he said.

"No. He'll see us." Vicky crouched closer to the ground.

He gripped her arm hard and pulled her sideways a few feet up the mountain. The rifle exploded behind them, and the bullets slammed into a nearby boulder, blasting off one corner. Fragments of granite bit his face and neck, and Vicky screamed into the rain.

He had to let go of her arm to push the shrubbery to one side. As soon as she saw the narrow space between the boulders, Vicky slipped inside and he followed, allowing the branches to fall slowly back into place. There was the sound of boots squishing in mud and scratching against rocks. He held his breath and closed his eyes in the darkness. It was dry in the tunnel, and quiet, as if the storm had disappeared. He leaned against the rough, cold granite, afloat in pain. His arm hung loose in its sling, like a raft floundering on a river.

After a few moments he began inching his way along the tunnel, so narrow in one place he had to turn sideways. Then he saw the faint light ahead. Vicky was already in the little room, just big enough for a boy to sleep in, to live in, while he waited for the eagle. Boulders arched overhead forming a solid roof, except for one spot the size of a saddle that was covered with brush. Gray daylight filtered through, and water ran along the branches and dripped onto the dirt floor.

Vicky had slumped down against the wall. In the faint light he could see the smears of mud on her face. He crouched beside her. "The eagle catch," she whispered. "How did you know?"

He didn't say anything. It hurt to talk.

"Tell me later." Still a whisper. "You wouldn't happen to have a cigarette on you?"

He laughed silently, which sent the muscles of his arm into paroxysms of pain. God, this woman was full of surprises.

"I know you're here. I'll find you. You're gonna die." The rancher was shouting from somewhere above them, only a few feet away. Father John knew he could push through the brush and grab Ned's feet, but he was having trouble just breathing with the pain. And he only had one arm. And he didn't want anyone to die here. He could see the outline of Vicky's face. She was staring straight ahead, holding her breath. No more jokes.

"You can't hide from me." The rancher shouted again, his voice further away, muffled in the rain. Father John could picture where Ned was standing now: On the flat surface of the highest boulder, where he and Anthony had stood looking out over the plains. The mountain fell away on the other side, a sheer thousand-foot drop into the canyon below.

The rifle cracked again, then again, then again. "Jesus," Vicky whispered, hunching toward him. Suddenly the rock Father John and Vicky were leaning against reverberated with the explosion of thunder. Lightning flashed through the brush roof. A thousand lights seemed to turn on around them, and electricity buzzed around the rock walls. The thunder crashed again. Then quiet. They waited, not speaking, barely breathing.

After a long while—he couldn't have guessed how long—Father John pushed himself up with his good arm, wincing with pain. "Wait here," he whispered as he started to edge back down the corridor. He pulled the branches aside and looked out. The rain fell in enormous drops, but it was less furious. Staying low, he slipped through the opening and started up the boulder field, looking around, half expecting the rancher to jump out, slam the bolt, and pull the trigger.

It was all he could do to climb over the wet granite. His cowboy boots slipped, and he fell backwards, clipping his dislocated shoulder. Fighting the blackness that threatened to engulf him, he crawled a few feet before he got himself upright, gripping his shoulder the whole time to keep it from flying away from some centrifugal force of pain. Slowly he worked his way upward until finally he was on top. The rain had settled into a fine drizzle, and the sky was beginning to lighten; there was a strip of sunlight across the plains in the distance. He moved slowly toward the far edge of the boulders and looked down. Ned's body, arms, and legs akimbo like those of a disjointed rag doll, lay on a little cliff that jutted out from the granite wall. "May God have mercy on your soul," Father John whispered.

"It's over." Vicky's voice startled him, and he whirled about. She had climbed up the boulders and was standing next to him, and he hadn't known she was there.

He put his arm around her to help her down the mountain, but he knew she was the one helping him, with her arm around his waist. The storm was over, and the last of the gloomy daylight almost gone, but the sky was dark and ominous with more rain. They were halfway down when Father John heard the sirens screaming up the canyon. The road below filled with BIA and Fremont County sheriff patrol cars, their red and blue lights flashing. Then he saw Anthony zigzagging toward them, waving both arms. He was hollering that Melissa was okay.

Walking with them down the last hundred feet of the slope, Anthony kept up a steady patter. Dorothy had defied her brother. For the first time in her life, she'd stood up to him and said that Melissa was free to marry anyone she chose. Ned Cooley went crazy and locked Melissa and her mother in the old cabin. Anthony had to break down the door to get them out. They were scared to death. They said Ned had gone crazy. They didn't know what he might do next.

Close to the bottom, Anthony stopped and turned toward them. "Geez, you two don't look so good," he said.

Banner ran up as they came out of the stand of aspens, his face flushed the color of ripened berries. "Where's Cooley?"

"On the other side of the mountain," Father John said. "Dead."

Before he could say anything else, the police chief held up one hand. "Anthony told me all about Cooley. I just hope you got the proof."

"You'll find it there," Father John said, nodding at the blue pickup as they made their way toward the patrol cars. A whole army of policemen milled about, boots squishing in the muddy shoulder of the road. A police radio was squawking. Banner opened the back door to a patrol car, and Vicky crawled inside. Just as Father John was about to get in beside her, he spotted the FBI agent wearing a silver slicker and floppy plastic hat. There were questions in his eyes as he came around the car.

"You want your murderer, Miller?" Father John called. "You'll need a helicopter."

Then, to the BIA police chief standing beside him, Father John said, "Get me to the hospital, will you?"

∾ 33 ∾

THREE MONTHS LATER, the Toyota bounced across the field, careening over the ruts and sagebrush. Father John hit the brakes and brought it to a stop behind several other pickups and a few rusted-out sedans. The crowd was already gathered at the Ethete powwow grounds. It was nearly the end of October, the Moon of Falling Leaves, and the thistles and scrub brush across the reservation were tinged with red. Even the ground had taken on red tones. The sky was low, fading into gray-blue with the approach of winter.

Father John slammed the door to the Toyota and started toward the Arapahos, aware he was late. He knew, though, that they wouldn't start the ceremony until everyone was there and ready. He'd been in a meeting most of the morning with the adult education teachers at St. Francis Mission, and then he'd stopped by the hospital to see Lucy Elkhorn. He'd anointed the old lady last week. There would probably be another wake and funeral in a few days. The Provincial had promised him a new assistant before Christmas, but Father John could have used the help now.

He'd gotten a postcard from Father Brad a few days ago.

He was teaching freshman English at the Kansas City Jesuit prep school, charged with the mission of preparing scion sons for future scion positions. He liked it, but he'd asked about the people on the reservation and said he hoped everything was going well.

After the news about Ned Cooley had taken over the headlines—CNN had sent it around the world—the Provincial had been vague about Father John's next assignment, and Father John hadn't asked for clarification. He was at St. Francis Mission on the Wind River Reservation for now, and that was enough. He didn't want to know what the future might hold.

Father John made his way through the crowd to Harvey's family. The musicians had already taken their places around two kettle drums. A campfire was burning where Harvey's tipi had stood, and a large frying pan sat on the fire grate. Several elders huddled around Will Standing Bear, preparing the blessing. Father John missed Vicky at gatherings like this. She'd been in L.A. for almost two months now. The last he'd heard she had landed a good job with a downtown law firm.

First Father John paid his respects to Maria who was sitting in a lawn chair near the campfire. He could see she was still in the half-life. Perhaps she would never leave. Perhaps she was too old to live only with the living.

Then he shook hands with Rita and with Anthony, who clapped him on the shoulder and thanked him for coming. Father John winced. His shoulder was like a raw wound, slow to heal, but then, he was no longer the promising young pitcher at Boston College who threw out his shoulder from time to time and confidently waited for it to be as good as new. Medical school was great, Anthony was saying. He was working hard and learning a lot. He'd be back at Wind

River Reservation as a pediatrician soon, the way time flew. The young man seemed more serious, more thoughtful.

"Heard from Melissa?" Father John asked.

"A few postcards." Anthony shrugged. "Melissa and her mother are in Italy."

Instinctively Father John placed his hand on the young man's shoulder. "You know, Melissa's not responsible for what her uncle did."

"I've told myself that a thousand times, ten thousand times." Anthony was looking out across the plains. "Harvey was like a father to me. It's hard. I don't know, maybe in time . . ."

"Heard about Vicky?" Rita asked, taking a new direction.

Father John shook his head. He wasn't sure he wanted to move on to this subject.

"She's spending a lot of time with her kids out in L.A. They're gettin' to know each other again, and she's glad." Rita took a deep breath, keeping her eyes on him. "I really miss her. It's good she's comin' back. This is where she belongs."

"She's coming back?" Father John asked. He couldn't believe the news hadn't flashed over the moccasin telegraph. Maybe he hadn't wanted to hear it, and yet, now that he had heard, he was glad.

Suddenly the drumbeats started up, loud thuds punctuating the air. The singers began to chant as the crowd formed a circle around the ground where Harvey had been killed. Will Standing Bear lifted the frying pan from the fire grate and walked into the circle. Allowing the cedar smoke to waft through the air, he prayed in Arapaho, his voice rising over the drums and the chanting.

Father John lifted his heart in prayer along with the elder who beseeched Shining Man Above to reclaim this place from the evil that had defiled it, to make it holy again for human beings and other creatures. The sacred cedar smoke crawled over the ground like fog, then rose and drifted through the crowd, symbolizing respect for life, for all living things.

Berkley Prime Crime Mysteries by Margaret Coel